Anne Douglas Sedgwick

The Dull Miss Archinard

Anne Douglas Sedgwick

The Dull Miss Archinard

ISBN/EAN: 9783337002299

Printed in Europe, USA, Canada, Australia, Japan

Cover: Foto ©Andreas Hilbeck / pixelio.de

More available books at **www.hansebooks.com**

The

Dull Miss Archinard

By
Anne Douglas Sedgwick

New York
Charles Scribner's Sons
1898

TO

MY GRANDMOTHER

B. M. D.

Prologue
PETER ODD

The Dull Miss Archinard

CHAPTER I.

PETER ODD was fishing. He stood knee-deep in a placid bend of stream, whipping the water deftly, his eyes peacefully intent on the floating fly, his mind in the musing, impersonal mood of fisherman reverie, no definite thought forming from the appreciative impressions of sunlit meadows, cool stretches of shade beneath old trees, gleaming curves of river. For a tired man, fishing is an occupation particularly soothing, and Peter Odd was tired, tired and sad. His pleasure was now, perhaps, more that of the lover of nature than of the true sportsman, the pastoral feast of the landscape with its blue distance of wooded hill, more to him than the expected flashing leap of a scarlet-spotted beauty; yet the attitude of receptive intentness was pleasant in all its phases, no one weary thought could become dominant while the eyes rested on the water, or were raised to such loveliness of quiet English country. So much of what he saw his own too; the sense of proprietorship is, under such circumstances, an intimately pleasant thing, and although, where Odd stood at a wide curve of water, a line of hedge and tall beech-trees sloping down to the river marked the confines of his property just here, the woods and meadows before him were all his—to the blue hills on the sky almost, the park behind him stretched widely about Allersley Manor, and to the left the river ran for a very respectable number of miles through woods and meadows as beautiful. The sense of proprietorship was still new enough to give a little thrill, for the old squire had died only two years before, and the sorrow of loss had only recently roused itself to the realization of bequeathed responsibilities, to the realization that energies so called forth may perhaps make of life a thing well worth living. A life of quiet utility; to feel oneself of some earthly use; what more could one ask? The duties of a landowner in our strenuous days may well fill a man's horizon, and Odd was well content that they should do so; for the present at least; and he did not look beyond the present.

In his tweeds and waterproof knee-breeches and boots, a sun-burnt straw hat shading his thin brown face, his hand steady and dexterous, as brown and thin, he was a pleasing example of the English country-gentleman type. He was tall, with the flavor of easy strength and elegance that an athletic youth gives to the most awkwardly made man. His face was at once humorous and sad; it is strange how a humorous character shows itself through the saddest set of feature. Odd's long, rather acquiline nose and Vandyke beard made a decidedly melancholy silhouette on the sunlit water, yet all the lines of the face told of a kindly contemplation of the world's pathetic follies;

the mouth was sternly cut yet very good-tempered, and its firm line held evident suggestions of quiet smiling.

Poor Peter Odd had himself committed a pathetic folly, and, as a result, smiles might be tinged with bitterness.

A captured trout presently demanded concentrated attention. The vigorous fish required long playing until worn out, when he was deftly secured in the landing-net and despatched with merciful promptitude ; indeed, a little look of nervous distaste might have roused in an unsympathetic looker-on conjectures as to a rather weak strain—a foolish width of pity in Peter Odd's character.

" A beauty," he mentally ejaculated. He sat down in the shade. It was hot ; the long, thick grass invited a lolling rest.

On the other side of the hedge was a rustic bathing-cabin, and from it Odd heard the laughing chatter of young voices. The adjoining property was a small one belonging to a Captain Archinard. Odd had seen little of him ; his wife was understood to be something of an invalid, and he had two girls —these their voices, no doubt. Odd took off his hat and mopped his forehead, looking at the little landing-wharf which he could just see beyond the hedge, and where one could moor boats or dive off into the deepness of the water. The latter form of aquatic exercise was probably about to take place, for Odd heard—

" I can swim beautifully already, papa," in a confident young voice—a gay voice, quiet, and yet excited too by the prospect of a display of prowess.

9

A tall, thin girl of about fourteen stepped out on to the landing. A bathing-dress is not as a rule a very graceful thing, yet this child, her skirt to her knee, a black silk sash knotted around her waist, with her slim white legs and charming feet, was as graceful as a young Amazon on a Grecian frieze. A heavy mass of braids, coiled up to avoid a wetting, crowned her small head. She was not pretty ; Odd saw that immediately, even while admiring the well-poised figure, its gallantly held little torso and light energy. Her profile showed a short nose and prominent chin, inharmoniously accentuated. She seemed really ugly when her sister joined her ; the sister was beautiful. Odd roused himself a little from his half recumbency to look at the sister appreciatively. Her slimness was exaggerated to an extreme—an almost fluttering lightness ; her long arms and legs seemed to flash their whiteness on the green ; she had an exquisite profile, and her soft black hair swept up into the same coronet of coils. Captain Archinard joined them as they stood side by side.

" You had better race," he said, looking down into the water, and then away to the next band of shadow. " Dive in, and race to that clump of aspens. This is a jolly bit for diving."

" But, papa, we shall wet our hair fearfully," said the elder girl—the ugly one—for so Odd already ungallantly designated her. " We usually get in on this shallower side and swim off. We have never tried diving, for it takes so long to dry our hair. Taylor would not like it at all."

" It is so deep, too," said the beauty in rather

a faltering voice—unfortunately faltering, for her father turned sharply on her.

"Afraid, hey? You mustn't be a coward, Hilda."

"I am not afraid," said the elder girl; "but I never tried it. What must I do? Put my arms so, and jump head first?"

"There is nothing to do at all," said the Captain, with some acidity of tone. "Keep your mouth shut and strike out as you come up. You'll do it, Katherine, first try. Hilda is in a funk, I see."

"Poor Hilda," Odd ejaculated mentally. She was evidently in a funk. Standing on the edge of the landing, one slim foot advanced in a tentative effort, she looked down shrinking into the water— very deeply black at this spot—and then, half entreatingly, half helplessly, at her father.

"Oh, papa, it is so deep," she repeated.

The Captain's neatly made face showed signs of peevish irritation.

"Well, deep or not, in you go. I must break you of that craven spirit. What are you afraid of? What could happen to you?"

"I—don't like water over my head—I might strike —on something."

Tears were near the surface.

What asses people made of themselves, thought Odd, with their silly shows of authority. The more the father insisted, the more frightened the child became; couldn't the idiot see that? The tear-filled eyes and looks that showed a struggle between fear of her father's anger and fear of the deep, black pool, moved Odd to a sudden though half-amused

resentment, for the little girl was certainly somewhat of a coward.

"Let me go in first, papa, and show her. Hilda,
dear, it's nothing; being frightened will make it
something, though, so don't be frightened, and watch
me."

"Yes, go in first, Katherine; show her that I
have a girl who isn't a coward—and how one of my
daughters came to be a coward I don't understand.
I am ashamed of you, Hilda."

Hilda evidently only controlled her sobs by a
violent effort; her caught-in under-lip, wide eyes,
and heaving little chest affected Odd painfully. He
frowned, sat up, put his hat on, and watched Miss
Katherine with a lack of sympathy that was certainly
unfair, for the plucky little person went through the
performance most creditably, stretched out and up
her thin pretty arms, curved forward her pretty
body, and made the plunge with a lithe elegance
that left her father gazing with complacent approval
after the white flash of her feet.

"Bravo! First-rate! There, Hilda, you see
what can be done. Come on, little white feather."
He spoke more kindly; the elder sister's prowess put
him more in humor with his less creditable offspring.

"Oh, papa!" The child shrank on the edge of
the platform—she would go bundling in, and hurt
herself. "But, papa," and her voice held a sharp
accent of distress, "where is Katherine?"

Indeed Katherine had not reappeared. Only a
moment had passed, but a moment under water is
long. Captain Archinard's eyes searched the surface of the river.

" But she can swim ? "

" Papa! papa! She is drowned, *drowned!* "
Hilda's voice rose to a scream. With a wild look
of resolve she sprang into the river just as Odd
dashed in, knee-deep, and as Katherine's head appeared at some distance down the current—an angry
little head, half choked, and gasping. Katherine
swam and waded to the shore, falling on her knees
upon the bank, while Odd dived into the hole—
very bad hole, deep and weedy—after Hilda.

He groped for the child among a tangle of roots,
touched her hair, grasped her round the waist, and
came to the surface with some difficulty, his strokes
impeded by sinuous cord-like weeds. Captain Archinard was too much astonished by the whole matter to do more than exclaim, " Upon my word! "
as his younger daughter was deposited at his feet.

" A nasty hole that. The weeds have probably
grown since any one has dived."

Odd spoke shortly, having lost his breath, and
severely; the child looked half drowned, and Katherine was still gasping.

" Why, Mr. Odd! Upon my word! "—the Captain recognized his neighbor—" I don't know how
to thank you."

The Captain had not recovered from his astonishment, and repeated with some vehemence : " Upon
my word! "

" Well, papa, you nearly drowned me! " Katherine was struggling between pride and anger. She
would not let the tears come, but they were near
the surface. " Those horrible snaky things got hold
of me and I almost screamed, only I remembered

13

that I must n't open my mouth, and I thought I would *never* come to the top." The self-pitying retrospect brought the tears to her eyes, but she held up her head and looked and spoke her resentment, " I think you might have gone in first yourself. And Hilda! Why did n't you wait until I came to the surface before you made her do it?"

Captain Archinard looked more vague under these reproaches than one would have expected after his exhibition of rather fretful autocracy.

" Made her!" he repeated, seizing with a rather mean haste at the error; " made her? She went in herself! Like a rocket, after you. By Jove! she showed her blood after all."

" Hilda! you tried to save my life!"

Odd still held the younger girl on his arm, supporting her while she choked and panted, for she had evidently had not shown her sister's *aplomb* and had opened her mouth. Katherine took her into her arms and kissed her with a warmth quite dramatic.

" Darling Hilda! And you were so frightened, too. I would have gone in after *her*," she added, looking up at Odd with a bright, quick glance, " but there would have been nothing to my credit in that."

" And *I* would have gone in after her, it goes without saying, Mr. Odd," said the Captain, when Katherine had led away to the bathing-cabin her still dazed sister, " but you seemed to drop from the clouds. Really, you have put me under a great obligation."

" Not at all. I have spent most of the day in

the river. I merely went in a bit deeper to fish out that plucky little girl."

"I 've dived off that spot a hundred times. I 'd no idea there were weeds. I've never known weeds to be there. I 'll send down one of the men directly after lunch and have it seen to. Really I feel a sense of responsibility." The Captain went on with an air of added self-justification, " Though, of course, I 'm not responsible. I could n't have known about the weeds."

Weeds or no weeds, Odd could not forgive him for the child's fright, though he replied good-humoredly to the invitation to the house.

"Mrs. Archinard would have called on Mrs. Odd before this, but my wife is an invalid—never leaves the house or grounds. She sees a good deal of Miss Odd. I knew your father myself as well as one may know such a recluse ; spent some pleasant hours in his library—magnificent library you 've got. Peculiarly satisfactory it must be, as you go in for that sort of thing. Won't you come in to tea this afternoon? And Mrs. Odd? Miss Odd? I was sorry to find them out when I called the other day. I have n't seen Mrs. Odd. I don't see her at church."

"No; we have hardly settled down to our duties yet, and my wife only got back from the Riviera a few weeks ago."

"Well, I hope we shall keep you at Allersley now that your *wanderjahre* are over, and that you are married. I was wandering myself during your boyhood. My brother bought the place, you know ; liked the country here immensely. Poor old Jack! Only lived ten years to enjoy it—and died a bach-

15

elor—luckily for me. But we've missed one ai
other, have n't we? Neighbors too. I have see
Mrs. Odd—at a dance in London, Lady Bartl
bury's, I remember; and I remember that she wa
the prettiest girl in the room. Miss Castleton—th
beautiful Alicia Castleton."

Miss Castleton's fame had indeed been so wid
that the title was quite public property, and th
Captain's reminiscent tone of admiration most na
ural and allowable. Odd accepted the invitation t
tea, waded back round the hedge, gathered up hi
basket and rod, and made his way up through th
park to Allersley Manor.

CHAPTER II

M RS. ODD and Miss Odd, Peter's eldest and unmarried sister, were having an only half-veiled altercation when Odd, after putting on dry clothes, came into the morning-room just before lunch. Miss Odd sat by the open French window cutting the leaves of a review. There were several more reviews on the table beside her, and with her eyeglasses and fine, severe profile, she gave one the impression of a woman who would pass her mornings over reviews and disagree with most of them for reasons not frivolous.

Mrs. Odd lay back in an easy-chair. She was very remarkable looking. The adjective is usually employed in a sense rather derogatory to beauty pure and simple, yet Mrs. Odd's dominant characteristic was beauty, pure and simple; beauty triumphantly certain of remark, and remarkable in the sense that no one could fail to notice her, as when one had noticed her it was impossible not to find her beautiful. It was not a loveliness that admitted of discussion. In desperate rebellion against an almost tame conformity, a rash person might assert that to him her type did not appeal; but the type was resplendent. Perhaps too resplendent; in this extreme lay the only hope of escape from conformity. The long figure in the uniform-

2

like commonplace of blue serge and shirt-waist was almost too uncommonplace in elegance of outline ; the white hand too slender, too pink as to finger-tips and polished as to nails ; the delicate scarlet splendor of her mouth, the big wine-colored eyes, too dazzling.

Mrs. Odd's red-brown hair was a glory, a bur-nished, well-coiffed, well-brushed glory; it rippled, coiled, and curved about her head. Her profile was bewildering—lazily, sweetly petulant. " Is this the face ? " a man might murmur on first seeing Alicia.

Odd had so murmured when she had flashed upon his vision over a year ago. He was still young and literary, and, as he was swept out of himself, had still had time for a vague grasp at self-expres-sion.

Mrs. Odd was speaking as he entered the room.

" I don't really see, Mary, what duty has got to do with it." Without turning her head, she turned her eyes on Odd : " How wet your hair is, Peter ! "

Mary Odd looked up from the review she was cutting rather grimly, and her cold face was irradi-ated with a sudden smile.

" Well, Peter," she said quietly.

" I fished a little girl out of the river," said Odd, taking a seat near Alicia, and smiling responsively at his sister. " Captain Archinard's little girl." He told the story.

" An interesting contrast of physical and moral courage."

" I have seen the children. They are noticeable children. They always ride to hounds." Hunting had been Miss Odd's favorite diversion during her father's lifetime. "But the pretty one, as I remember, has not the pluck of her sister—physical, as you say, Peter, no doubt."

"What sort of a person is Mrs. Archinard?"

"Very pretty, very lazy, very selfish. She is an American, and was rich, I believe. Captain Archinard left the army when he married her, and immediately spent her money. Luckily for him poor Mr. Archinard died—Jack Archinard; you remem-him, Peter? A nice man. I go to see Mrs. Archinard now and then. I don't care for her."

"You don't care much for any one, Mary," said Mrs. Odd, smiling. "Your remarks on your Allersley neighbors are very pungent and very true, no doubt. People are so rarely perfect, and you only tolerate perfection."

"Yet I have many friends, Alicia."

"Not near Allersley?"

"Yes; I think I count Mrs. Hartley-Fox, Mrs. Maynard, Lady Mainwaring, and Miss Hibbard among my friends."

"Mrs. Maynard is the old lady with the caps, isn't she? What big caps she does wear! Lady Mainwaring I remember in London, trying to marry off her eighth daughter. You told me, I recollect, that she was an inveterate matchmaker."

"She has no selfish eagerness, if that is what you understood me to mean."

"But she does interfere a great deal with the course of events, when events are marriageable young men, does n't she?"

"Does she?"

"Well, you said she was a matchmaker, Mary.

19

There was no disloyalty in saying so, for it is known by every one who knows Lady Mainwaring."

" And, therefore, my friends are not, and need not be, perfect."

During this little conversation, Odd sat with the unhappy, helpless look men wear when their women-kind are engaged in such contests.

" I am awfully hungry. Isn't it almost lunch-time?" he said, as they paused.

Mrs. Odd looked at her watch. " It only wants five minutes."

Odd walked to the window and looked out at the sweep of lawn, with its lime-trees and copper beeches. The flower-beds were in all their glory.

" How well the mignonette is getting on, Mary," he said, looking down at the fragrant greenness that came to the window. Alicia got up and joined her husband, putting her arm through his.

"Let us take a turn in the garden, Peter," she smiled at him ; and although he understood, with the fatal clearness that one year of life with Alicia had given him, that the walk was only proposed as a slight to Mary, he felt the old pleasure in her beauty—a rather sickly, pallid pleasure—and an inner qualm was dispersed by the realization that he and Mary understood one another so well that there need be no fear of hurting her.

After one year of married life, he and Mary knew the nearness of the sympathy that allows itself no words.

There seemed to Odd a perverse pathos in Alicia's lonely complacency—a pathos emphasized by her indifferent unconsciousness.

"Mary is so disagreeable to-day," said Alicia, as they walked slowly across the lawn. "She has such a strong sense of her own worth and of other people's worthlessness."

Odd made no reply. He never said a harsh word to his wife. He had chosen to marry her. The man who would wreak his own disillusion on the woman he had made his wife must, thought Odd, be a sorry wretch. He met the revealment of Alicia's shallow selfishness with humorous gentleness. She had been shallow and selfish when he had married her, and he had not found it out—had not cared to find it out. He contemplated these characteristics now with philosophic, even scientific charity. She was born so.

"It will be dull enough here, at all events," Alicia went on, pressing her slim patent-leather shoe into the turf with lazy emphasis as she walked, for Alicia was not bad-tempered, and took things easily; "but if Mary is going to be disagreeable—"

"You know, Alicia, that Mary has always lived here. It is in a truer sense her home than mine, but she would go directly if either you or she found it disagreeable. Had you not assented so cordially she would never have stayed."

"Don't imply extravagant things, Peter. Who thinks of her going?"

"She would—if *you* made it disagreeable."

"I? I do nothing. Surely Mary won't want to go because she scolds me."

"Come, Ally, surely you don't get scolded—more than is good for you." Odd smiled down at her. Her burnished head was on a level with his eyes.

" Like everybody else, you are not perfection, and, as Mary is somewhat of a disciplinarian, you ought to take her lectures in a humble spirit, and be thankful. I do. Mary is so much nearer perfection than I am."

" I am afraid I shall be bored here, Peter." Alicia left the subject of Mary for a still more intimate grievance.

" The art of not being bored requires patience, not to say genius. It can be learned though. And there are worse things than being bored."

" I think I could bear anything better."

" What would you like, Ally?" Odd's voice held a certain hopefulness. " I 'll do anything I can, you know. I believe in a woman's individuality and all that. Does your life down here crush your individuality, Alicia?"

Again Odd smiled down at her, conscious of an inward bitterness.

" Joke away, Peter. You know how much I care for all that woman business—rights and movements and individualities and all that ; a silly claiming of more duties that do no good when they 're done. I am an absolutely banal person, Peter ; my mind to me is n't a kingdom. I like outside things. I like gayety, change, diversion. I don't like days one after the other—like sheep—and I don't like sheep !"

They had passed through the shrubbery, and before them were meadows dotted with the harmless animals that had suggested Mrs. Odd's simile.

" Well, we won't look at the sheep. I own

that they savor strongly of bucolic immutability.
You've had plenty of London for the past year,
Ally, and Nice and Monte Carlo. The sheep are
really the change."

"You had better go in for a seat in Parliament,
Peter."

"Longings for a political salon, Ally? I have
hardly time for my scribbling and landlording as
it is."

"A salon! Nothing would bore me so much as
being clever and keeping it up. No, I like seeing
people and being seen, and dancing and all that. I
am absolutely banal, as I tell you."

"Well, you shall have London next year. We'll
go up for the season."

"You took me for what I was, Peter," Mrs. Odd
remarked as they retraced their steps towards the
house. "I have never pretended, have I? You
knew that I was a society beauty and that only. I
am a very shallow person, I suppose, Peter; I certainly can't pretend to have depths—even to give
Mary satisfaction. It would be too uncomfortable.
Why *did* you fall in love with me, Peter? It
wasn't *en caractère* a bit, you know."

"Oh yes, it was, Ally. I fell in love with you
because you were beautiful. Why did you fall in
love with me?"

The mockery with which Alicia's smile was
tinged deepened into a good-humored laugh at her
own expense.

"Well, Peter, I don't think any one before made
me feel that they thought me so beautiful. I am
vain, you know. Your enthusiasm was awfully

flattering. I am very sorry you idealized me, Peter.
I am sure you idealized me. Shall we go in?
Lunch must be ready, and you must be hungrier
than ever."

24

CHAPTER III

A T four that afternoon Odd, his wife, and Mary
started for the Archinards' house. Mary had
offered to join her brother; the prospect of the walk
together was very pleasant. She could not object
when Alicia, at the last moment, announced her intention of going too.

" I have never been to see her. I should like the
walk, and Mary will approve of the fulfilment of my
duty towards my neighbor."

Mary's prospects were decidedly nipped in the
bud, as Alicia perhaps intended that they should
be; but Alicia's avowed motive was so praiseworthy
that Mary allowed herself only an inner discontent,
and, what with her good-humored demeanor, Odd's
placid chat of crops and tenantry, and Alicia's ac-
quiescent beauty, the trio seemed to enjoy the mile
of beechwood and country road and the short sweep
of prettily wooded drive that led to Allersley Priory,
a square stone house covered with vines of magnolia
and wisteria, and incorporating in its walls, according to tradition, portions of the old Priory which
once occupied the site. From the back of the house
sloped a wide expanse of lawn and shrubberies, and
past it ran the river that half a mile further on flowed
out of Captain Archinard's little property into Odd's.

The drawing-room was on the groundfloor, and its windows opened on this view.

Mrs. Archinard and the Captain were talking to young Lord Allan Hope, eldest son of Lord Mainwaring. Mrs. Archinard's invalidism was evidently not altogether fictitious. She had a look of at once extreme fragility and fading beauty. One knew at the first glance that she was a woman to have cushions behind her and her back to the light. There was no character in the delicate head, unless one can call a passive determination to do or feel nothing that required energy, character.

The two little girls came in while Odd talked to their father. They were dressed alike in white muslins. Katherine's gown reached her ankles; Hilda's was still at the *mi-jambe* stage. Their long hair fell about their faces in childlike fashion. Katherine's was brown and strongly rippled; Hilda's softly, duskily, almost bluely black; it grew in charming curves and eddies about her forehead, and framed her little face and long slim neck in straightly falling lines.

Katherine gave Odd her hand with a little air that reminded him of a Velasquez Infanta holding out a flower.

"You were splendid this morning, Mr. Odd. That hole was no joke, and Hilda swallowed lots of water as it was. She might easily have been drowned,"

Katherine was certainly not pretty, but her deeply set black eyes had a dominant directness. She held her head up, and her smile was charming—a little girl's smile, yet touched with the conscious power of a clever woman. Odd felt that the child was

clever, and that the woman would be cleverer. He
felt, too, that the black eyes were lit with just a spice
of fun as they looked into his as though she knew
that he knew, and they both knew together, that
Hilda had not been in much danger, and that his
ducking had been only conventionally " splendid."

" Hilda wants to thank you herself, don't you,
Hilda ? She had such a horrid time altogether ; you
were a sort of Perseus to her, and papa the sea monster!" Then Katherine, having, as it were, introduced and paved the way for her sister, went back
across the room again, and stood by young Allan
Hope while he talked to the beautiful Mrs. Odd.

Hilda seemed really in no need of an introduction.
She was not shy, though she evidently had not her
sister's ready mastery of what to say, and how to
say it. Odd was rather glad of this; he had found
Katherine's *aplomb* almost disconcerting.

" I do thank you very much." She put her hand
into Odd's as he spoke, and left it there ; the con-
fiding little action emphasized her childlikeness.

" What did you think of as you went down ? " he
asked her.

" In the river? " A shade of retrospective terror
crossed her face.

" No, no ! we won't talk about the river, will we ? "
Odd said quickly. However funny Katherine's
greater common sense had found the incident, it had
not been funny to Hilda. " Have you lived here
long ? " he asked. Captain Archinard had joined
Mrs. Odd, and with an admirer on either side, Alicia
was enjoying herself. " I have never seen you before, you know."

"We have lived here since my uncle died; about eight years ago, I think."

"Yes, just about the time that I left Allersley."

"Did n't you like Allersley?" Hilda asked, with some wonder.

"Oh, very much; and my father was here, so I often came back; but I lived in London and Paris, where I could work at things that interested me."

"I have been twice in London; I went to the National Gallery."

"You liked that?"

"Oh, very much." She was a quiet little girl, and spoke quietly, her wide gentle gaze on Odd.

"And what else did you like in London?"

Hilda smiled a little, as if conscious that she was being put through the proper routine of questions, but a trustful smile, quite willing to give all information asked for.

"The Three Fates."

"You mean the Elgin Marbles?"

"Yes, with no heads; but one is rather glad they have n't."

"Why?" asked Odd, as she paused. Hilda did not seem sure of her own reason.

"Perhaps they would be *too* beautiful with heads," she suggested. "Do you like dogs?" she added, suddenly turning the tables on him.

"Yes, I love dogs," Odd replied, with sincere enthusiasm.

"Three of our dogs are out there on the verandah, if you would care to know them?"

"I should very much. Perhaps you 'll show me the garden too; it looks very jolly."

It was a pleasure to look at his extraordinarily pretty little Andromeda, and he was quite willing to spend the rest of his visit with her. They went out on the verandah, where, in the awning's shade, lay two very nice fox terriers. A dachshund sat gazing out upon the sunlit lawn in a dog's dignified reverie.

" Jack and Vic," Hilda said, pointing out the two fox terriers. " They just belong to the whole family, you know. And this dear old fellow is Palamon; Arcite is somewhere about; they are mine."

" Who named yours ? "

" I did—after I read it ; they had other names when they were given to me, but as I had never called them by them, I thought I had a right to change them. I wanted names with associations, like Katherine's setters ; they are called Darwin and Spencer, because Katherine is very fond of science."

" Oh, is she ? " said Odd, rather stupefied. " You seem to have a great many dogs in couples."

" The others are not ; they are more general dogs, like Jack and Vic."

Hilda still held Odd's hand : she stooped to stroke Arcite's pensive head, giving the fox terriers a pat as they passed them.

" So you are fond of Chaucer ? " Odd said. They crossed the gravel path and stepped on the lawn.

" Yes, indeed, he is my favorite poet. I have not read all, you know, but especially the Knight's Tale."

" That's your favorite ? "

" Yes."

" And what is your favorite part of the Knight's Tale ? "

" The part where Arcite dies."

" You like that? "

" Oh ! so much ; don't you ? "

" Very much ; as much, perhaps, as anything ever written. There never was a more perfect piece of pathos. Perhaps you remember it." He was rather curious to know how deep was this love for Chaucer.

" I learnt it by heart; I have n't a good memory, but I liked it so much."

" Perhaps you would say it to me."

Hilda looked up a little shyly.

" Oh, I can't ! " she exclaimed timidly.

" *Can't* you ? " and Odd looked down at her a humorously pleading interrogation.

" I can't say things well; and it is too sad to say —one can just bear to read it."

" Just bear to say it—this once," Odd entreated.

They had reached the edge of the lawn, and stood on the grassy brink of the river. Hilda looked down into the clear running of the water.

" Is n't it pretty? I don't like deep water, where one can't see the bottom ; here the grasses and the pebbles are as distinct as possible, and the minnows —don't you like to see them ? "

" Yes, but Arcite. Don't make me tease you."

Hilda evidently determined not to play the coward a second time. The quiet pressure of Odd's hand was encouraging, and in a gentle, monotonous little voice that, with the soft breeze, the quickly running sunlit river, went into Odd's consciousness as a quaint, ineffaceable impression of sweetness and sadness, she recited :—

> " Allas the wo! allas the peynes stronge,
> That I for you have suffered, and so longe!
> Allas the deth! allas myn Emelye!
> Allas departing of our companye!
> Allas myn hertes quene! allas, my wyf!
> •   Myn hertes lady, endere of my lyf!
> What is this world?   What asketh man to have?
> Now with his love, now in his colde grave
> Allone, withouten any companye."

Odd's artistic sensibilities were very keen. He felt that painfully delicious constriction of the throat that the beautiful in art can give, especially the beautiful in tragic art.   The far-away tale; the far-away tongue; the nearness of the pathos, poignant in its " white simplicity."   And how well the monotonous little voice suited its melancholy.

> " Allone, withouten any companye,"

he repeated. He looked down at Hilda; he had tactfully avoided looking at her while she spoke, fearing to embarrass her; her eyes were full of tears.

" Thanks, Hilda," he said.   It struck him that this highly strung little girl had best not be allowed to dwell too long on Arcite and, after a sympathetic pause (Odd was a very sympathetic person), he added :

" Now are you going to take me into the garden ? "

" Yes." Hilda turned from the river.   " You know he had just gained her, that made it all the worse. If he had not loved her he would not have minded dying so much, and being alone.   One can hardly bear it," Hilda repeated.

" It is intensely sad.   I don't think you ought to have learned it by heart, Hilda.   That 's ungrateful of me, is n't it? But I am old enough to take an impersonal pleasure in sad things; I am afraid they make you sad."

Hilda's half-wondering smile was reassuringly childlike.

" Oh, but it 's *nice* being sad like that."

Odd reflected, as they went into the garden, that she had put herself into his category.

After the shadow of the shrubberies through which they passed, the fragrant sunlight was dazzling. Rows of sweet peas, their mauves and pinks and whites like exquisite musical motives, ran across the delicious old garden. A border of deep purple pansies struck a beautifully meditative chord. Flowers always affected Odd musically; he half closed his eyes to look at the sweeps of sun-flooded color. A medley of Schumann and Beethoven sang through his head as he glanced down, smiling at Hilda Archinard; her gently responsive little smile was funnily comprehensive; one might imagine that tunes were going through her head too.

" Is n't it jolly, Hilda?"

" Very jolly," she laughed, and, as they walked between the pansy borders she kept her gentle smile and her gentle stare up at his appreciative face.

She thought his smile so nice; his teeth, which crowded forward a little, lent it perhaps its peculiar sweetness; his eyelids, drooping at the outer corners, gave the curious look of humorous sadness to the expression of his brown eyes. His moustache was cut shortly on his upper lip, and showed the rather quizzical line of his mouth. Hilda, unconsciously, enumerated this catalogue of impressions.

"What fine strawberries," said Odd. "I like the fragrance almost more than the flavor."

"But won't you taste them?" Hilda dropped his hand to skip lightly into the strawberry bed. "They are ripe, lots of them," she announced, and she came running back, her outstretched hands full of the summer fruit, red, but for the tips, still untinted. The sunlit white frock, the long curves of black hair, the white face, slim black legs, and the spots of crimson color made a picture—a sunshiny Whistler.

Odd accepted the strawberries gratefully; they were very fine.

"I don't think you can have them better at Allersley Manor," said Hilda, smiling.

"I don't think mine are as good. Won't you come some day to Allersley Manor and compare?"

"I should like to very much."

"Then you and Miss Katherine shall be formally invited to tea, with the understanding that afterwards the strawberry beds are to be invaded."

"I should like to very much," Hilda repeated.

"Hullo! Don't make me feel a pig! Eat some yourself," said Odd, who had finished one handful.

"No, no, I picked them for you."

Odd took her disengaged hand in his as they walked on again, Hilda resisting at first.

"It is so sticky."

"I don't mind that: it is very generous." She laughed at the extravagance.

"And what do you do all day besides swimming?" Odd asked.

"We have lessons with our governess. She is

3   33

strict, but a splendid teacher. Katherine is quite a first-rate Latin scholar."

" Is Katherine fond of Chaucer? "

"Katherine cares more for science and—and philosophy." Hilda spoke with a respectful gravity. "That's why she called her dogs Darwin and Spencer. She has n't read any of Spencer yet, but of course he is a great philosopher. She knows that, and she has read a good deal of a big book by Darwin, ' The Origin of Species,' you know."

" Yes, I know." Odd found Katherine even more startling than her sister.

" I tried to read it, but it was so confusing— about selection and cabbages—I don't see how cabbages *can* select, do you? " Hilda's voice held a reminiscent vagueness. " Katherine says that she did not care for it *much*, but she thought she ought to look through it if she wanted a foundation; she is very keen on foundations, and she says Darwin is the foundation-key—or corner-stone—no, keystone to the arch of modern science—at least she did not say so, but she read me that from her journal."

" Oh! Katherine wrote that, did she? "

"Yes; but you must n't think that Katherine is a blue-stocking." Something in Odd's tone made Hilda fear misunderstanding. " She loves sports of all kinds, and fun. She goes across country as well as any woman—that is what Lord Mainwaring said of her last winter during fox-hunting. She is n't afraid of anything."

" And what else do you do besides lessons? "

" Well, I read and walk; there are such famous walks all about here, walks in woods and on hills.

I don't care for roads, do you? And I stay with mamma and read to her when she is tired."

" And Katherine?"

"She is more with papa." In her heart Hilda said: " He loves her best," but of that she could not speak, even to this new friend who seemed already so near; to no one could she hint of that ache in her heart of which jealousy formed no part, for it was natural that papa should love Katherine best, that every one should; she was so gay and courageous; but though it was natural that Katherine should be loved best, it was hard to be loved least.

"You are by yourself a good deal, then?" said Odd. "Do you walk by yourself, too?"

"Yes, with the dogs. I used to have grandmamma, you know; she died a year ago."

" Oh, yes! Mrs. Archinard's mother."

Hilda nodded; her grasp on Odd's hand tightened and they walked in silence. Odd remembered the fine portrait of a lady in the drawing-room; he had noticed its likeness and unlikeness to Mrs. Archinard; a delicate face, but with an Emersonian expression of self-reliance, a puritan look of stanchness and responsibility.

35

CHAPTER IV

O N the way home, cool evening shadows slant-
ing across the road, Alicia declared that she
had really enjoyed herself.

"Captain Archinard is quite jolly. He has seen
everybody and everything under the sun. He is
most entertaining, and Lord Allan is remarkably
uncallow."

" He thinks of standing for Parliament next year.
A nice, steady, honest young fellow. How do you
like the Archinards, Peter?"

" The child—Hilda—is a dear child."

"She is awfully pretty," said Alicia, who could
afford to be generous; " I like that colorless type."

"She is delicate, I am afraid," said Mary.

" She has the mouth of a Botticelli Madonna and
the eyes of a Gainsborough; you know the portrait
of Sheridan's wife at Dulwich?"

Alicia had never been to Dulwich. Mary assented.

" The other one—the ugly one—is very clever,"
Alicia went on ; she was in a good temper evidently.
Not that Alicia was ever exactly bad-tempered.
"She said some very clever things and looked
more."

"She is too clever perhaps," Mary remarked.
" As for Mrs. Archinard, I should like to slap her.
I think that my conventionality is of a tolerant

order, but Mrs. Archinard's efforts at æsthetic originality make me feel grimly conventional."

" Mary ! Mary ! how delightful to hear such uncharitable remarks from you. *I* should rather like
to slap her too, though she struck me as awfully
conventional."

" Oh, she is, practically. It is the artistic *argot*
that bores one so much."

" She is awfully self-satisfied too. Dear me,
Peter, I wish we had driven after all. I hate the
next half-mile. It is just uphill enough to be irritating—fatigue without realizing exactly the cause
of it. Why did n't we drive, Peter ? "

" I thought we all preferred walking. You are a
very energetic young person as a rule."

" Not for tiresome country roads. They should
be got over as quickly as possible."

" Well, we will cut through the beech-woods as
we came."

" Oh dear," Alicia yawned, " how tired I am
already of those tiresome beech-woods. I wish it
were autumn and that the hunting had begun.
Captain Archinard gives me glowing accounts, and
promises me a lead for the first good run. We must
fill the house with people then, Peter."

" The house shall be filled to overflowing. Perhaps you would like some one now. Mrs. Laughton
and her girls; you like them, don't you ? "

Alicia wrinkled up her charming nose.

" Can't say I do. I 've stopped with them too
much perhaps. They bore me. I am afraid no one
would come just now, everything is so gay in
London. I wish I were there."

Alicia was not there because the doctor had strongly advised country air and the simple inaction of country life. Alicia had lost her baby only three weeks after its birth—two months ago—and had herself been very ill.

" But I think I shall write to some people and ask them to take pity on me," she added, as they walked slowly through the woods. " Sir John, and Mr. and Mrs. Damian, Gladys le Breton, and Lord Calverly."

" Well ! " Peter spoke in his usual tone of easy acquiescence.

Mary walked on a little ahead. What good did it do to trouble her brother uselessly by her impatient look? But how could Peter yield so placidly ? Mary respected him too much to allow herself an evil thought of his wife ; but Alicia was a person to be talked about. Mary did not doubt that she had been talked about already, and would be more so if she were not careful.

Lord Calverly and Sir John dangling attendance would infallibly cause comment on any woman— let alone the beautiful Mrs. Odd. Yet Peter said, " Well ! "

CHAPTER V

THE evening did not pass pleasantly at the
Priory. Captain Archinard's jolliness did not
extend to family relationships; he often found
family relationships a bore, and the contrasted
stodginess of his own surroundings seemed greater
after Mrs. Odd's departure.

He muttered and fumed about the drawing-room
after dinner.

He was confoundedly pinched for money, and
upon his word he would not be surprised if he
should have to sell the horses. "And what my
life will be stuck down here without the hunting, I
can't imagine. Damnable!"

The Captain growled out the last word under his
breath in consideration of Katherine and Hilda,
who had joined their father and mother after their
own tea and a game of lawn-tennis. But Mrs.
Archinard was not the woman to allow to pass un-
noticed such a well-founded cause of grievance.

With a look of delicate disgust she laid down the
volume of Turgenieff that she was reading.

"Shall I send the children away, Charles? Either
they or you had best go, if you are going to talk
like that."

"Beg pardon," said the Captain shortly. "No,
of course they don't go."

"I am sure I have few enough enjoyments with-

39

out being made to suffer because you are to lose one of yours."

"Who asks you to suffer, Kate? But you don't wait for the asking. You 're only too willing to offer yourself as a *souffre-douleur* on all occasions."

Then Mrs. Archinard retired behind her book in scornful resignation and, after twenty minutes of silence, the little girls were very glad to get away to bed.

Hilda was just undressed when Mrs. Archinard sent for her to come to her room. Her head ached, and Hilda must brush her hair; it was early yet. This was a customary task, and one that Hilda prided herself upon accomplishing with sovereign beneficence. Taylor's touch irritated Mrs. Archinard; Hilda only was soothing.

In dressing-gown and slippers she ran to her mother's room.

Mrs. Archinard's long hair—as black and as fine as Hilda's—fell over the back of the large arm-chair in which she reclined.

"Such a headache!" she sighed, as Hilda took up the brush and began to pass it slowly and gently down the length of hair. "It is really brutal of your father to forget my head as he does."

Hilda's heart sank. The unideal attitude of her father and mother toward one another was one of her great sorrows. Papa was certainly fond of his pretty wife, but he was so fretful and impatient, and mamma so continually grieved. It was all wrong. Hilda had already begun to pass judgment, unconsciously, on her father; but her almost maternal tenderness for her mother as yet knew no doubt.

"It would be very dreadful if the horses had to go, would n't it?" she said. Her father's bad temper might be touching if its cause were suggested.

"Of course it would; and so are most things dreadful. I am sure that life is nothing but dreadfulness in every form." Yet Mrs. Archinard was not at all an unhappy woman. Her life was delicately epicurean. She had few wants, but those few were never thwarted. From the early cup of exquisite tea brought to her bedside, through all the day of dilettante lounging over a clever book— a day relieved from monotony by pleasant episodes —dainty dishes especially prepared, visits from acquaintances, with whom she had a reputation for languid cynicism and quite awesome literary and artistic cleverness—to this hour of hair-brushing, few of her moments were not consciously appreciative of the most finely flavored mental and physical enjoyment. But the causes for enjoyment certainly seemed so slight that Mrs. Archinard's graceful pessimism usually met with universal sympathy. Hilda was very sorry for her mother. To lie all· day reading dreary books; condemned to an inaction that cut her off from all the delights of outdoor life, seemed to her tragic. Mrs. Archinard did not undeceive her; indeed, perhaps, the most fascinating of Mrs. Archinard's artistic occupations was to fancy herself very tragic. Hilda went back to her room much depressed.

The girls slept together, and Katherine was sitting up in her night-gown writing her journal by candlelight and enjoying a sense of talent flowing at all costs—for writing by candlelight was strictly forbidden—as she dotted down what she felt to be a very original and pungent account of the day and the people it had introduced.

When, however, she heard the patter of Hilda's heedless slippers in the corridor, she blew out the candle in a hurry, pinched the glowing wick, and skipped into bed. She might take an artistic pleasure in braving rules, but Katherine knew that Hilda would have shown an almost dull amazement at her occupation; and although Katherine characterized it as dull, she did not care to arouse it. She wished to stand well in Hilda's eyes in all things. Hilda must find nothing to criticise in her either mentally or morally.

" What shall we do if the horses are sold ? " she exclaimed, as Hilda got into the little bed beside hers. " Only imagine ! no hunting next winter ! at least, none for us ! "

" Poor papa," Hilda sighed.

" Oh, you may be sure that he will keep one hunter at least, but of course he will be dreadfully cut off from it with only one, and of course our horses will have to go if the worst comes to the worst. You won't miss it as much as I will, Hilda ; the riding, yes, no doubt, but not the hunting. Still Lord Mainwaring will give us a mount, and now that Mr. Odd is here, he will be sure to have a lot of horses. The old squire let everything of that sort run down so, Miss Odd had only two hunters. Well, Hilda, and what do you think of Mr. Odd ? "

" Oh, I love him, Katherine ! " Hilda lay looking with wide eyes into the soft darkness of the room.

The windows were open, and the drawn chintz curtains flapped gently against the sills.

" I would n't say that if I were you, Hilda," Katherine remarked, with some disapproval.

" Why not?" Hilda's voice held an alarmed note. Katherine was, to a great extent, her mentor.

" It does n't sound very—dignified. Of course you are only a little girl, but still—one does n't say such things."

" But I do love him ; how can one help loving a person who treats one so kindly. And then—anyway—even if he had not been kind to me I should love him, I think."

Hilda would have liked to be able properly to analyze her sensations and win her sister's approval ; but how explain clearly ?

" That would be rather foolish," Katherine said, in a tone of kind but restraining wisdom ; " one should n't let one's feelings run away with one like that. Shall I tell you what *I* think about Mr. Odd ?"

" Oh yes, please."

" I think he is like the river where we jumped in to-day—ripples on the top, kindness and smiles, you know—but somewhere in his heart a big hole —a hole with stones and weeds in it." Katherine was quoting from her journal, but Hilda might as well think the simile improvised : Katherine felt some pride in it ; it certainly justified, she thought, the conventionally illicit act of the candle.

Hilda lay in silent admiration.

" Oh, Katherine, I never know how I feel things till you tell me like that," she said at last. " How beautiful ! Yes, I am sure he has a hole in his

43

heart." And tears came into Hilda's eyes and into her mind the line :—

"Allone, withouten any companye."

" As for Mrs. Odd," Katherine continued, pleased with the success of her psychology, "she has no heart to make a hole in."

" Katherine, do you think so? How dreadful!"

" She is a thorough egotist. She does n't know much either, Hilda, for when Darwin came in she laughed a lot at the name and said she would n't be paid to read him—the real Darwin."

" Perhaps she likes other things best."

" Herself," said Katherine decisively. " Miss Odd of course we have had time to make up our minds about."

" I like her; don't you? She has such a clear, trustful face."

" She is rather rigid; about as hard on other people as she would be on herself. She could never do anything wrong."

"I don't quite like *that;* being hard on other people, I mean. One could be quite sure about one's own wrongness, but how can one about other people's? It is rather uncharitable, is n't it, Katherine?"

" She is n't very charitable, but she is very just. As for Lord Allan, he is a sort of type, and, therefore, not very entertaining."

"A type of what?"

" Oh, just the eldest son type; very handsome, very honest, very good, with a strong sense of responsibility. Jimmy Hope is just like him, which is a great pity, as one expects a difference in the younger son—more interest."

44

Katherine went to sleep with a warmly comfortable sense of competence. She doubted whether many people saw things as clearly as she did.

She was wakened by an unpleasant dreaming scream from Hilda.

" What is the matter, Hilda?" She spoke crossly. " How you startled me."

" Oh, such a horrid dream!" Hilda half sobbed. " How glad I am that it is n't so!"

" What was it?" Katherine asked, still crossly; severity she thought the best attitude towards Hilda's fright.

" About the river, down in the hole; I was choking, and my legs and arms were all tangled in roots."

" Well, go to sleep now," Katherine advised.

Hilda was obediently silent, but presently a small, supplicating voice was heard.

" Katherine—I 'm so sorry—don't be angry— might I come to you? I 'm so frightened."

" Come along," said Katherine, still severely, but she put her arms very fondly around her shivering sister, snuggled her consolingly and kissed her.

" Silly little Hilda," she said.

45

CHAPTER VI

THREE days before the arrival of Gladys le Breton, Mrs. Marchant, Lord Calverly, and Sir John (the Damians only did not accept Alicia's invitation), Mary Odd astonished her brother.

She came into the library early one morning before breakfast. Odd was there, writing.

"Peter," she said, "last night, before going to bed, I wrote to Mr. Apswith and accepted him."

Mary always spoke to the point. Peter wheeled round his chair in amazement.

"Accepted Mr. Apswith, Mary?"

"Yes. I always intended to at some time, and I felt that the time had come."

Mr. Apswith, a clever, wealthy M. P., had for years been in love with Miss Odd. Mary was now one-and-thirty, two years older than her brother, and people said that Mr. Apswith had fallen in love when she first came out twelve years ago. Mr. Apswith's patience, perseverance, and fidelity were certainly admirable, but Peter, like most people, had thought that as Mary had, so far, found no difficulty in maintaining her severe independence, it would, in all probability, never yield to Mr. Apswith's ardor.

Mary, however, was a person to keep her own counsel. During her father's lifetime, when much

46

responsibility and many duties had claimed her, she had certainly doubted more than once the possibility of Mr. Apswith's ultimate success; there was a touch of the Diana in Mary, and a great deal of the Minerva. But, since her father's death, since Peter's bridal home-coming, Mary often found herself thinking of Mr. Apswith, her fundamental sympathy with him on all things, her real loneliness and his devotion. They had corresponded for years, and often saw one another. Familiarity had not bred contempt, but rather strengthened mutual trust and dependence. A certain tone of late in Mary's letters had called forth from Mr. Apswith a most domineering and determined love-letter. Mary had yielded to it—gladly, as she now realized. Yet her heart yearned over Peter. He got up now, and kissed her.

"Mary, my dear girl"—he could hardly find words—"may you be very, very happy. You deserve it ; so does he."

Neither touched, as they talked of the wonderful decision, on the fact that by it Peter would be left to the solitary companionship of his wife ; it was not a fact to be touched on. Mary longed to fling her arms around his neck and cry on his shoulder. Her happiness made his missing it so apparent, but she shrank from emphasizing their mutual knowledge.

"We must ask Apswith down at once," said Odd. "It's a busy session, but he can manage a few days."

"Well, Peter, that is hardly necessary. I shall go up to London within the week. Lady Mainwaring asked me to go to Paris with her on the 20th. She

47

stops in London for three days. I shall see Mr.
Apswith there, get my trousseau in Paris, and be
married in July, in about six weeks' time. Delay
would be rather silly—he has waited so long."

"You take my breath away, Mary. I am selfish,
I own. I don't like to lose you."

"It is n't losing me, Peter dear. We shall see a
lot of one another. I shall be married from here,
of course. Mr. Apswith will stop with the Main-
warings."

When Mary left him, Peter resumed his seat, and
even went on writing for a few moments. Then he
put down the pen and stretched himself, as one
does when summoning courage. He did not lack
courage, yet he owned to himself that Mary's pros-
pective departure sickened him. Her grave, even
character had given him a sense of supporting sympathy; he needed a sympathetic atmosphere; and
Alicia's influence was a very air-pump. Poor Alicia,
thought Odd. The sense of his own despair struck
him as rather unmanly. He looked out of the open
window at the lawn, its cool, green stretches
whitened with the dew; the rooks were cawing in
the trees, and his thoughts went back suddenly to
a certain morning in London, not two months ago,
just after the baby's death and just before Alicia's
departure for the Riviera.

Alicia was lying on the sofa—Peter staring at the
distant trees, did not see them but that scene—her
magnificent health had made lying on sofas very
uncharacteristic, and Odd had been struck with a
gentle sort of compunction at the sight of the bronze
head on the pillow, the thin white cheek. His heart

was very heavy. The paternal instincts are not
said to be strong; Odd had not credited himself
with possessing them in any elevated form. Yet,
now that the poor baby was dead, he realized how
keen had been his interest in the little face, how
keen the half-animal pleasure in the clinging of the
tiny fingers, and as he looked at the baby in its small
white coffin, he had realized, too, with a pang of
longing that the little white face, like a flower among
the flowers about it, was that of his child—dead.

On that morning he bent over Alicia with something of the lover's tenderness in his heart, though
Alicia had very nearly wrung all tenderness out of it.

" My dear girl, my poor, dear girl," he said, kiss-
ing her; and he sat down beside her on the sofa and
smoothed back her hair. Alicia looked up at him
with those wonderful eyes—looked up with a smile.

" Oh, I shall be all right soon enough, Peter."

Peter put his arm under her head and looked hard
at her—her beauty entranced him as it had done
from the beginning.

" Alicia, Alicia, do you love me ? " His earnest-
ness pleased her ; she felt in it her own power.

" What a thing to ask, Peter. Did you ever
imagine I did n't ? "

" Shall it bring us together, my wife, the death of
our child ? Will you feel for my sorrow as I feel for
yours, my poor darling ? "

" Feel for you, Peter ? Why, of course I do. It
is especially hard on you, too, losing your heir."

Her look, her words crushed all the sudden impulse of resolve, hope, love even.

" My heir ? " Peter repeated, in a stumbling tone.

4   49

"That has nothing to do with it. I was n't thinking of that."

"Were n't you?" said Alicia, rather wearily. She
felt her weakness, it irked her, and her next words
were more fretfully uttered—

"Of course I know you feel for me. Such a lot
to go through, too, and for nothing." She saw the
pain setting her husband's lips sternly. "I suppose
now, Peter, that you are imagining I care nothing
about baby," she remarked.

"I hope I am not a brute," said Peter gloomily.

"You hope *I 'm* not, too, no doubt."

"Don't, don't, Alicia."

"I felt awfully about it; simply awfully," Alicia
declared.

Odd, retracing the sorry little scene as he looked
from his library windows, found that from it unconsciously he had dated an epoch, an epoch of resignation that had donned good-humor as its shield.
Alicia could disappoint him no longer.

In the first month of their married life, each revelation of emptiness had been an agony. Alicia was
still mysterious to him, as must be a nature centered
in its own shallowness to one at touch on all points
with life in all its manifestations; her mind still
remained as much a thing for conjecture as the
mind of some animals. But Alicia's perceptions
were subtle, and he only asked now to keep from her
all consciousness of his own marred life; for he had
marred it, not she. He was carefully just to Alicia.

Mary remained at the Manor until all Alicia's
guests had arrived. Mrs. Marchant, an ugly, "smart,"
vivacious widow, splendid horsewoman, and good

singer ; Gladys le Breton, who was very blonde and
fluffy as to head, just a bit made-up as to skin,
harmless, pretty, silly, and supposed to be clever.

" Clever, I suppose," Mary said to Lady Mainwaring, " because she has the reputation of doing
foolish things badly—dancing on dinner-tables and
thoroughly *bête* things like that. She has not danced
on Peter's table as yet."

Miss le Breton skirt-danced in the drawing-room,
however, very prettily, and Peter's placid contemplation of her coyness irritated Mary. Miss le
Breton's coyness was too mechanical, too well worn
to afford even a charitable point of view.

" Poor little girl," said Peter, when she expressed
her disapproval with some severity; " it is her
nature. Each man after his own manner ; hers is
to make a fool of herself," and with this rather unexpected piece of opinion Mary was fully satisfied.
As for Lord Calverly, she cordially hated the big
man with the good manners and the coarse laugh.
His cynical observation of Miss le Breton aroused
quite a feeling of protecting partisanship in Mary's
breast, and his looks at Alicia made her blood boil.
They were not cynical. Sir John Fleetinge was
hardly more tolerable ; far younger, with a bonnie
look of devil-may-care and a reputation for reckless-
ness that made Mary uneasy. Peter was indifferent
good-humor itself, but she thought the time might
come when Peter's good-humor might fail.

The thought of Mr. Apswith was cheering ; but
she hated to leave Peter *dans cette galère.*

Peter, however, did not much mind the *galère.*
His duties as host lay lightly on him. He did not

mind Calverly at billiards, nor Fleetinge at the river, where they spent several mornings fishing silently and pleasantly together. Fleetinge had only met him casually in London clubs and drawing-rooms, but at close quarters he realized that literary tastes, which might have indicated a queer twist according to Sir John and an air of easy confidence in Mrs. Odd, would not make a definite falling in love with Mrs. Odd one whit the safer; he rather renounced definiteness therefore, and rather liked Peter.

Mary departed for London with Lady Mainwaring, and Alicia, as if to show that she needed no chaperonage, conducted herself with a little less gayety than when Mary was there.

She rode in the mornings with Lord Calverly and Captain Archinard—who had not, as yet, put into execution the hideous economy of selling his horses. In the evening she played billiards in a manly manner, and at odd hours she flirted, but not too forcibly, with Lord Calverly, Sir John, and with Captain Archinard in the beech-woods, or by lamplight effects in the drawing-room.

Peter had not forgotten Hilda and the strawberry beds, and one day Captain Archinard, who spent many of his hours at the Manor, was asked to bring his girls to tea.

Hilda and Katherine found Lord Calverly and Mrs. Marchant in the drawing-room with Mrs. Odd, and their father, after a cursory introduction, left them to sit, side by side, on two tall chairs, while he joined the trio. Mrs. Marchant moved away to a sofa, the Captain followed her, and Alicia and Lord Calverly were left alone near the two children.

Katherine was already making sarcastic mental notes as to the hospitality meted out to Hilda and herself, and Hilda stared hard at Mrs. Odd. Mrs. Odd was more beautiful than ever this afternoon in a white dress; Hilda wondered with dismay if Katherine could be right about her. Alicia, turning her head presently, met the wide absorbed gaze, and, with her charming smile, asked if they had brought their dogs—

" I saw such a lot of them about at your place the other day."

" We did n't know that you expected them to tea. We should have liked to bring them," said Katherine, and Hilda murmured with an echo-like effect : " We *should* have liked to ; Palamon howled dreadfully."

That Palamon's despair had been unnecessary made regret doubly keen.

" Hey ! What 's that ? " Lord Calverly had been staring at Hilda and heard the faint ejaculation ; "what is your dog called ? "

" Palamon." Hilda's voice was reserved ; she had already thought that she did not like Lord Calverly, and now that he looked at her, spoke to her, she was sure of it.

" What funny names you give your dogs," said Alicia. " The other is called Darwin," she added, looking at Lord Calverly with a laugh ; "but Palamon is pretty—prettier than the monkey gentleman. What made you call him that ? "

" It is out of ' The Knight's Tale,' " said Katherine ; " Hilda is very fond of it, and called her dogs after the two heroes, Palamon and Arcite."

Lord Calverly had been trying to tease Hilda by

53

the open admiration of his monocled gaze; the fixed gravity of her stare, like a pretty baby's, hugely amused him.

"So you like Chaucer?" Hilda averted her eyes, feeling very uncomfortable. "Strong meat that for babes," Lord Calverly added, looking at Alicia, who contemplated the children with pleasant vagueness.

"Never read it," she replied briskly; "not to remember. If I had had literary tastes in my infancy I might have read all the improper books without understanding them ; now I am too old to read them innocently."

Katherine listened to this dialogue with scorn for the speakers (she did not care for Chaucer, but she knew very well that to dispose of him as "improper" showed depths of Philistinism), and Hilda listened in alarm and wonder. Alicia's expressive eyebrows and gayly languid eyes made her even more uncomfortable than Lord Calverly's appreciative monocle —the monocle turning on her more than once while its wearer lounged with abrupt, lazy laughs near Alicia. Hilda wondered if Mrs. Odd liked a man who could so laugh and lounge, and a vague disquiet and trouble, a child's quick but ignorant sense of sadness stirred within her, for if Katherine had been right, then Mr. Odd must be unhappy. She sprang up with a long breath of relief and eagerness when he came in. Odd, with a half-humorous, half-cynical glance, took in the situation of his two little guests ; Alicia was evidently taking no trouble to claim them hers. He appreciated, too, Hilda's glad face.

"I'm sorry I have kept you waiting; are you ready for strawberries?"

He shook hands, smiling at them.

" Don't, please, put yourself out, Odd, in looking after my offspring," called the Captain; "they can find their way to the garden without an escort."

" But it won't put me out to take them ; it would put me out very much if I could n't," and Odd smiled his kindliest at Hilda, who stood dubious and hesitating.

Katherine thought it rather babyish to go into the garden for strawberries. She preferred to await tea in this atmosphere of unconscious inferiority; these grown-up people who did not talk to her, and who were yet so much duller than she and Hilda. When Hilda went out with Mr. Odd she picked up some magazines, and divided her attention between the pictures and the couples. Papa and Mrs. Marchant did not interest her, but she found Alicia's low, musical laughter, and the enjoyment with which she listened to Lord Calverly's half-muffled utterances, full of psychological suggestions that would read very well in her journal.

" He is probably flattering her," thought Katherine ; " that is what she likes best."

Meanwhile Hilda had forgotten Lord Calverly's stare and Alicia's frivolity ; she was so glad, so glad to be with her big friend again. He took her first to the picture gallery—having noticed as they went through a room that her eyes swerved to a Turner water-color with evident delight. Hilda was silent before the great Velasquez, the Holbein drawings, the Chardin and the Corot ; but as they went from picture to picture, she would look up at Odd with her confident, gentle smile, so that, after the half-

55

hour in the fine gallery, he felt sure that the child cared for the pictures as much as he did ; her silence was singularly sympathetic. As they went into the garden she confessed, in answer to his questions, that she would love to paint, to draw.

"All the beautiful, beautiful things to do!" she said ; "almost everything would be beautiful, would n't it, if one were great enough?"

The strawberry beds were visited, and—

"Shall we go down to the river and have a look at the scene of our first acquaintance?" asked Peter ; "we have plenty of time before tea." But, seeing the half-ashamed reluctance in Hilda's eyes, " Well, not there, then, but to the river ; there are even prettier places. Our boating-house is a mile from yours, and I 'll give you a paddle in my Canadian canoe,— such a pretty thing. You must sit very still, you know, or you 'll spill us both into the river."

"I should n't mind, as you would be there," laughed Hilda ; and so they went through the sunlit golden green of the beechwoods, and Hilda made the acquaintance of the Canadian canoe and of a mile or so of river that she had never seen before, and she and Peter talked together like the best and oldest of friends.

56

CHAPTER VII

ODD'S life of melancholy and good-humored resignation was cut short with an abruptness so startling that the needlessness of further resignation deepened the melancholy to a lasting habit of mind.

The melancholy that lies in the resignation to a ruinous mistake, the acceptance of ruin, and the nerving oneself to years of self-control and kindly endurance may well become a fine and bracing stoicism, but the shock of the irretrievably lost opportunity, the eternally irremediable mistake, gave a sensitive mind a morbid faculty of self-questioning and self-doubt that sapped the very springs of energy and confidence.

Mary's wedding came off in July, and when Mr. and Mrs. Apswith were gone for two months' cruising in a friend's yacht about the North Sea, Peter set to work with vigor. " The Sonnet " was in a year's time to make him famous in the world of letters. In September, Mary and her husband went to their house in Surrey, and there Peter paid her a visit. Alicia found a trip to Carlsbad with friends more desirable. The friends were thoroughly irreproachable—a middle-aged peer and his young and pretty but very sensible wife.

Peter, in allowing her to enjoy herself after her

57

own fashion, felt no weight of warning responsibility. But Alicia died suddenly at Carlsbad, and the horror of self-reproach, of bitter regret, that fell upon Odd when the news reached him at his sister's, was as unjust as it was poignant. At Allersley the general verdict was that Mrs. Odd's death had broken her husband's heart, and Allersley, though arguing from false premises, was not far wrong. Odd was nearly heart-broken. That Alicia's death should have lifted the weight of a fatal mistake from his life was a fact that tortured and filled him with remorse. Doubts and conjectures haunted him. Alicia might have dumbly longed for a sympathy for which she was unable to plead, and he to guess her longing. She had died away from him, without one word of mutual understanding, without one look of the love he once had felt and she accepted; and bitterest of all came the horrid realism of the thought that his absence had not made death more bitter to her. He shut himself up in the Manor for three weeks, seeing no one, and then, in sudden rebellion against this passive suffering, determined to go to India. He had a second sister married there. The voyage would distract him, and change, movement, he must have. The news spread quickly over Allersley, and Allersley approved of the wisdom of the decision.

At the Priory little Hilda Archinard was suffering in her way—the dreary suffering of childhood, with its sense of hopeless finality, of helpless inexperience. Chasms of desolation deepened within her as she heard that her friend was going away.

The sudden blossoming of her devotion to Odd

had widened her capabilities for conscious loneliness. Her loneliness became apparent to her,
and the immense place his smile, his kindness, her
confident sense of his goodness had filled in her
dreaming little life. Her aching pity for him was
confused by a vague terror for herself. She could
hardly bear the thought of his departure. Every
day she walked all along the hedges and walls that
divided the Priory from the Manor estate; but she
never saw him. The thought of not seeing him
again, which at first had seemed impossible, now
fixed upon her as a haunting obsession.

" Odd goes to-morrow," the Captain announced
one evening in the drawing-room. Katherine was
playing, not very conscientiously but rather cleverly,
a little air by Grieg. Hilda had a book on her lap,
but she was not reading, and her father's words
seemed to stop her heart in its heavy beating.

" I met Thompson "—Mr. Thompson was Peter's
land-agent—" and everything is settled. Poor chap!
Thompson says he 's badly broken up."

" How futile to mourn over death," Mrs. Archinard
sighed from her sofa. " Tangled as we are in the
webs of temperament, and environment, and circumstance, should we not rather rejoice at the release
from the great illusion ? " Mrs. Archinard laid down
a dreary French novel and vaguely yawned, while
the Captain muttered something about talking " rot "
before the children.

" Move this lamp away, Hilda," said Mrs. Archinard. " I think I can take a nap now, if Katherine
will put on the soft pedal."

It was a warm autumn night, and the windows

were open. Hilda slipped out when she had moved the lamp away.

She could not go by the country road, nor scramble through the hedge, but to climb over the wall would be an easy matter. Hilda ran over the lawn, across the meadows, and through the woods. In the uncanny darkness her white dress glimmered like the flitting wings of a moth. As she came to the wall the moon seemed to slide from behind a cloud. Hilda's heart stood still with a sudden terror at her loneliness there in the wood at night. The boy-like vault over the wall gave her an impetus of courage, and she began to run, feeling, as she ran, that the courage was only mechanical, that the moon, the mystery of a dimly seen infinity of tree trunks, the sorrow holding her heart as if in a physical pressure, were all terrible and terrifying. But Hilda, on occasions, could show an indomitable moral courage even while her body quaked, and she ran all the half-mile from the boundary wall to Allersley Manor without stopping. There was a light in the library window; even at a distance she had seen it glowing between the trees. She ran more slowly over the lawn, and paused on the gravel path outside the library to get her breath. Yes, *he* was there alone. She looked into the dignified quiet of the fine old room. A tall lamp threw a strong light on the pages of the book he held, and his head was in shadow. The window was ajar, and Hilda pushed it open and went in.

At the sound Odd glanced up, and his face took on a look of half incredulous stupefaction. Hilda's white face, tossed hair, the lamentable condition of her muslin frock, made of her indeed a startling apparition.

" My dear Hilda!" he exclaimed.

Hilda pressed her palms together, and stared silently at him. Mr. Odd's face looked so much older; its gravity made her heart stand still with an altogether new sense of calamity. She stood helplessly before him, tears brimming to her eyes.

" My dear child, what is the matter? You positively frightened me."

" I came to say 'Good-bye,' " said Hilda brokenly.

Peter's gravity was mere astonishment and sympathetic dismay. The tear-brimmed eyes, after his weeks of solitary brooding, filled him with a most exquisite rush of pity and tenderness.

"Come here, you dear child," he said, holding out his arms to her; "you came to say ' Good-bye?' I am very grateful to you."

Hilda leaned her head against his shoulder and wept. After the frozen nightmare moment, the old kindness was a delicious contrast ; she almost forgot the purport of her journey, though she knew that she was crying. Odd stroked her long hair; her tears slightly amused and slightly alarmed him, even while the pathos of the affection they revealed touched him deeply.

" Did you come alone ? " he asked.

Hilda nodded.

" That was a very plucky thing to do. I thank you for it. There, can't you smile at me? Don't cry."

"Oh, I love you *so* much, I can hardly bear it."

Peter felt uncomfortable. The capacity for suffering revealed in these words gave him a sense of responsibility. Poor child! Would her lot in life be to cry over people who were not worth it?"

"I shall come back some day, Hilda." Hilda stopped crying, and Peter was relieved by the sobs' cessation. "I have a wandering fit on me just now; you understand that, don't you?"

She held his hand tightly. She could not speak; her heart swelled so at his tone of mutual understanding.

"I am going to see my sister. I haven't seen her for five years; but long before another five years are passed I shall be here again, and the thing I shall most want to see when I get back will be your little face."

"But you will be different then, I will be different, we will both be changed." Hilda put her hands before her face and sobbed again. Peter was silent for a moment, rather aghast at the child's apprehension of the world's deepest tragedy. He could not tell her that they would be unchanged—he the man of thirty-five, she the girl of seventeen. Poor little Hilda! Her grief was but too well founded, and his thoughts wandered for a moment with Hilda's words far away from Hilda herself. Hilda wiped her eyes and sat upright. Odd looked at her. He had a keen sense of the unconventional in beauty, and her tears had not disfigured her small face—had only made it strange. He patted her cheek and smiled at her.

"Cheer up, little one!" She evidently tried to smile back.

"I am afraid you have idealized me, my child—

it 's a dangerous faculty. I am a very ordinary sort of person, Hilda; you must not imagine fine things about me nor care so much. I 'm not worth one of those tears, poor little girl ! "

It was difficult to feel amused before her solemn gaze; a sage prophecy of inevitable recovery would be brutal; to show too much sympathy equally cruel. But the reality of her feeling dignified her grief, and he found himself looking gravely into her large eyes.

" You 're not worth it ? " she repeated.

" No, really."

" I don't imagine things about you."

" Well, I am glad of that," said Peter, feeling rather at a loss.

" I love you dearly,"said Hilda, with a certain air of dreary dignity ; "you are you. I don't have to imagine anything."

Odd put her hand to his lips and kissed it gently.

" Thank you, my dear child. I love you too, and certainly I don't have to imagine anything."

Hilda's eyes, with their effect of wide, almost unseeing expansion, rested on his for a moment longer. She drew herself up, and a look of reso-lution, self-control, and fidelity hardened her young face. Odd still felt somewhat disconcerted, some-what at a loss.

" I must go now; they don't know that I am here."

" They did n't know that you were coming, I suppose ? "

" No ; they would n't have let me come if I had told them before, but I will tell them now."

63

"Well, we will tell them together."

"Are you going to take me home?"

"Did you imagine that I would let you go alone?"

"You are very kind."

"And what are you, then? Your shoes are wringing wet, my child. Your dress is thin, too, for this time of year. Wrap this coat of mine around you. There! and put on this hat."

Peter laughed as he coiffed her in the soft felt hat that came down over her ears; she looked charming and quaint in the grotesque costume. Hilda responded with a quiet, patient little smile, gathering together the wide sleeves of the covert coat. Odd lit a cigar, put on his own hat, took her hand, and they sallied forth.

"You came across, I suppose?"

"Yes, by the woods."

"And you were n't frightened?"

He felt the patient little smile in the darkness as she replied—

"You know already that I am a coward."

"I know, on the contrary, that you are amazingly courageous. The flesh may be weak, but the spirit is willing with a vengeance. Eh, Hilda?"

"Yes," said Hilda vaguely.

They walked in silence through the woods. Clouds hid the moon, and the wind had risen.

Peter had dreary thoughts. He felt like a ghost in the ghost-like unreality of existence. The walk through the melancholy dimness seemed symbolical of a wandering, aimless life. The touch of Hilda Archinard's little hand in his was comforting. When they had passed through the Priory shrubbery and were nearing the house, Hilda's step beside him paused.

"Will you kiss me 'Good-bye' here, not before them all?"

"What beastly things 'Good-byes' are," Odd said, looking down at the glimmering oval of her uplifted face; "what thoroughly beastly things." He took the little face between his hands and kissed her: "Good-bye, dear little Hilda."

"Thank you so much—for everything," she said.

"Thank you, my child. I shall not forget you."

"Don't be different. *Try* not to change."

"Ah, Hilda! Hilda!"

That she, not he, would change was the inevitable thing. He stooped and kissed again the child beside him.

5   65

Part I
KATHERINE

CHAPTER I

ODD knew that he was late as he drove down the Champs Elysées in a rattling, closed *fiacre*. He and Besseint had talked so late into the evening that he had barely had time to get to his hotel in the Marbœuf quarter and dress.

Besseint was one of the cleverest French writers of the day ; he and Peter had battled royally and delightfully over the art of writing, and as Besseint was certainly more interesting than would be the dinner at the Embassy, Peter felt himself excusable.

Lady —— welcomed him unresentfully—

" Just, only just in time. I am going to send you down with Miss Archinard—over there talking to my husband—she is such a clever girl."

Peter was conscious of a shock of surprise ; a shock so strong that Lady —— saw a really striking change come over his face. Peter himself was startled by his own pleasure and eagerness.

" Evidently you know her ; and evidently you *were* going to be bored and are *not* going to be now ! Your change of expression is really unflattering ! " Lady —— laughed good humoredly.

" I have n't seen her for ten years ; we were the greatest chums. Oh ! it is n't Hilda, then ! " Odd caught sight of the young lady.

" I am *very* sorry it is n't 'Hilda.' Hilda is the

69

beauty; she is, unfortunately, almost an unknown quantity; but Katherine will be a stepping-stone, and I assure you that she is worth cultivation on her own account."

Yes, Katherine was a stepping-stone; that atoned somewhat for the disappointment that Odd felt as he followed his hostess across the room.

"Miss Archinard—an old friend. Mr. Odd tells me he has not seen you for ten years."

"Mr. Odd!" cried Miss Archinard. She was evidently very glad to see him.

"It is astonishing, isn't it?" said Peter. "Ten years does mean something, doesn't it?"

"So much and yet so little. It hasn't changed you a bit," said Katherine. "And here is papa. Papa, isn't this nice? Mr. Odd, do you remember the day you fished Hilda out of the river? Poor Hilda! And her romantic farewell escapade?"

Captain Archinard was changed; his hair had become very white, and his good looks well worn, but his greeting had the cordiality of old friendship.

"And Hilda?" Peter questioned, as he and Katherine went into the dining-room together. "Hilda is well? And as lovely as ever?"

"Well, and as lovely as ever," Katherine assured him. "She is not here because she rarely goes out. Papa and I are the frivolous members of the family. Mamma goes in for culture, and Hilda for art." Peter had a good look at her as they sat side by side.

Katherine was no more beautiful than in childhood, but she was distinctly interesting and—yes—distinctly charming. Her black eyes, deeply set under broad eyebrows, held the same dominant

significance; humorous, cynical, clever eyes. Her
white teeth gave a brilliant gayety to her smile.
There was distinction in her coiffure—the thick
deeply rippled hair parted on one side, and coiled
smoothly from crown to neck; and Peter recognized
in her dress a personal taste as distinctive—the long
unbroken lines of her nasturtium velvet gown were
untinged by any hint of so-called artistic dowdiness,
and yet the dress wrinkled about her waist as she
moved with a daring elegance far removed from
the moulded conventionality of the other women's
bodices. This glowing gown was cut off the shoulders; Katherine's shoulders were beautiful, and
they were triumphantly displayed.

"And now, please tell me," said Peter, "how it
comes that I haven't seen you for ten years?"

"How comes it that we have not seen *you?* You
have been everywhere, and so have we; really it is
odd that we should never have met. Of course
you know that we left the Priory only a year after
you went to India?"

Peter nodded.

"I was dismayed to find you gone when I got
back. I heard vague rumors of Florence, and when
I went there one winter you had disappeared."

"We must have been in Dresden. How I hated
it! All the shabby second-rate culture of the world
seems to gravitate to Dresden. We had to let the
Priory, you know. We are so horribly poor."

Katherine's smiling assertion was not carried out
in her appearance, yet the statement put a bond of
familiarity between them; Katherine spoke as to
an old friend who had a right to know.

" Then we had a year or two at Dinard—loathsome place I think it ! Then Florence again, and at last Paris, and here we have been for over three years, and here we shall probably stick for who knows how long ! Hilda's painting gives us a reasonable background ; at least as reasonable as such exiles can hope for."

" But you don't mean to say that your exile is indefinite ? "

Katherine nodded, with eyebrows lifted and a suggestion of shrug in the creamy expanse of shoulder.

" And Hilda paints ? Well ? "

" Hilda paints really well. She has always painted, and her work is really individual, unaffectedly individual, and that's the rare thing, you know. Over four years of atelier work did n't scotch Hilda's originality, and she has a studio of her own now, and is never happy out of it."

" What kind of work does she go in for ? " Peter was conscious of a vague uneasiness about Hilda. " Portraits ? "

" No ; Hilda is not very good at likenesses. Her things are very decorative—not Japanese either— except in their air of choice and selection ; well, you must see them, they really are original, and, in their own little way, quite delightful ; they are, perhaps, a wee bit like baby Whistlers—not that I intimate any real resemblance—but the sense of color, the harmony ; but you must see them," Katherine repeated.

" And Mrs. Archinard ? " Peter felt some remorse at having forgotten that rather effaced personality.

" Mamma is just the same, only stronger than

she used to be in England. I think the Continent suits her better. And now *you*, Mr. Odd. The idea of talking about such nobodies as we are when you have become such a personage ! You have become rather cynical too, have n't you ? As a child you did not make a cynical impression on me, and your ' Dialogues ' did. I think you are even more cynical than Renan. Some stupid person spoke to me of a *rapport* between your ' Dialogues ' and his ' Dialogues Philosophiques.' I don't imply that, except that you are both sceptical and both smiling, only your smile is more bitter, your scepticism less frivolous."

" I 'm sceptical as to people, not as to principles," said Peter, smiling not bitterly.

" Yet you are not a misanthrope, you do not hate people."

" I don't admire them."

" You would like to help them to become more admirable. Ah ! The Anglo-Saxon is strong within you. You are not at all like Renan. And then you went in for Parliamentary honors too ; three years ago, was n't it ? Why did n't you keep on ? "

" Because I did n't keep my seat when my party went out. The honors were dubious, Miss Archinard. I cut a very ineffective figure."

" I remember meeting a man here at the time who said you were n't ' practical,' and I liked you for it too. If only you had kept in we should surely have met. Hilda and I were in London this spring."

" Were you ? And I was in Japan. I only got back three weeks ago."

" How you do dash about the globe. But you have been to Allersley since getting back ? "

" Only for a day or two. But tell me about your spring in London."

" We were with Lady Mainwaring."

" Ah, I did not see her when I was at Allersley. That accounts for my having had no news of you. You did not see my sister in London ; she has been in the country all this year. You went to Court, I suppose ? "

" Yes, Lady Mainwaring presented us."

" And Hilda enjoyed herself ? "

Katherine smiled : " How glad you will be to see Hilda. Yes, enjoyed herself after a fashion, I think. She only stopped a month. She does n't care much for that sort of thing really."

Katherine did not say, hardly knew perhaps, that the reproachful complaint of Mrs. Archinard's weekly letter had cut short Hilda's season, and brought her back to the little room in the little *appartement*, *3ième au dessus de l'entresol*, where Mrs. Archinard spent her days as she had spent them at Allersley, at Dresden, at Dinard, at Florence. Change of surroundings made no change in Mrs. Archinard's lace-frilled recumbency, nor in the air of passive long-suffering that went with so much appreciation of her own merits and other people's deficiencies.

" But Hilda's month meant more than other girls' years," Katherine went on ; " you may imagine the havoc she played, all unconsciously, poor Hilda ! Hilda is the most unconscious person. She fixes one with those big vague eyes of hers. She fixed, among other people, another old friend," and Katherine smiled, adding with lowered tone, " Allan Hope."

74

Peter was not enough conscious of a certain inner irritation to attempt its concealment.

"Allan Hope?" he repeated. "It is impossible for me to imagine little Hilda with lovers; and Allan Hope one of them!"

"Allan Hope is very nice," Katherine said lightly.

"Nice? Oh, thoroughly nice. But to think that Hilda is grown up, not a child."

Odd looked with a certain tired playfulness at Katherine.

"And you are grown up too; have lovers too. What a pity it is."

"That depends." Katherine laughed. "But regrets of that kind are unnecessary as far as Hilda is concerned. I don't think little Hilda is much less the child than when you last saw her. Having lovers does n't imply that one is ready for them, and I don't think that Hilda is ready."

Odd had looked away from her again, and Katherine's black eyes rested on him with a sort of musing curiosity. She had not spoken quite truthfully in saying that the ten years had left him unchanged. A good deal of white in the brown hair, a good many lines about eyes and mouth might not constitute change, but Katherine had seen, in her first keen clear glance at the old friend, that these badges of time were not all.

There had been something still boyish about the Mr. Odd of ten years ago; the lines at the eye corners were still smiling lines, the quiet mouth still kind; but the whole face wore the weary, almost heavy look of middle age.

"His Parliamentary experience probably knocked

the remaining illusions out of him," Katherine reflected. "He was certainly very unsuccessful, he
tried for such a lot too, sought obstacles. He should
mellow a bit now (that smile of his is bitter) into
resignation, give up the windmill hunt (I think all
nice men go through the Quixotic phase), stop at
home and write homilies. And he certainly, certainly ought to marry; marry a woman who would
be nice to him." And it was characteristic of
Katherine that already she was turning over in her
mind the question as to whether it would be feasible,
or rather desirable—for Katherine intended to please
herself, and had not many doubts as to possibilities
if once she could make up her mind—to contemplate
that rôle for herself. Miss Archinard was certainly
the last woman in the world to be suspected of
matrimonial projects; her frank, almost manly bon-
homie, and her apparent indifference to ineligibility
had combined to make her doubly attractive ; and
indeed Katherine was no husband-hunter. She
would choose, not seek. She certainly intended to
get married, and to a husband who would make life
definitely pleasant, definitely successful ; and she
was very keenly conscious of the eligibility or unfitness of every man she met ; only as the majority
had struck her as unfit, Miss Archinard was still
unmarried. Now she said to herself that Peter Odd
would certainly be nice to his wife, that his position
was excellent — not glittering — Katherine would
have liked glitter, and the more the better; and yet
with that long line of gentlefolk ancestry, that old
Elizabethan house and estate, far above the shallow
splendor of modern dukedoms or modern wealth, fit

only to impress ignorance or vulgarity. He had money too, a great deal. Money was a necessity if one wanted a life free for highest flights; and she added very calmly that she might herself, after consideration, find it possible to be nice to him. Rather amusing, Katherine thought it, to meet a man whom one could at once docket as eligible, and find him preoccupied with a dreamy memory of such slight importance as Hilda's child friendship; but Katherine's certainty of the slightness—and this man of forty looked anything but sentimental— left her very tolerant of his preoccupation.

Hilda was a milestone, a very tiny milestone in his life, and it was to the distant epoch her good-bye on that autumn night had marked as ended, rather than to the little closing chapter itself, that he was looking. Indeed his next words showed as much.

"How many changes—forgive the truism, of course—in ten years! Did you know that my sister, Mrs. Apswith, had half-a-dozen babies? I find myself an uncle with a vengeance."

"I have n't seen Mrs. Apswith since she was married. It does seem ages ago, that wedding."

"Mary has drawn a lucky number in life," said Odd absently.

"She expects you to settle down definitely now, I suppose; in England, at Allersley?"

"Yes, I shall. I shall go back to Allersley in a few months. It is rather lonely."

"Why don't you fill it with people?"

"You forget that I don't like people," said Odd.

"You prefer loneliness, with your principles for company. There will be something of martyrdom,

77

then, when you at last settle down to your duty as landowner and country gentleman."

" Oh, I shall do it without any self-glorification. Perhaps you will come back to the Priory. That would mitigate the loneliness."

" The sense of our nearness. Of course you would n't care to see us! No, I think I prefer Paris to the Priory."

" What do you do with yourself in Paris?"

" Very little that amounts to anything," Katherine owned; " one can't very well when one is poor and not a genius. If one is n't born with them, one must buy weapons before one can fight. I feel I should be a pretty good fighter if I had my weapons!" and Katherine's dark eye, as it flashed round on him in a smile, held the same suggestion of gallant daring with which she had impressed him on that morning by the river ten years ago. He looked at her contemplatively; the dark eyes pleased him.

"Yes," he said, "I think you would be a good fighter. What would you fight?"

" The world, of course: and one only can with its own weapons, more's the pity."

" And the flesh and the devil," Odd suggested; "is this to be a moral crusade?"

" I 'm afraid I can't claim that. I only want to conquer for the fun of conquering; 'to ride in triumph through Persepolis,' like Tamburlaine, chain up people I don't like in cages! Oh, of course, Persepolis would be a much nicer place when once I held it, I should be delightful to the people I liked."

" And all the others would be in cages!"

78

" They would deserve it if I put them there ! I 'm very kind-hearted, very tolerant."
" And when you have conquered the world, what then ? As life is not all marching and caging."
" I shall live in it after my own fashion. I am ambitious, Mr. Odd, but not meanly so, I assure you."
" No ; not meanly so, I am sure." Odd's eyes were quietly scrutinizing, as, another sign of the ten years, he adjusted a pair of eyeglasses and looked at her, but not, as Katherine felt, unsympathetic.
" And meanwhile? you will find your weapons in time, no doubt, but, meanwhile, what do you do with yourself ? "
" Meanwhile I study my *milieu*. I go out a good deal, if one can call it going out in this dubious Parisian, Anglo-American *mélange ;* I read a bit, and I bicycle in the Bois with papa in the morning. It sounds like sentimentality, but I do feel that there is an element of tragedy in papa and myself bicy-cling. Oh, for a ride across country ! "
" You rode so well, too, Mary told me."
" Yes, I rode well, otherwise I should n't regret it." Katherine smiled with even more assurance under the added intensity of the *pince-nez*.
" You enjoy the excelling, then, more than the feeling."
" That sounds vain ; I certainly should n't feel pleasure if I were conscious of playing second fiddle to anybody."
" A very vain young lady," Odd's smile was quite alertly interested, " and a self-conscious young lady, too."

"Yes, rather, I think," Katherine owned; frankness became her, "but I am very conscious of everything, myself included. I am merely one among the many phenomena that come under my notice, and, as I am the nearest of them all, naturally the most intimately interesting. Every one is self-conscious, Mr. Odd, if they have any personality at all."

"And you are clever," Peter pursued, in a tone of enumeration, his smile becoming definitely humorous as he added: "And I am very impudent."

Katherine was not sure that she had made just the effect she had aimed for, but certainly Mr. Odd would give her credit for frankness.

It was agreed that he should come for tea the next afternoon.

"After five," Katherine said; "Hilda does n't get in till so late; and I know that Hilda is the *clou* of the occasion."

"Does Hilda take her painting so seriously as all that?"

"She does n't care about anything, *anything* else," Katherine said gravely, adding, still gravely, "Hilda is very, very lovely."

"I hope you were n't too much disappointed," Lady —— said to Odd, just before he was going; "is she not a charming girl?"

"She really is; the disappointment was only comparative. It was Hilda whom I knew so well. The dearest little girl."

"I have not seen much of her," Lady —— said, with some vagueness of tone. "I have called on Mrs. Archinard, a very sweet woman, clever, too;

but the other girl was never there. I don't fancy she is much help to her mother, you know, as Katherine is. Katherine goes about, brings people to see her mother, makes a *milieu* for her; such a sad invalid she is, poor dear! But Hilda is wrapt up in her work, I believe. Rather a pity, don't you think, for a girl to go in so seriously for a fad like that? She paints very nicely, to be sure; I fancy it all goes into that, you know."

"What goes into that?" Odd asked, conscious of a little temper; all seemed combined to push Hilda more and more into a slightly derogatory and very mysterious background.

"Well, she is not so clever as her sister. Katherine can entertain a roomful of people. Grace, tact, sympathy, the impalpable something that makes success of the best kind, Katherine has it."

Katherine's friendly, breezy frankness had certainly amused and interested Odd at the dinnertable, but Lady ——'s remarks now produced in him one of those quick and unreasoning little revulsions of feeling by which the judgments of a half-hour before are suddenly reversed. Katherine's cleverness was that of the majority of the girls he took down to dinner, rather *voulu*, banal, tiresome. Odd felt that he was unjust, also that he was a little cross.

"There are some clevernesses above entertaining a roomful of people. After all, success isn't the test, is it?"

Lady —— smiled, an unconvinced smile—

"You should be the last person to say that."

"I?" Odd made no attempt to contradict the

6   81

evident flattery of his hostess' tones, but his ejaculation meant to himself a volume of negatives. If success were the test, he was a sorry failure.

He was making his way out of the room when Captain Archinard stopped him.

"I have hardly had one word with you, Odd," said the Captain, whose high-bridged nose and finely set eyes no longer saved his face from its fundamental look of peevish pettiness. "Mrs. Brooke is going to take Katherine home. It's a fine night, won't you walk?"

Odd accepted the invitation with no great satisfaction; he had never found the Captain sympathetic. After lifting their hats to Mrs. Brooke and Katherine as they drove out of the Embassy Courtyard, the two men turned into the Rue du Faubourg St. Honoré together.

"We are not far from you, you know," the Captain said—"Rue Pierre Charron; you said you were in the Marbœuf quarter, did n't you? We are rather near the Trocadero, uphill, so I'll leave you at the door of your hotel."

They lit cigars and walked on rather silently. The late October night was pleasantly fresh, and the Champs Elysées, as they turned into it, almost empty between the upward sweep of its line of lights.

"Ten years is a jolly long time," remarked Captain Archinard, "and a jolly lot of disagreeable things may happen in ten years. You knew we'd left the Priory, of course?"

"I was very sorry to hear it."

"Devilish hard luck. It was n't a choice of evils,

though, if that is any consolation; it was that or
starvation."

" As bad as that ? "

" Just as bad; the horses went first, and then
some speculations—safe enough they seemed, and,
sure enough, went wrong. So that, with one thing
and another, I hardly knew which way to turn. To
tell the truth, I simply can't go back to England.
I have a vague idea of a perfect fog of creditors. I
have been able to let the Priory, but the place is
mortgaged up to the hilt; and devilish hard work
it is to pay the interest; and hard luck it is altogether," the Captain repeated. " Especially hard
on a man like me. My wife is perfectly happy. I
keep all worry from her; she does n't know anything about my troubles; she lives as she has always
lived. I make that a point, sacrifice myself rather
than deprive her of one luxury." The tone in which
the Captain alluded to his privations rather made
Peter doubt their reality. " And the two children
live as they enjoy it most; a very jolly time they
have of it. But what is my life, I ask you ? " The
Captain's voice was very resentful. Odd almost felt
that he in some way was to blame for the good
gentleman's unhappy situation. " What is my life,
I ask you ? I go dragging from post to pillar with
stale politics in the morning, and five o'clock tea
in grass widows' drawing-rooms for all distraction.
Paris is full of grass widows," he added, with an even
deepened resentment of tone ; "and I never cared
much about the play, and French actresses are so
deuced ugly, at least I find them so, even if I cared
about that sort of thing, which I never did—much,"

and the Captain drew disconsolately at his cigar, taking it from his lips to look at the tip as they passed beneath a lamp.

"I can hardly afford myself tobacco any longer," he declared, " smokable tobacco. Thought I 'd economize on these, and they 're beastly, like all economical things!" And the Captain cast away the cigar with a look of disgust.

Peter offered him a substitute.

"You are a lucky dog, Odd, to come to contrasts," the Captain paused to shield his lighted match as he applied it to the fresh cigar; "I don't see why things should be so deuced uneven in this world. One fellow born with a silver spoon in his mouth—and you 've got a turn for writing, too ; once one's popular, that 's the best paying thing going, I suppose—and the other hunted all over Europe, through no fault of his own either. Rather hard, I think, that the man who does n't need money should be born with a talent for making it."

"It certainly is n't just."

"Damned unjust."

Odd felt that he was decidedly a culprit, and smiled as he smoked and walked beside the rebellious Captain. He was rather sorry for him. Odd had wide sympathies, and found whining, feeble futility pathetic, especially as there was a certain amount of truth in the Captain's diatribes, the old eternal truth that things are not evenly divided in this badly managed world. It would be kinder to immediately offer the loan for which the Captain was evidently paving the way to a request. But he reflected that the display of such quickness of comprehension might make the request too easy; and in the future the Captain might profit by a discovered weakness a little too freely. He would let him ask. And the Captain was not long in coming to the point. He was in a devilish tight place, positively could n't afford a pair of boots (Peter's eyes involuntarily sought the Captain's feet, neatly shod in social patent-leather), could Odd let him have one hundred pounds? (The Captain was frank enough to make no mention of repayment) etc., etc.

Peter cut short the explanation with a rather unwise manifestation of sympathetic comprehension; the Captain went upstairs with him to his room when the hotel was reached, and left it with a check for 3000 francs in his pocket; the extra 500 francs were the price of Peter's readiness.

CHAPTER II

I T rained next day, and Peter took a *fiacre* from the Bibliothèque Nationale, where he had spent the afternoon diligently, and drove through the gray evening to the Rue Pierre Charron. It was just five when he got there, and already almost dark. There were four flights to be ascended before one reached the Archinards' apartment; four steep and rather narrow flights, for the house was not one of the larger newer ones, and there was no lift. Wilson, whom Odd remembered at Allersley, opened the door to him. Captain Archinard had evidently not denuded himself of a valet when he had parted with his horses; that sacrifice had probably seemed too monstrous, but Peter wondered rather whether Wilson's wages were ever paid, and thought it more probable that a mistaken fidelity attached him to his master. In view of year-long arrears, he might have found it safer to stay with a future possibility of payment than, by leaving, put an end forever to even the hope of compensation.

The little entrance was very pretty, and the drawing-room, into which Peter was immediately ushered, even prettier. Evidently the Archinards had brought their own furniture, and the Archinards had very good taste. The pale gray-greens of the room were

86

charming. Peter noticed appreciatively the Copenhagen vases filled with white flowers; he could find time for appreciation as he passed to Mrs. Archinard's sofa, for no one else was in the room, a fact of which he was immediately and disappointedly aware. Mrs. Archinard was really improved. Her husband's monetary embarrassments had made even less impression on her than upon the surroundings, for though the little salon was very pretty, it was not the Priory drawing-room, and Mrs. Archinard was, if anything, plumper and prettier than when Peter had last seen her.

" This is really quite too delightful! Quite too delightful, Mr. Odd! " Mrs. Archinard's slender hand pressed his with seemingly affectionate warmth. " Katherine told us this morning about the *rencontre*. I was expecting you, as you see. Ten years! It seems impossible, really impossible! " Still holding his hand, she scanned his face with her sad and pretty smile. " I could hardly realize it, were it not that your books lie here beside me, living symbols of the years."

Peter indeed saw, on the little table by the sofa, the familiar bindings.

" I asked Katherine to get them out, so that I might look over them again; strengthen my impression of your personality, join all the links before meeting you again. Dear, dear little books! " Mrs. Archinard laid her hand, with its one great emerald ring, on the " Dialogues," which was uppermost. " Sit down, Mr. Odd ; no, on this chair. The light falls on your face so. Yes, your books are to me among the most exquisite art productions of our age.

Pater is more *étincellant*—a style too jewelled perhaps—one wearies of the chain of rather heartless
beauty; but in your books one feels the heart, the
aroma of life—a chain of flowers, flowers do not
weary. Your personality is to me very sympathetic,
Mr. Odd, very sympathetic."

Peter was conscious of being sorry for it.

"I think we are both of us tired." Mrs. Archinard's smile grew even more sadly sweet; "both
tired, both hopeless, both a little indifferent too.
How few things one finds to care about! Things
crumble so, once touched, do they not? Everything crumbles." Mrs. Archinard sighed, and, as
Peter found nothing to say ("How dull a man who
writes quite clever books can be!" thought Mrs.
Archinard), she went on in a more commonplace
tone—

"And you talked with dear Katherine last night;
you pleased her. She told Hilda and me this morning that you really pleased her immensely. Katherine is hard to please. I am proud of my girl, Mr.
Odd, very, very proud. Did you not find her quite
distinctive? Quite significant? I always think of
Katherine as significant, many facetted, meaning
much." The murmuring modulations of Mrs. Archinard's voice irritated Odd to such a pitch of ill-tem-
per that he found it difficult to keep his own pleasant
as he replied—

"Significant is most applicable. She is a charming girl."

"Yes, charming; that too applies, and oh, what a
misapplied word it is! Every woman nowadays
is called charming. The daintily distinctive term is

flung at the veriest schoolroom hoyden, as at the hard, mechanical woman of the world."

Peter now said to himself that Mrs. Archinard was an ass—very unjustly—Mrs. Archinard was far from being an ass. She felt the atmosphere with unerring promptitude. Her effects were not to be made upon *ce type là.* She welcomed Katherine's entrance as a diversion from looming boredom. Katherine seemed to go in for a regal simplicity in dress. Her gown was again of velvet, a deep amethyst color. The high collar and the long sleeves that came over her white hands in points were edged with a narrow line of sable. A necklace of amethysts lightly set in gold encircled the base of her throat. Peter liked to see a well-dressed woman, and Katherine was more than well dressed. In the pearly tints of the room she made a picture with her purple gleams and shadows.

" I *am* glad to see you. Sit down. It is nice to have you in our little diggings. You are like a bit of England sitting there—a big bit ! "

" And you are a perfectly delightful condensation of everything delightfully Parisian."

" The heart is British. True oak ! " laughed Katherine ; " don't judge me by the foliage."

" Ah, but it needs a good deal of Gallic genius to choose such foliage."

" No, no. I give the credit to my American blood, to mamma. But thanks, very much. I am glad you are appreciative." Katherine smiled so gayly, and looked so charmingly in the amethyst velvet, that Peter forgot for a moment to wonder where Hilda was, but Katherine did not forget.

89

" I expect Hilda every moment. I have told them to wait tea until she comes, poor dear! 'Them ' is Wilson, whom you saw, I suppose ; Taylor, our old maid ; and the cook! The cook is French, otherwise our staff is shrunken, but of the same elements. One does n't mind having no servants in a little box like this. Yes, mamma, I have paid *all* the calls, and only two people were out; so I deserve petting and tea. I hope Hilda will hurry." Mrs. Archinard's face took on a look of ill-used resignation.

" We all pay dearly for Hilda's egotism," she remarked, and for a moment there was a rather uncomfortable silence. Odd felt a queer indignation and a queerer melancholy rising within him.

The Hilda of to-day seemed far further away than the Hilda of ten years ago. They talked in a rather desultory fashion for some time. Mrs. Archinard's presence was damping, and even Katherine's smile was like a flower seen through rain. The little clock on the mantelpiece struck the quarter.

" Almost six ! " exclaimed Katherine ; " we must have tea."

" Yes, we may sacrifice ourselves, but we must not sacrifice Mr. Odd," said Mrs. Archinard with distinct fretfulness. Taylor answered the bell, and Peter, with a quickness of combination that surprised himself, surmised that Hilda was out alone. Had she become emancipated ? Bohemian ? His melancholy grew stronger. Tea was brought, a charming set of daintiest white and a little silver teapot of a quaint and delicate design.

" Hilda designed it in Florence," said Katherine, seeing him looking at it; " an Italian friend had it made for her after her own model and drawings. Yes, Hilda goes in for decorative work a good deal. People who know about it have admired that teapot, as you do, I see."

"It's a lovely thing," said Peter, as Katherine turned it before him; "the simplicity of the outline and the delicate bas-relief"—he bent his head to look more closely—"exquisite." And he thought it rather rough on Hilda; to pour the tea from her own teapot without waiting for her.

Still, he owned, when at last the door-bell rang at fully half-past six, that he might have been asking for too much patience.

"There she is," said Katherine; "I must go and tell her that you are here." Katherine went out, and Odd heard a murmured colloquy in the entrance. He was conscious of feeling excited, and unconsciously rose to his feet and looked eagerly toward the door. But only Katherine came in.

"I don't believe I shall ever see Hilda!" he exclaimed, with an assumption of exasperation that hid some real nervousness. Katherine laughed.

"Oh yes, you shall, in five minutes. She had to wash her face and hands. Artists are untidy people, you know," and Odd, with that same strange acuteness of perception with which he seemed dowered this afternoon, felt that Hilda had been coming in in all her artistic untidiness, and that Katherine had seen to a more respectable *entrée*.

It rather irritated him with Katherine, and that tactful young lady probably guessed at his disappointment, for she went to the piano and began to play a sad aria from one of Schumann's Sonatas that sighed and pled and sobbed. She played very well, with the same perfect taste that she showed in her gowns, and Peter was too fond of music, too fond of Schumann especially, not to listen to her.

In the middle of the aria Hilda came in. It was over in a moment, the meeting, as the most exciting things in life are. Peter had not realized till the moment came how much it would excite him.

Hilda came in and walked up to him. She put her hand in his with all the pretty gravity he remembered in the child. Odd took the other hand too and stared at her. He was conscious then of being very much excited, and conscious that she was not.

Her eyes were "big and vague," but they were the most beautiful eyes he had ever seen, and the vagueness was only in a certain lack of expression, for they looked straight into his. Carried along by that first impulse of excitement, despite the little shock of half-felt disappointment, Peter bent his head and kissed her on each cheek.

" Bravo ! " said Katherine, still striking soft chords at the piano, " Bravo, Mr. Odd ! considering your first meeting and your last parting, you have a right to that ! " And Katherine laughed pleasantly, though she was a trifle displeased.

" Yes, I have, have n't I ? " said Peter, smiling. He still held Hilda's hands. The little flush that had come to her cheeks when he had kissed her was gone, and she looked very white.

" Are you glad to see me, Hilda ? " he asked ; " I beg your pardon, but it comes naturally to call you that."

" I am very glad to see you, Mr. Odd," Hilda

smiled. Her voice was very like the child's voice saying, "I thank you very much," ten years ago. The same voice, grave and gentle. Odd had expected some little warmth, some little embarrassment even, in the girl, considering the parting from the child. But Hilda did not show any warmth, neither did she seem at all embarrassed, and Odd felt rather as one does when an unnecessary downward stride reveals level ground where one expected another step. He had stumbled a little, and now, half ruefully, half humorously, he considered the child Hilda grown up. She sat down near her mother.

"I am so sorry. I am afraid you waited for me," she said, bending towards her; "I really couldn't help it, mamma."

"No, I think it kindest to consider you irresponsible; there is certainly an element of insanity in your exaggerated devotion to your work." Mrs. Archinard smiled acidly, and Hilda, Odd thought, did look a little embarrassed now. He had adjusted himself to the reality of the present, and was able to study her. The same Botticelli Madonna mouth, the same Gainsborough eyes; the skin of dazzling whiteness—an almost unnatural white—but she was evidently tired.

Certainly her black gown looked strangely beside Katherine's velvet, Mrs. Archinard's silk and laces. Odd saw that there was mud on the skirt, a very short skirt, and Hilda's legs were very long. She had walked, then. His own paternal solicitude struck him as amusing, and rather touching, as he glanced at her slim feet, to see with satis-

93

faction that wet boots had been replaced by patent-leather shoes—heelless little shoes.

"I am afraid you work too much, you tire yourself," he said, for after her mother's rebuff she had sunk back in her chair with a weary lassitude of pose. Hilda immediately sat up straightly, giving him an almost frightened glance. How unchanged the little face, though the cloud of her hair no longer framed it. Hilda's hair was as smooth as her sister's, only it was brushed straight back, and the soft blue-black coils were massed from ear to ear, and showed, in a coronet-like effect above her head, almost too much hair; it emphasized the pale fragility of her look.

"Oh no, I am not tired," she said, "not particularly. I walked home, you see. I am very fond of walking."

"Hilda is fond of such funny things," said Katherine, coming from the piano, "of walking in the mud and rain for instance. She is the most persistently, consistently energetic person I ever knew." Katherine paused pleasantly as though for Hilda to speak, but Hilda said nothing and looked even more vague than before, almost dull in fact.

"Well, she has had no tea," said Odd, "and after mud and rain that is rather cruel, even as a punishment."

Again Hilda gave him the alarmed quick glance; his eyes were humorously kind, and she smiled a slight little smile.

"Some tea!" Katherine cried; "my poor Hilda, I'm afraid it is hard-boiled by this time"—she laid her hand on the teapot—"and *almost* cold. Shall I heat some more water, dear?"

"Oh! don't think of it, Katherine, it is almost dinner-time."

"Must I be off?" asked Odd, laughing.

"How absurd; we don't dine till eight," Katherine said.

"It wasn't a hint to me, then, Hilda?" Hilda looked helplessly distressed.

"A hint? Oh no, no. How could you think that?"

"I was only joking. I didn't really believe you so anxious to get rid of an old friend." Odd, with some determination, crossed the room and sat down beside her.

"I want to see a great deal of you if you will let me."

"No one sees much of Hilda, not even her own mother," said Mrs. Archinard from her sofa. "It is terrible indeed to feel oneself a cumberer of the earth, unable to suffice to oneself, far less to others. With my failing eyesight I simply cannot read by lamplight, and there are three or four hours at this season when I am absolutely without resources. Yet even those hours Hilda cannot give me."

Hilda now looked so painfully embarrassed that Odd was perforce obliged, for very pity's sake, to avert his eyes from her face.

"Ah, Mr. Odd," Mrs. Archinard went on, "you do not know what that is. To lie in the gray dusk and watch one's own gray, gray thoughts."

"It must be very unpleasant," Odd owned unwillingly, feeling that his character of old friend was

95

being rather imposed upon ; this degree of intimacy was certainly unwarranted.

" Now, mamma, you usually have friends every afternoon," said Katherine, in her pleasant, even voice. She was preparing some fresh tea. " You make me as well as Hilda feel a culprit."

" No, my dear." Mrs. Archinard's deep sense of accumulated injury evidently got quite the better of her manners. " No, my dear, you never *could* read aloud and never *did*. I never asked it of you. You are really occupied as a girl should be. At all events you fulfil your social duties. You see that people come to see me. As I cannot go out, as Hilda will not, I really don't know what I should do were it not for you. And, as it is, no one came this afternoon until Mr. Odd made his welcome appearance."

" But Mr. Odd came at five, and you always read till then." Katherine's voice was gently playful. Hilda had not said one word, and her expression seemed now absolutely dogged.

" At this season, Katherine ! You forget that it is night by four ! And how a girl with any regard for her mother's wishes can walk about the streets of Paris alone after that hour it passes my comprehension to understand."

" Do you care about bicycling, Mr. Odd ? " The change was abrupt but welcome. " Because I am going to the Bois to-morrow morning, and alone for once." Katherine smiled at him over the kettle which she was lifting. " Papa has deserted me."

" I should enjoy it immensely. And you," he looked at Hilda, " won't you come ? "

" Oh, I can't," said Hilda, with a troubled look. "Thanks so much."

" Oh no, Hilda can't," laughed Mrs. Archinard.

"And where is the Captain off to?" queried Peter hastily. He felt that he would like to shake Mrs. Archinard. Hilda's stubborn silence might certainly be irritating, and Odd had sympathy for parental claims and wishes, especially concerning the advisability of a beautiful girl walking in the streets at night unescorted, sacrificed to youthful conceit; but Mrs. Archinard's personality certainly weakened all claims, and her taste was as certainly atrocious.

" Papa," said Katherine, pouring out the tea, " is going to-morrow morning to the Riviera. Lucky papa!" Odd thought with some amusement of the £120 that constituted papa's "luck." " I have only been once to Monte Carlo, and I won such a lot. Only imagine how forty pounds turned my head. I revelled in hats and gloves for a whole year. Then we go to-morrow, Mr. Odd? I have my own bicycle. I have kept it near the Porte Dauphine, and you can hire a very nice one at the same place."

" May I call for you here at ten, then? Will that suit you?"

" Very well." Odd watched Katherine as she carried the tea and cake to her sister. Hilda gave a little start.

" O Katherine, how good of you! I did n't realize what you were doing."

" It is you who are good, my pet," said Katherine in a low, gentle voice. Peter thought it a pretty little scene.

" A great deal of latitude must be granted to the

97

young person who invented that teapot," he said to
Hilda. "One must work hard to do anything in
art, must n't one? A most lovely teapot, Hilda."

" I am glad you like it." Hilda smiled her thanks,
but her eyes still expressed that distance and reserve that showed no consciousness of the past, no
intention of admitting it as a link to the present.
She did not seem exactly shy, but her whole manner was passive—negative. Katherine probably
thought that Mr. Odd had by this time realized the
futility of an attempt to draw out the unresponsive
artist, for she seated herself between Odd and the
sofa, thus protecting Hilda from Mrs. Archinard's
severities and Odd from the ineffectual necessity for
talking to Hilda. Odd thought that were Katherine and Mrs. Archinard not there he might have
" come at " Hilda, but the sense of ease Katherine
brought with her was undeniable. She was charmingly mistress of herself, made him talk, appealed
prettily to her mother, who even gave more than
one melancholy laugh, and, with a tactful give and
take, yet kept the reins of conversation well within
her own hands.

Odd found her a nice girl, but the undercurrent
of his thought dwelt on Hilda, and at every gayety
of Katherine's, his eyes sought her sister's face;
Hilda's eyes were always fixed on Katherine, and
she smiled a certain dumbly admiring smile. As he
sat near her, he could see that the little black dress
was very shabby. He could not have associated
Hilda with real untidiness, and indeed the dress with
its white linen cuffs and collar, its inevitable grace
of severely simple outline, was neat to an almost

painful degree.   Hilda's artistic proclivities perhaps
showed themselves in shiny seams and careful darns
and patches.

When he rose to go he took her hands again ; he
hoped that his persistency did not make him appear
rather foolish.

" I am sorry you won't come to-morrow.   May I
hope for another day ? "

" I can't come to-morrow "—there was a touch of
self-defence in Hilda's smile—" but perhaps some
other day.   I should love to," she finished rather
abruptly.

" But you will be different—I will be different.
We will both be changed," repeated itself in Odd's
mind as he walked down the Rue Pierre Charron.
Poor little child-voice ! how sadly it sounded.   How
true had been the prophecy.

99

PETER ODD, at this epoch of his life, felt that he was resting on his oars and drifting. He had spent his life in strenuous rowing. He had seen much, thought much, done much; yet he had made for no goal, and had won no race; how should he, when he had not yet made up his mind that racing for anything was worth while?

Perhaps the two years in Parliament had most closely savored of consciously applied contest, and in that contest Odd considered himself beaten, and its efforts as though they had never been. Every one had told him that to bring the student's ideals into the political arena was to insure defeat; one's friends would consider a carefully discriminating honesty and broad-mindedness mere disloyal luke-warmness, foolish hair-splitting feebleness; one's enemies would rejoice and triumph in the impartiality of an opponent. Certainly he had been defeated, and he could not see that his example had in any way been effectual. At all events, he had held to the ideals.

His fine critical taste found even his own books but crude and partial expressions of still groping thoughts. His unexpressed intention, good indeed, if one might so call its indefiniteness, had been to make the world better for having lived in it; better,

or at least wiser. But he doubted the saving power
of his own sceptical utterances; the world could not
be saved by the balancings of a mind that saw the
tolerant point of view of every question, a mind
itself so unassured of results. A strong dash of
fanaticism is necessary for success, and Odd had
not the slightest flavor of fanaticism. Perhaps he
had given a little pleasure in his more purely literary
studies, and Peter thought that he would stick to
them in the future, but he had put the future away
from him just now. He had only returned from the
great passivity of the Orient a few weeks ago, and
its example seemed to denote drifting as the supreme wisdom. No effort, no desire; a peaceful
receptivity, a peaceful acceptance of the smiles or
buffets of fate ; that was Odd's ideal—for the present.
He was a little sick of everything. The Occidental's
energy for combat was lulled within him, and the
Occidental's individualistic tendencies seemed to
stretch themselves in a long yawn expressive of an
amused and tolerant observation free from striving;
and, for an Occidental, this mood is dangerous.
Odd also did a good deal of listening to very modern
and very clever French talk. He knew many clever
Frenchmen. He did not agree with all of them,
but, as he was not sure of his own grounds for dis-
agreement, he held his peace and listened smilingly.
Certainly the exclusively artistic standpoint was a
most comforting and absorbing plaything to fall
back on.

Peter's friends talked of the amusing and touching
spectacle of the universe. The representation of
each man's illusion on the subject, and the manner

of that representation, were never-ceasing sources of interest. Peter also read a little at the Bibliothèque Nationale, paid a few calls, dined out pretty constantly, and bicycled a great deal in the mornings with Katherine Archinard. She understood things well, and her taste was as sure and as delicate as even Odd could ask. Katherine had absorbed a great deal of culture during her wanderings, and it would have taken a long time for any one to find out that it was of a rather second-hand quality, and sought more for attainment than for enjoyment. Katherine talked with clever people and read clever reviews, and being clever herself, with a very acute critical taste, she knew with the utmost refinement of perception just what to like and just what to dislike; and as she tolerated only the very best, her liking gave value. Yet *au fond* Katherine did not really care even for the very very best. Her appreciation was negative. She excelled in a finely smiling, superior scorn, and could pick flaws in almost any one's enjoyment, if she chose to do so. Katherine, however, was kind-hearted and tactful, and did not arouse dislike by displaying her cleverness except to people who would like it. Enthusiasm was banal, and Katherine was not often required to feign where she did not feel it; her very rigor and exclusiveness of taste implied an appreciation too high for expression; but Katherine had no enthusiasm.

Her rebellious and iconoclastic young energy amused Odd. He thought her rather pathetic in a way. There was a look of daring and revolt in her eye that pleased his lazy spirit. Meanwhile Hilda troubled him.

Would she never bicycle? Katherine, wheeling
lightly erect beside him, gave the little shake of
the head and shrug of the shoulders characteristic
of her. She evidently found no fault with Hilda.
Others might do so—the shrug implied that,
implied as well that Katherine herself perhaps
owned that her sister's impracticable unreason gave
grounds for fault-finding—but Hilda was near her
heart.

When could he see her? That, too, seemed
wrapped in the general cloud of vagueness, un-
accountableness that surrounded Hilda. Odd called
twice in the evening; once to be received by Katherine alone, Hilda was already in *dèshabille* it seemed,
and once to find not even Katherine; she was dining
out, and Miss Hilda in bed. In bed at nine!
"Was she ill?" he asked of Taylor. Wilson had
evidently accompanied the Captain.

"No wonder if she were, sir," Taylor had replied,
with a touch of the grievance in her tone that Hilda
always seemed to arouse in those about her; "but
no, she 's only that tired!" and Odd departed with
a deepened sense of Hilda's wilful immolation.
Katherine brought him home to lunch on several
occasions after the bicycling, but Hilda was never
there. She lunched at her studio.

On a third call Hilda appeared, but only as he
was on the point of going. She wore the same
black dress, and the same look of unnatural
pallor.

"Hilda," said Odd, for amid these unfamiliar conditions he still used the familiar appellation, "I must
see the cause of all this."

"Of what?" Her smile was certainly the sweet smile he remembered.

"Of this unearthly devotion ; these white cheeks."

"Hilda is naturally pale," put in Mrs Archinard ; "she has my skin. But, of course, now she is a ghost."

"Well, I want to see the haunted studio. I want to see the masterpieces." Odd spoke with a touch of gentle irony that did not seem to offend Hilda.

"You will see nothing either uncanny or unusual."

"Well, at all events, when can I come to see you in your studio ?" The vague look crossed Hilda's smile.

"You see—I work very hard ;" she hesitated, seemed even to cast a beseeching glance at Katherine, standing near. Katherine was watching her.

"She is getting ready her pictures for the Champs de Mars. But, Hilda, Mr. Odd may come some morning."

"Oh yes. Some morning. I thought you always bicycled in the morning. I wish you *would* come, it would be so nice to see you there !" she spoke with a gay and sudden warmth ; "only you must tell me when to expect you. My studio must be looking nicely and my model presentable."

"I will take Mr. Odd to-morrow," said Katherine, "he would never find his way."

"Thanks, that will be very jolly," said Odd, conscious that an unescorted visit would have been more so, yet wondering whether Hilda alone might not be more disconcerting than Hilda aided and abetted by her sister.

So the next morning he called for Katherine, and

they walked to a veritable nest of *ateliers* near the Place des Ternes, where they climbed interminable stairs to the very highest studio of all, and here, in very bare and business-like surroundings, they found Hilda. She left her easel to open the door to them. A red-haired woman was lying on a sofa in a far, dim corner, a vase of white flowers at her head. There was a big linen apron of butcher's blue over the black dress, and Hilda looked very neat, less pallid, too, than Odd had seen her look as yet. Her skin had blue shadows under the chin and nose, and a blue shadow made a mystery beneath the long sweep of her eyebrows and about her beautiful eyes. But when she turned her head to the light, Odd saw that the lips were red and the cheeks freshly and faintly tinted.

He was surprised by the picture on the big easel; the teapot had not prepared him for it. A rather small picture, the figure flung to its graceful, lazy length, only a fourth life-size. It was a picture of elusive shadows, touched with warmer lights in its grays and greens. The woman's half-hidden face was exquisite in color. The sweep of her pale gown, half lost in demi-tint, lay over her like the folded wings of a tired moth. The white flowers stood like dreams in the dreamy atmosphere.

"Hilda, I can almost forgive you." Odd stood staring before the canvas; he had put on his eye-glass. "Really this atones."

"Isn't it wonderfully simple, wonderfully decorative?" said Katherine, "all those long, sleepy lines. My clever little Hilda!"

"My clever, clever little Hilda!" Odd repeated,

turning to look at the young artist. Her eyes met his with their wide, sweet gaze that said nothing. Hilda was evidently only capable of saying things on canvas.

" It is lovely."

" You like it really ? "

" I really think it is about as charming a picture as I have seen a woman do. So womanly too." Odd turned to Katherine, it was difficult not to merge Hilda in her art, not to talk about her talent as a thing apart from her personality : " She expresses herself, she does n't imitate."

"Perhaps that is rather unwomanly," laughed Katherine : " a crawling imitativeness seems unfortunately characteristic. Certainly Hilda has none of it. She has inspired me with hopes for my sex."

" Really cleverer than Madame Morisot," said Odd, looking back to the canvas, " delightful as she is ! She could touch a few notes surely, gracefully ; Hilda has got hold of a chord. Yes, Hilda, you are an artist. Have you any others ? "

Hilda brought forward two. One was a small study of a branch of pink blossoms in a white porcelain vase ; the other a woman in white standing at a window and looking out at the twilight. This last was, perhaps, the cleverest of the three ; the lines of the woman's back, shoulder, *profil perdu*, astonishingly beautiful.

"You are fond of dreams and shadows, are n't you ? "

" I have n't a very wide range, but one can only try to do the things one is fitted for. I like all sorts

of pictures, but I like to paint demi-tints and twi-
lights and soft lamplight effects."

"'Car nous voulons la nuance encor—
pas la couleur, rien que la nuance,'"

chanted Katherine. " Hilda lives in dreams and
shadows, I think, Mr. Odd, so naturally she paints
them. ' *L'art c'est la nature, vue à travers un temperament.* Excuse my spouting."

"So your temperament is a stuff that dreams are
made of. Well, Hilda, make as many as you can.
Hello! is that another old friend I see?" On turning to Hilda he had caught sight of a dachshund—
rather white about the muzzle, but very luminous
and gentle of eye—stretching himself from a nap
behind the little stove in the corner. He came toward them with a kindly wag of the tail.

" Is this Palamon or Arcite?"

A change came over Hilda's face.

" That is Palamon ; poor old Palamon. Arcite
fulfilled his character by dying first."

" And Darwin and Spencer? "

" Dead, too ; Spencer was run over."

" Poor old Palamon ! Poor old dog ! " Odd had
lifted the dog in his arms, and was scratching the
silky smooth ears as only a dog-lover knows how.
Palamon's head slowly turned to one side in an
ecstasy of appreciation. Odd looked down at
Hilda. Katherine was behind him. " Poor Palamon, 'allone, withouten any companye.'" Hilda's
eyes met his in a sad, startled look, then she dropped
them to Palamon, who was now putting out his
tongue towards Odd's face with grateful emotion.

" Yes," she said gently, putting her hand caress-

THE DULL MISS ARCHINARD

ingly on the dog's head; her slim, cold fingers just brushed Odd's; "yes, poor Palamon." She was silent, and there was silence behind them, for Katherine, with her usual good-humored tact, was examining the picture. The model on the sofa stretched her arms and yawned a long, scraping yawn. Palamon gave a short, brisk bark, and looked quickly and suspiciously round the studio. Both Odd and Hilda laughed.

"But not 'allone,' after all," said Odd. "Is he a great deal with you? That is a different kind of company, but Palamon is the gainer."

"We must n't judge Palamon by our own standards," smiled Hilda, "though highly civilized dogs like him don't show many social instincts towards their own kind. He did miss Arcite though, at first, I am sure; but he certainly is not lonely. I bring him here with me, and when I am at home he is always in my room. I think all the walking he gets is good for him. You see in what good condition he is."

Palamon still showing signs of restlessness over the yawn, Odd put him down. He was evidently on cordial terms with the model, for he trotted affably toward her, standing with a lazy, smiling wave of the tail before her, while she addressed him with discreetly low-toned, whispering warmth as "*Mon chou! Mon bijou! Mon petit lapin à la sauce blanche!*"

"Don't you get very tired working here all day?" Odd asked.

"Sometimes. But anything worth doing makes one tired, does n't it?"

"You take your art very seriously, Hilda?"

"Sometimes—yes—I take it seriously." Hilda smiled her slight, reserved smile.

"Well, I can't blame you ; you really have something to say."

"Hilda, I am afraid we are becoming *de trop*. I must carry you off, Mr. Odd. Hilda's moments are golden."

"That is a sisterly exaggeration," said Hilda. Had all her personality gone into her pictures? was she a self-centred little egotist? Odd wondered, as he and Katherine walked away together. Katherine's warmly human qualities seemed particularly consoling after the chill of the abstract one felt in Hilda's studio.

CHAPTER IV

"PETER, she is a nice, a clever, a delightful girl," said Mary Apswith.

Mrs. Apswith sat in a bright little salon overlooking the Rue de la Paix. For her holiday week of shopping Peter's hotel was not central enough, but Peter himself was at her command from morning till night. He stood before her now, his back to the flaming logs in the fireplace, looking alternately down at his boots and up at his sister. Peter's face wore an amused but pleasant smile. Katherine must certainly be nice, clever, and delightful, to have won Mary, usually so slow in friendship.

"Whether she is deep—deeply good, I mean—I don't know; one can't tell. But, at all events, she is sincere to the core." Mary had called on the Archinards some days ago, and had seen Katherine every day since then.

Mary's stateliness had not become buxom. The fine lines of her face had lost their former touch of heaviness. Her gray hair—grayer than Peter's—and fresh skin gave her a look of merely perfected maturity. Life had gone well with her; everybody said that; yet Mary knew the sadness of life. She had lost two of her babies, and sorrow had softened, ripened her. The Mary of ten years ago had not had that tender look in her eyes, those lines of sympathetic sensibility about the lips. Her decisively friendly sentence was followed by a little sigh of disapprobation.

" As for Hilda ! "

" As for Hilda ? "

" I am disappointed, Peter. Yes ; we went to her studio this morning ; Katherine took me there ; Katherine's pride in her is pretty. Yes ; I suppose the pictures are very clever, if one likes those rather misty things. They look as though they were painted in the back drawing-room behind the sofa ! " Peter laughed. " I don't pretend to know. I suppose *au fond* I am a Philistine, with a craving for a story on the canvas. I don't really appreciate Whistler, so of course I have n't a right to an opinion at all. But however clever they may be, I don't think those pictures should fill her life to the exclusion of *everything*. The girl owes a duty to herself ; I don't speak of her duty to others. I have no patience with Mrs. Archinard, she is simply insufferable ! Katherine's patience with her is admirable ; but Hilda is completely one-sided, and she is not great enough for that. But she will fancy herself great before long. Lady —— told me that she was never seen with her sister—there is that cut off, you see— how natural that they should go out together ! Of course she will grow morbidly egotistic, people who never meet other people always do ; they fancy themselves grandly misunderstood. So unhealthy, too ! She looked like a ghost."

" Poor little Hilda ! She probably fancies an artist's mission the highest. Perhaps it is, Mary."

" Not in a woman's case "—Mrs. Apswith spoke

with a vigorous decision that would have stamped
her with ignominy in the eyes of the perhaps mythical New Woman; "woman's art is never serious
enough for heroics."

" Perhaps it would be, if they would show a con-
sistent heroism for it." Peter opposed Mary for the
sake of the argument, and for the sake of an old
loyalty. *Au fond* he agreed with her.

" A female Palissy would revolutionize our ideas
of woman's art."

" A pleasant creature she would be ! Tearing up
the flooring and breaking the chairs for firewood!
An abominable desecration of the housewifely instincts! I don't know what Allan Hope will do
about it," Mary pursued.

" Ah ! That is an accepted fact, then ? " ·

" Dear me, yes. Lady Mainwaring is very anxious
for it. It shows what Allan's steady persistency has
accomplished. The child has n't a penny, you know."

" You think she 'd have him ? "

" Of course she will have him. And a lucky girl
she is for the chance ! But, before the definite acceptance, she will, of course, lead him the usual
dance; it 's quite the thing now among girls of that
type. Individuality ; their own life to be lived,
their Art—in capitals—to be lived for ; home, husband, children, degrading impediments. Such tiresome rubbish ! I am very sorry for poor Allan."
Peter studied his boots.

" Allan probably accounts for that general absent-
mindedness I observed in her ; perhaps Allan accounts for more than we give her credit for ; this
desperate devotion to her painting, her last struggle

to hold to her ideal. Really the theory that she is badly in love explains everything. Poor child ! "

" Why poor, Peter? Allan Hope is certainly the very nicest man I know, barring yourself and Jack. He has done more than creditably in the House, and now that he is already on the Treasury Bench, has only to wait for indefinite promotion. He is clever, kind, honest as the day. He will be an earl when the dear old earl dies, and that that is a pretty frame to the picture no one can deny. What more can a girl ask ? "

" This girl probably asks some impossible dream. I 'm sorry for people who have n't done dreaming."

" Between you and me, Peter, I don't think Hilda is really clever enough to do much dreaming—of the pathetic sort. Her eyes are clever ; she sees things prettily, and puts them down prettily ; but there is nothing more. She struck me as a trifle stupid— really dull, you know."

Odd shifted his position uncomfortably.

"That may be shyness, reserve, inability for self-expression." He leaned his arm on the mantelpiece and studied the fire with a puzzled frown. "That exquisite face must *mean* something."

" I don't know. By the law of compensation Katherine has the brains, the heart, and Hilda the beauty. *I* did n't find her shy. She seemed perfectly mistress of herself. It may be a case of absorption in her love affair, as you say. I am not sure that he has asked her yet. He is a most modest lover."

Mary saw a great deal of Katherine during her stay, and her first impression was strengthened.

8   113

Katherine shopped with her; they considered gowns together. Katherine's taste was exquisite, and the bonnets of her choice the most becoming Mrs. Apswith had ever worn. The girl was not above liking pretty things—that was already nice in her—for the girl was clever enough to pose indifference. Mary saw at once that she was clever. Katherine was very independent, but very attentive. Her sincerity was charmingly gay, and not priggish. She said just what she thought; but she thought things that were worth saying. She made little display of learning, but one felt it—like the silk lining in a plain serge gown. She did not talk too much; she made Mrs. Apswith feel like talking. Mary took her twice to the play with Peter and herself. Hilda was once invited and came. Odd sat in the back of the box and watched for the effect on her face of the clever play interpreted by the best talent of the Théâtre Français. The quiet absorption of her look might imply much intelligent appreciation; but Katherine's little ripples of glad enjoyment, clever little thrusts of criticism, made Hilda's silence seem peculiarly impassive, and while between the acts Katherine analyzed keenly, woke a scintillating sense of intellectual enjoyment about her in flashes of gay discussion, Hilda sat listening with that same smile of admiration that almost irritated Odd by its seeming acceptance of inability—inferiority.

The smile, from its very lack of all self-reference, was rather touching; and Mary owned that Hilda was "sweet," but the adjective did not mitigate the former severity of judgment—that was definite.

When Mary went, she begged Katherine to accept the prettiest gown Doucet could make her, and Katherine accepted with graceful ease and frankness. The gown was exquisite. Mary sent to Hilda a fine Braun photograph, which Hilda received with surprised delight, for she had done nothing to make Mrs. Apswith's stay in Paris pleasant. She thought such kindness touching, and Katherine's gown the loveliest she had ever seen.

CHAPTER V

MARY gone, the bicycling *tête-à-têtes* were resumed, and Odd, too, began to call more frequently at the houses where he met Katherine. They were *bon camarades* in the best sense of the term, and Peter found it a very pleasant sense. He realized that he had been lonely, and loneliness in his present *désœuvrée* condition would have been intolerable. The melancholy of laziness could not creep to him while this girl laughed beside him. The frank, sympathetic relation—almost that of man to man—was untouched by the faintest infusion of sentiment; delicious breeziness and freedom of intercourse was the result. Peter listened to Katherine, laughed at her sometimes, and liked her to laugh at him. He told her a good many of his thoughts; she criticised them, approved of them, encouraged him to action. But Odd felt his present contemplativeness too wide to be limited by any affirmation. He had never felt so little sure of anything nor so conscious of everything in general. Writing in such a mood seemed folly, and he continued to drift. He still read in an objectless way at the Bibliothèque, hunting out old references, pleasing himself by a circuit through the points of view of all times. Katherine offered to help him, and in the morning he would bring her his notes to

116

look over; her quick comprehension formed another link. He was very sorry for Katherine too. She had no taste for drifting. In her eye he read a dissatisfaction, a thirst for wider vision, wider action, a restless impatience with the narrowness, the ineffectiveness of her lot, that made him muse on her probable future with a sense of pathos. Hilda's wide gaze showed no such rebellion with the actual ; her art had filled it with a distant content that shut strife and the defeat of yearnings from her: or was it merely the placid consciousness of Allan Hope— a future assured and fully satisfactory ? Under Katherine's gayety there was a fierce beating of caged wings, and Odd fancied at times that, freed, the imprisoned birds might be strong and beautiful. He fancied this especially when she played to him ; she played well, with surprising sureness of taste, and, as the winter came and it grew too cold for bicycling, Peter often spent the morning in listening to her. Mrs. Archinard did not appear until the afternoon in the drawing-room, and in the evenings he usually met her dining out or at some reception ; their intimacy once noticed, they were invited together. Lady —— was especially anxious that Odd should have every opportunity for meeting her favorite.

But with all this intimacy, to Peter's consciousness thoroughly, paternally platonic, under all its daily interests and quiet pleasure lay a half-felt hurt, a sense of injury and loss. The little voice, seldom thought of during the last ten years, now repeated often : " But you will be different ; I will be different ; we will both be changed."

Captain Archinard returned from the Riviera in

a temper that could mean but one thing; he had gambled at Monte Carlo, and he had lost. He did not mention the fact in the family circle; indeed, by a tacit agreement, money matters were never alluded to before Mrs. Archinard. Her years of successful invalidism had compelled even her husband's acquiescence in the decision early arrived at by Hilda and Katherine: mamma must be spared the torments to which they had grown accustomed. But to Katherine the Captain freed his querulous soul, never to Hilda. There was a look in Hilda's eyes that made the Captain very uncomfortable, very angry; conscious of those cases of wonderful champagne, the races, the clubs, the boxes at the play, and all the infinite array of his wardrobe—a sad, wondering look. Katherine's scoldings were far preferable, for Katherine was not so devilish superior to human weaknesses; she had plenty of unpaid bills on her own conscience, and understood the necessities of an aristocratic taste. He and Katherine had their little secrets, and were mutually on the defensive. Hilda never criticised, to be sure, but her very difference was a daily criticism. The Captain thought his younger daughter rather dull; Katherine, of finer calibre than her father, admired such dulness, and found some difficulty in stilling self-reproachful comparisons; temperament, circumstance, made a comforting philosophy. And then Hilda's art made things easy for Hilda; with such a refuge, would she, Katherine, ask for more? Katherine rather wondered now, after her father's exasperated recountal of ill-luck, where papa had got the money to lose; but papa on this point was prudently reticent, and borrowed two one-hundred-franc notes from Peter while the latter waited in the drawing-room for Katherine one morning.

Katherine and her father were making a round of calls one day, and the Captain stopped at his bank to cash a check. Katherine stood beside him, and, although he manœuvred concealment with hand and shoulder, her keen eyes read the name.

Her mouth was stern as they walked away—the Captain had folded the notes and put them in his pocket.

" A good deal of money that, papa."

" I suppose I owe twice as much to my tailor," Captain Archinard replied, with irritation.

" Has Mr. Odd lent you money before this? "

" I really don't know that Mr. Odd's affairs—or mine—are any business of yours, Katherine."

"Yours certainly are, papa. When a father puts his daughter in a false position, his affairs decidedly become her business."

" What rubbish, Katherine. Better men than Odd have been glad to give me a lift. I can't see that Odd has been ill-used. He is rolling in money."

" I don't quite believe that, papa. Allersley is not such a rich property. But it is not of Mr. Odd's ill-usage I complain, it is of mine ; for if this borrowing goes on, I hardly think I can continue my relations with Mr. Odd. It would rather look like—decoying."

The Captain stopped and fixed a look of futile dignity on his daughter.

" That 's a strange word for you to use, Katherine.

I would horsewhip the man who would suggest it. Odd is a gentleman."

" Decidedly. I did not speak of his point of view but of mine. All frankness of intercourse between us is impossible if you are going to sponge on him."

" Katherine! I can't allow such impertinence! Outrageous! It really is! Sponge! Can't a man borrow a few paltry hundreds from another without exposing himself to such insulting language?—especially as Odd is to become my son-in-law, I suppose. He is always hanging about you."

" That is what I meant, papa." Katherine's tone was icy. "Your suppositions were apparent to me, you drain Mr. Odd on the strength of them. Borrow from any one else you like as much as you can get, but, if you have any self-respect, you won't borrow from Mr. Odd in the hope that I will marry him."

" Devilish impertinent! Upon my word, devilish impertinent!" the Captain muttered. He drew out his cigar-case with a hand that trembled. Katherine's bitter look was very unpleasant.

Katherine expected Odd the next morning; he was reading a manuscript to her, and would come early.

She was waiting for him at ten. She had put on her oldest dress. The severe black lines, a silk sash, knotted at the side, suggested a *soutane*—the slim buckled shoes with their square tips carried out the monastic effect, and Katherine's strong young face was cold and stern.

" Shall we put off our work for a little while? I want to speak to you," she said, after Odd had come, and greetings had passed between them.

"*Shall* we? You have been too patient all along, Miss Archinard." Odd smiled down at her as he held her hand. "You make me feel that I have been driving you—arrantly egotistic."

"No; I like our work immensely, as you know." Katherine remained standing by the fireplace. She leaned her arm on the mantelpiece, and turned her head to look directly at him. "I am not at all happy this morning, Mr. Odd." Odd's kind eyes showed an almost boyish dismay.

"What is it? Can I help you?" His tone was all sympathetic anxiety and friendly warmth.

"No; just the contrary. Mr. Odd, I am ashamed that you should have seen the depths of our poverty. It is not a poverty one can be proud of. Poverty to be honorable must work, and must not borrow."

Odd flushed.

"You exaggerate," he said, but he liked her for the exaggeration.

"I did not know till yesterday that papa owed to you his Riviera trip."

"Really, Katherine"— he had not used her name before, it came now most naturally with this new sense of intimacy—"you mustn't misunderstand, misjudge your father. He couldn't work; his life has unfitted him for it; it would be a false pride that would make him hesitate to ask an old friend for a loan; an old friend so well able to lend as I am. You women judge these things far too loftily." And Peter liked her for the loftiness.

"Would you mind telling me how much you lent him last time? I was with him when he cashed the check. I saw the name, not the amount."

"It was nothing of any importance," said Odd shortly. He exaggerated now. The Captain had told him that the furniture would be seized unless some creditors were satisfied, and, with a very decided hint as to the inadvisability of another trip for retrievement to the Riviera, Peter had given him the money, ten thousand francs ; a sum certainly of importance, for Odd was no millionaire.

Katherine looked hard at him.

"You won't tell me because you want to spare me."

" My dear Katherine, I certainly want to spare you anything that would add a straw's weight to your distress; you have no need, no right to shoulder this. It is your father's affair—and mine. You must not give it another thought."

" That is so easy ! " Katherine clenched her hand on the mantelpiece. She was not given to vehemence of demonstration ; the little gesture showed a concentration of bitter rebellion. Odd, standing beside her, put his own hand over hers ; patted it soothingly.

" It 's rather hard on me, you know, a slur on my friendship, that you should take a merely conventional obligation so to heart."

Katherine now looked down into the fire.

" Take it to heart? What else have I had on my heart for years and years ? It is a mere variation on the same theme, a little more poignantly painful than usual, that is all ! What a life to lead. What a future to look forward to. I wonder what else I shall have to endure." Odd had never seen her before in this mood of fierce hopelessness.

"Our poverty has poisoned everything, *everything*. I have had no youth, no happiness. Every moment of forgetfulness means redoubled keenness of gnawing anxiety. Debts! Duns! harassing, sordid cares that drag one down. Mr. Odd, I have had to coax butchers and bakers; I have had to plead with horrible men with documents of all varieties! I have had to pawn my trinkets, and all with surface gayety; everything must be kept from mamma, and papa's extravagance is incorrigible."

Odd was all grave amazement, grave pity, and admiration.

"You are a brave woman, Katherine."

"No, no; I am not brave. I am frightened—frightened to death sometimes. I see before me either a hideous struggle with want or—a *mariage de convenance*. I have none of the classified, pigeon-holed knowledge one needs nowadays to become a teaching drudge, and I can't make up my mind to sell myself, though, in spite of my lack of beauty and lack of money, that means of escape has often presented itself. I have had many offers of marriage. Only I *can't*."

Odd was silent under the stress of a new thought, an entirely new thought.

"For Hilda I have no fear," Katherine continued, still speaking with the same steady quiet voice, still looking into the fire. "In the past her art has absorbed and protected her, and her future is assured. She will marry a good husband." A flash as of Hilda's beauty crossed the growing definiteness of Peter's new thought. That old undoing, that mirage of beauty; he put it aside with some self-

123

disgust, feeling, as he did so, a queer sense of impersonality as though putting away himself as he put
away his weakness. He seemed to contemplate
himself from an outside aloofness of observation.
The trance-like feeling of the illusion of all things
which he had felt more than once of late made him
hold more firmly to the tonic thought of a fine com-
mon-sense.

"Of course, mamma will be safe when Hilda is
Lady Hope," Katherine said; "perhaps I shall be
forced to accept the same charity." Her voice broke
a little, and she turned the sombre revolt of her look
on Peter; her eyes were full of tears.

"Katherine," he said, "will you marry me?"

Odd, five minutes before, had not had the remot-
est idea that he would ask Katherine Archinard to
be his wife. Yet one could hardly call the sudden
decision that had brought the words to his lips, impulsive. While Katherine spoke, the bitter struggle
of the fine young life, surely meant for highest
things; the courage of the cheerfulness she never
before had failed in; the pride of that repulsion for
the often offered solution to her difficulties—a solution many women would have accepted with a sense
of the inevitable—became admirably apparent to
Odd. Their mutual sympathy and good-fellowship
and, almost unconsciously, Hilda's assured future—
Allan Hope—had defined the thought. He felt
none of that passion which, now that he looked back
on it, made of the miserable year of married life that
followed but the logical retribution of its reckless
and wilful blindness. The very lack of passion now
seemed an added surety of better things. His life

with Katherine could count on all that his life with
Alicia had failed in. He did not reason on that un-
excited sense of impersonality and detachment. He
would like her to accept him. He would like to help
this fine, proud young creature; he would like sympathetic companionship. He was sure of that. He
had not surprised Katherine; she had seen, as clearly
as he now saw, what Peter Odd would do. She had
not exactly intended to bring him to a realization of
this by the morning's confession, for on the whole
Katherine had been perfectly sincere in all that she
had said, but she felt that she could rely on no better
opportunity. Now she only turned her head towards
him, without moving from her position before the
fireplace. Katherine never took the trouble to act.
She merely aimed at the most advantageous line of
conduct and let taste and instinct lead her. Her
taste now told her that quiet sincerity was very suit-
able; she felt, too, a most sincere little dash of
proud hesitation.

" Are you generously offering me another form of
charity, Mr. Odd? My distress was not conscious
of an appeal."

" You know your own value too well, Katherine,
to ask me that. *I* appeal."

" Yet the apropos of your offer makes me smart.
Another joy of poverty. One can't trust."

" It was apropos because a man who loves you
would not see you suffer needlessly." Peter, too,
was sincere; he did not say " loved."

" Shall I let you suffer needlessly?" asked Katherine, smiling a little. " I sha'n't, if that implies that
you love me."

125

"Suppose I do. And suppose I stand on my dignity. Pretend to distrust your motives. Refuse to be married out of pity?"

"That sort of false dignity would n't suit you; you have too much of the real."

"Would you be good to me, Mr. Odd?"

"Very, very good, Katherine."

Odd took her hand and kissed it, and Katherine's smile shone out in all its frank gayety. "I think I can make you happy, dear."

"I think you can, Mr. Odd."

"You must manage 'Peter' now."

"I think you can, Peter," Katherine said obediently.

"And Katherine—I would not have dared say this before, you would have flung it back at me as bribery—but I can give you weapons."

"Yes, I shall be able to fight now." She looked up at him with her charming smile. "And you will help me, you must fight too. You must be great, Peter, great, *great!*"

"With such a fiery little engine throbbing beside my laggard bulk, I shall probably be towed into all sorts of combats and come off victorious."

They sat down side by side on the sofa. Katherine was a delightfully comfortable person; no change, but a pleasant development of relation seemed to have occurred.

"You won't expect any flaming protestations, will you, Katherine," said Peter; "I was never good at that sort of thing."

"Did you never flame, then?"

"I fancy I flamed out in about two months—a

long time ago ; that is about the natural life of the feeling."

" And you bring me ashes," said Katherine, rallying him with her smile.

" You must n't tease me, Katherine," said Peter. He found her very dear, and kissed her hand again.

Part II
HILDA.

CHAPTER I

" WELL, Hilda, we have some news for you ! "
With these words, spoken in the triumphant
tone of the news-breaker, the Captain greeted his
daughter as she came into the drawing-room at half-
past six. Odd had been paying his respects to his
future parents-in-law, and was sitting near Mrs.
Archinard's sofa. He rose to his feet as Hilda entered and looked at her, smiling a trifle nervously.

" Guess what has happened, my dear," said the
Captain, whose good humor was apparent, while
Mrs. Archinard murmured, "*She* would never guess.
Hilda, only look at your hat in the mirror." It was
windy, and Hilda's shabby little hat was on the back
of her head.

" What must I guess ? Is it about you? " she
asked, turning her sweet bewildered eyes from Odd
to her father, to her mother, and back to Odd again.

" Yes, about me and another person."

" You are going to marry Katherine ! " Her eyes
dilated and their sweetness deepened to a smile ;
" you are going to marry Katherine, that *must* be it."

" That is it, Hilda. Congratulate me." He took
her hands in his and kissed her. " Welcome me,
and tell me you are glad."

" Oh ! I am very glad. I welcome you. I congratulate you ! "

131

" You will like your brother ? "

" A brother is dearer than a friend, and you have always been a friend, have n't you, Mr. Odd ? "

" Always, always, Hilda ; I did n't know that you realized it."

" Did *you* realize it ? "

" *Did* I, my dear Hilda! I did, I do, I always will." Hilda's face seemed subtly irradiated. Her listless look of pallor had brightened wonderfully. No one could have said that the lovely face was dull with this sudden change upon it. Peter felt that he himself was grave in comparison.

" And I am going to claim all a brother's rights immediately, Hilda."

" What are a brother's rights ? "

" I am going to look after you, to scold you, to see you don't overwork yourself."

" I give you leave, but you must n't presume *too* much on the new rights."

" Ah ! but I have old ones as well."

" You must n't be tyrannical ! " she still laughed gently as she withdrew her hands ; " I must go and see Katherine."

" Yes, go and dress now, Hilda." Mrs. Archinard spoke from the sofa, having watched the scene with a slight air of injury ; Hilda's unwonted gayety constituted a certain grievance. " Mr. Odd dines with us, and I really can't bear to see you in that costume. The skirt especially is really ludicrous, my dear. I am glad that I don't see you walking through the streets in it."

" Hilda knows that her feet bear showing," remarked the Captain, crossing his own with com-

132

placency; "she has her mother's foot in size and mine in make—the Archinard foot; narrow, arched instep, and small heel.

"Really, Charles, I think the Maxwells will bear the comparison!" Mrs. Archinard, though she smiled, looked distinctly distressed.

Hilda found her sister before the long mirror in her room, Taylor fastening the nasturtium velvet. Katherine always had a commanding air, and it was quite regally apparent to-night; all things seemed made to serve her, and Taylor's crouching attitude symbolic.

Hilda put her arms around her neck.

"My dear, dear Kathy, I am so glad! To think that good things *do* come true!"

"You like my choice, pet?"

"*No* one else would have done," cried Hilda; "he is the only man I ever saw whom I could have thought of for you. Why, Katherine, from that first day when you told me you had met him at the dinner, I *knew* it would happen."

"Yes, I certainly felt a prophetic sense of proprietorship from the first," Katherine owned musingly. She looked over her sister's shoulder at the fine outline of her own head and neck in the glass.

"Aren't you rather splashed and muddy, pet?" Poor people can't afford an affection that puts their velvet gowns in danger. There, I mustn't rumple my lace."

"I haven't hurt, have I?" Hilda stood back hastily. "I forgot, I *am* rather muddy. And, Katherine, you will help one another so much; that makes it so ideal."

THE DULL MISS ARCHINARD

" Idealistic little Hilda ! "

" But that is evident, is n't it ? You with all your energy and cleverness and general *sanity*, and he so widely sympathetic that he is a bit impersonal. I mean that he doubts himself because he doubts everything rather; he sees how relative everything is; he probably thinks too much; I am sure that is dangerous. You will make him act."

"I am to be the concrete to his abstract. He certainly does lack energy. I wonder if even I shall be able to prod him into initiative."

Katherine patted down the fine old lace that edged her bodice, and looked a smiling question from her own reflection in the mirror to her sister. "Suppose I fail to arouse him."

" You will understand him. He will have something to live for; that is what he needs. He won't be able to say, ' Is it worth while ? ' about *your* happiness. As for initiative, you will probably have to have that for both. After all, he has made his name and place. He has the nicest kind of fame; the more apparent sort made up by the admiration of mediocrities is n't half as nice."

" Ah, pet, you are an intellectual aristocrat. My *pâte* is coarser. I like the real thing; the donkey's brayings make a noise, and one must take the whole world with all its donkeys conscious of one, to be famous. I like noise." Katherine smiled as she spoke, and Hilda smiled, too, a little smile of humorous comprehension, for she did not take Katherine in this mood at all seriously. She was as stanch in her belief of Katherine's ideals as she was in sticking to her own.

HILDA

" We will be married in March," said Katherine, pausing before her dressing-table to put on her rings—a fine antique engraved gem and a splendid opal. " You may go, Taylor; and Taylor, you may put out my opera-cloak after dinner. I think, Hilda, I will go to the opera ; papa has a box. He and I and Peter might care about dropping in for the last two acts. You don't care to come, do you ? "

" Well, mamma expects me to read to her ; it 's a charming book, too," added Hilda, with tactful delicacy.

" Well, I shall envy you your quiet evening. I can't ask Peter to spend his here in the bosom of my family. Yes, March, I think, unless I decide on making that round of visits in England ; that would put it off for a month. I hope the ravens will fetch me a trousseau—for I don't know who else will."

" I shall have quite a lot by that time, Katherine. I have n't heard from the dealer in London yet, but those two pictures will sell, I hope. And, at all events, with the other things, you know, I shall have about a hundred pounds."

Katherine flushed a little when Hilda spoke of " other things," and looked round at her sister.

" I *hate* to think of taking the money, Hilda."

" My dear, why should you ? Except, of course —the debts," Hilda sighed deeply : " but I think on *this* occasion you have a right to forget them." Katherine's flush perhaps showed a consciousness of having forgotten the debts on many occasions less pressing.

" I meant, in particular, taking the money from you."

THE DULL MISS ARCHINARD

Hilda opened her wide eyes to their widest.
"Kathy! as if it were not my pleasure! my joy!
I am lucky to be able to get it for you. *Can* you
get a trousseau for that much, Kathy?"

"Well, linen, yes. I don't care how little I get,
but it must be good—good lace. I shall manage;
I don't care about gowns, I can get them afterwards.
Peter, I know, will be an indulgent husband." A
pleasant little smile flickered across Katherine's
lips. "He *is* a dear! I only hope, pet, that you
will be able to hold on to the money. Don't let
the duns worry it out of you!" The weary, pallid
look came to Hilda's face.

"I'll try, Kathy dear. I'll do my very best."

"My precious Hilda! You need not tell me
that! Run quickly and dress, dear, it must be
almost dinner-time. What *have* you to wear?
Shall I lend you anything?"

"Why, you forgot my gray silk! My fichu! Insulting Kathy!"

"So I did! And you look deliciously pretty in
that dress, though she *did* make a fiasco of the
back; let the fichu come well down over it. You
really shouldn't indulge your passion for *petites
couturières*, child. It doesn't pay."

136

CHAPTER II

ODD climbed the long flight of stairs that led to
Hilda's studio. The concièrge below at the
entrance to the court had looked at him with the
sourness common to her class, as she stood spa-
ciously in her door. The gentleman had, evidently,
definite intentions, for he had asked her no questions, and Madame Prinet felt his independence as
a slur upon her Cerberus qualifications.

Odd was putting into practice his brotherly principles. He had spent the morning with Katherine
—the fifth morning since their engagement—and
time hanging unemployed and heavy on his hands
this afternoon, a visit to Hilda seemed altogether
desirable. It really behoved him to solve Hilda's
dubious position and, if possible, help her to a more
normal outlook; he felt the task far more feasible
since that glimpse of gayety and confidence. Indeed he was quite unconscious of Madame Prinet's
suspicious observation as he crossed the court, and
the absorption in his pleasant duty held his mind
while he wound up the interminable staircase.

His knock at Hilda's door—there was no mis-
taking it, for a card bearing her name was neatly
nailed thereon—was promptly answered, and Odd
found himself face to face with a middle-aged maiden

137

of the artistic type with which Paris swarms ; thin, gray-haired, energetic eyes behind eyeglasses, and a huge palette on her arm, so huge that it gave Odd the impression of a misshapen table and blocked the distance out with its brave array of color. Over the lady's shoulder, Odd caught sight of a canvas of heroic proportions.

" Oh ! I thought it was the concièrge," said the artist, evidently disappointed ; " have you come to the right door ?   I don't think I know you."

" No ; I don't know you," Odd replied, smiling and casting a futile glance around the studio, now fully revealed by the shifting of the palette to a horizontal position.

" I expected to find Miss Archinard.   Are you working with her ?   Will she be back presently ? "

The gray-haired lady smiled an answering and explanatory smile.

" Miss Archinard rents me her studio in the afternoon.   She only uses it in the morning ; she is never here in the afternoon."

Odd felt a huge astonishment.

" Never here ? "

" No ; can I give her any message ?   I shall probably see her to-morrow if I come early enough."

" Oh no, thanks.   Thanks very much."   He realized that to reveal his dismay would stamp Hilda with an unpleasantly mysterious character.

" I shall see her this evening—at her mother's. I am sorry to have interrupted you."

" Oh !   Don't mention it ! "   The gray-haired lady still smiled kindly ; Peter touched his hat and descended the stairs.   Perhaps she worked in a large atelier in the afternoon ; strange that she had never mentioned it.

Madame Prinet, who had followed the visitor to the foot of the staircase and had located his errand, now stood in her door and surveyed his retreat with a fine air of impartiality ; people who consulted her need not mount staircases for nothing.

" Monsieur did not find Mademoiselle."

Odd paused ; he certainly would ask no questions of the coèncirge, but she might, of her own accord, throw some light on Hilda's devious ways.

" No ; I had hoped to find her. Mademoiselle was in when I last called with her sister. I did not know that she went out every afternoon."

Odd thought this tactful, implying, as it did, that Miss Archinard's friends were not in ignorance of her habits.

" Every afternoon, monsieur ; *elle et son chien.*"

" Ah, indeed ! " Odd wished her good day and walked off. He had stumbled upon a mystery only Hilda herself might divulge : it might be very simple, and yet a sense of anxiety weighed upon him.

At five he went to call on a pleasant and pretty woman, an American, who lived in the Boulevard Haussmann. He was to dine with the Archinards, and Katherine had said she might meet him at Mrs. Pope's ; if she were not there by five he need not wait for her. She was not there, and Mr. Pope took possession of him on his entrance and led him into the library to show him some new acquisitions in bindings. Mrs. Pope was not a grass widow, and her husband, a desultory dilettante, was always in evidence in her graceful, crowded salon. He was a very tall, thin man, with white hair and a mild, almost timid manner, dashed with the collector's eagerness.

" Now, Mr. Odd, I have a treasure here ; really a perfect treasure. A genuine Grolier ; I captured it at the La Hire sale. Just look here, please ; come to the light. Is n't that a beauty ? "

Mrs. Pope, after a time, came and captured Peter ; she did not approve of the hiding of her lion in the library. She took him into the drawing-room, where a great many people were drinking tea and talking, and he was passed dexterously from group to group ; Mrs. Pope, gay and stout, shuffling the pack and generously giving every one a glimpse of her trump. It was a fatiguing process, and he was glad to find himself at last in Mrs. Pope's undivided possession. He was sitting on a sofa beside her, talking and drinking a well-concocted cup of tea, when a picture on the opposite wall attracted his attention. He put down the cup of tea and put up his eyeglasses to look at it. A woman in a dress of Japanese blue, holding a paper fan ; pink azaleas in the foreground. The decorative outline and the peculiar tonality made it unmistakable. He got up to look more closely. Yes, there was the delicate flowing signature : " Hilda Archinard."

He turned to Mrs. Pope in pleased surprise.

" I did n't know that Hilda had reached this degree of popularity. You are very lucky. Did she give it to you ? "

Katherine's engagement was generally known, and Mrs. Pope reproached herself for having failed to draw Mr. Odd's attention before this to the work of his future sister.

"Oh no; she is altogether too distinguished a
little person to give away her pictures. That was
in the Champs de Mars last year. I bought it. The
two others sold as well. I believe she sells most of
her things; for high prices, too. Always the way,
you know; a starving genius is allowed to starve,
but material success comes to a pretty girl who
does n't need it. Katherine is so well known in
Paris that Hilda's public was already made for her;
there was no waiting for the appreciation that is her
due. Her work is certainly charming."

Peter felt a growing sense of anxiety. He could
not share Mrs. Pope's feeling of easy pleasantness.
Hilda *did* need it. Certainly there was nothing
pathetic in doing what she liked best and making
money at it. Yet he wondered just how far Hilda's
earnings helped the family; kept the butcher and
baker at bay. With a new keenness of conjecture
he thought of the black serge dress; somewhere
about Hilda's artistic indifference there might well
lurk a tragic element. Did she not really care to
wear the amethyst velvets that her earnings perhaps went to provide? The vague distress that
had never left him since his first disappointment at the Embassy dinner, that the afternoon's
discovery at the atelier had sharpened, now became
acute.

" I always think it such a pretty compensation of
Providence," said Mrs. Pope, gracefully anxious to
please, "that all the talent that Hilda Archinard
expresses, puts on her canvas, is more personal in
Katherine; is part of herself as it were, like a perfume about her."

"Yes," said Odd rather dully, not particularly pleased with the comparison.

"She is such a brilliant girl," Mrs. Pope added, "such a splendid character. I can't tell you how it delighted me to hear that Katherine had at last found the rare some one who could really appreciate her. It strengthened my pet theory of the fundamental fitness of things."

"Yes," Odd repeated, so vaguely that Mrs. Pope hurriedly wondered if she had been guilty of bad taste, and changed the subject.

When Peter reached the Archinards' at half-past six that evening, he found the Captain and Mrs. Archinard alone in the drawing-room.

"Hilda not in yet?" he asked. His anxiety was so oppressive that he really could not forbear opening the old subject of grievance. Indeed, Odd fancied that in Mrs. Archinard's jeremiads there was an element of maternal solicitude. That Hilda should voluntarily immolate herself, have no pretty dresses, show herself nowhere—these facts perhaps moved Mrs. Archinard as much as her own neglected condition. At least, so Peter charitably hoped, feeling almost cruel as he deliberately broached the painful subject.

Mrs. Archinard now gave a dismal sigh, and the Captain shook his head impatiently as he put down *Le Temps*.

Odd went on quite doggedly—

"I didn't know that Hilda sold her pictures. I saw one of them at Mrs. Pope's this afternoon."

There could certainly be no indiscretion in the

statement, for Mrs. Pope herself had mentioned the fact of Hilda's success as well known. Indeed, although the Captain's face showed an uneasy little change, Mrs. Archinard's retained its undisturbed pathos.

"Yes," she said, "oh yes, Hilda has sold several things, I believe. She certainly needs the money. We are not *rich* people, Peter." Mrs. Archinard had immediately adopted the affectionate intimacy of the Christian name. "And we could hardly indulge Hilda in her artistic career if, to some extent, she did not help herself. I fancy that Hilda makes few demands on her papa's purse, and she must have many expenses. Models are expensive things, I hear. I cannot say that I rejoice in her success. It seems to justify her obstinacy—makes her independent of our desires—our requests."

Odd felt that there was a depth of selfish ignorance in these remarks. The Captain's purse he knew by experience to be very nearly mythical, and the Captain's expression at this moment showed to Peter's sharpened apprehension an uncomfortable consciousness. Peter was convinced that, far from making demands on papa's purse, Hilda had replenished it, and further conjectures as to Hilda's egotistic one-sidedness began to shape themselves.

"And a very lucky girl she is to be able to make money so easily," the Captain remarked, after a pause. "By Jove! I wish that doing what pleased me most would give me a large income!" and the Captain, who certainly had made most conscientious efforts to fulfil his nature, and had, at least, tried to do what most pleased him all his life long, and with the utmost energy, looked resentfully at his narrow well-kept finger-nails.

"Does she work all day long at her studio?" Peter asked, conscious of a certain hesitation in his voice. The mystery of Hilda's afternoon absences would now be either solved or determined. It was determined—definitely. There was no shade of suspicion in Mrs. Archinard's sighing, "Dear me, yes!" or in the Captain's, "From morning till night. Wears herself out."

Hilda, all too evidently, had a secret.

"She ought to go to two studios, it would tire her less. Her own half the day, and a large atelier the other." Assurance might as well be made doubly sure.

"Hilda left Julian's a long time ago. She has lived in her own place since then, really lived there. I have n't seen it; of course I could not attempt the stairs. Katherine tells me there are terrible stairs. Most shockingly unhealthy life she leads, I think, and most, *most* inconsiderate."

At the dinner-table Odd knew that Hilda had only him to thank for the thorough "heckling" she received at the hands of both her parents. Her silence, with its element of vacant dulness, now admitted many interpretations. It hedged round a secret unknown to either father or mother. Unknown to Katherine? Her grave air of aloofness might imply as much, or might mean only a natural disapproval of the scolding process carried on before her lover, a loyalty to Hilda that would ask no question and make no reproach.

"Any one would tell you, Hilda, that it is positively not *decent* in Paris for a young girl to be out alone after dusk," said the Captain. " Odd will tell you so ; he was speaking about it only this evening. You must come home earlier; I insist upon it."

Odd sat opposite to her, and Hilda raised her eyes and met his.

He smiled gravely at her, and shook his head.

" Naughty little Hilda ! " but his voice expressed all the tender sympathy the very sight of her roused in him, and Hilda smiled back faintly.

CHAPTER III

PETER brought Katherine the engagement ring a few days afterward. The drifting had ceased abruptly, and he felt the new sense of reality as most salutary. His personality and hers now filled the horizon; their relations demanded a healthy condensation of thoughts before expanded in wandering infinity, and he was thankful for the consciousness of definite duty and responsibility that made past years seem the refinement of egotism.

Katherine looked almost roguishly gay that afternoon, and, even after the ring was exclaimed over, put on, and Peter duly kissed for it, he felt that there was still an expression of happy knowingness not yet accounted for.

"The ring was n't a surprise, but you have one for me, Katherine."

Katherine laughed out at his acuteness.

"The ring is lovely ; clever, sensitive Peter ! "

"You have quite convinced me of your pleasure and my own good taste. What is the news ? "

"Well, Peter, a delightful thing has happened, or is *going* to happen, rather. Allan Hope is coming to Paris next week ! Peter, we may have a double wedding ! "

"Hilda has accepted him ? "

146

"Oh, we have not openly discussed it, you know. Mamma got his letter this morning; very short. He hoped to see us all by Wednesday. Of course, mamma is charmed. Hilda said nothing, and went off to the studio as usual; but Hilda never *does* say anything if she is really feeling."

"Does n't she?" There was a musing quality in Odd's voice.

"*I* think the child is in love with him; I thought so from the first. Wednesday! A week from to-morrow! Oh, of course she will have him!" Katherine said jubilantly.

"Allan is n't the man to fail in anything. He has a great deal of determination."

"Yes, he seems the very embodiment of success, does n't he? That is because he does n't try to see everything at once, like some people I know." And Katherine nodded her head laughingly at her *fiancé*. "Intellectual epicureanism is fatal. Allan Hope has no unmanageable opinions. His party can always count on him. He is always there, unchanged—unless they change! He pins his faith to his party, and verily he shall have his reward! By mere force of honest mediocrity he will mount to the highest places!"

"Venomous little Katherine! What are you trying to insinuate?"

"Why, that Lord Allan is n't particularly clever, nor particularly anything, except particularly useful to men who can be clever for him. He is the bricks they build with."

"Allan is as honest as the day," said Peter, a little shortly.

147

"Honest? Who's a denygin' of it, pray? His honesty is part of his supreme utility. My simile holds good; he is a brick; a dishonest man is a mere tool, fit only to be cast away, once used."

"How rhetorical we are!" said Odd, smiling at her with a touch of friendly mockery.

"Lord Allan most devoutly believes that in his party lies the salvation of his country," Katherine pursued. "Oh, I have talked to him!"

"You have, have you? Poor chap!" ejaculated Peter. "Will you ever serve me up in this neatly dissected way, as a result of our confidential conversations?"

"Willingly! but only to yourself. Don't be afraid, Peter. I could dissect myself far more neatly, far more unpleasantly. I have a genius for the scalpel! And I have said nothing in the least derogatory to Allan Hope. He couldn't disagree with his party, any more than a pious Catholic could disagree with his church. It is a matter of faith, and of shutting the eyes."

If Hilda was so soon to pass to the supreme authority of an accepted lover, Peter felt that for his own satisfaction he must make the most of the time left him, and solve the riddle of her occupations. That delicate sense of loyal reticence had held him from a hinted question to even Katherine. If Katherine were as ignorant as he, a question would arouse and imply suspicion. Odd could suspect Hilda of nothing worse than a silly disobedience founded on a foolish idea of her own artistic worth; a dull self-absorption, unsaved by a touch of humor. Yet this very suspicion irritated Odd profoundly; it seemed

logical and yet impossible. He felt, in his very revulsion from it, a justification for a storming of her
barriers.

That very evening, while Katherine played Schumann, the Captain having gone out and Mrs. Archinard dozing on the sofa, he determined to have the
truth if possible.

Hilda stood behind her sister, listening. Her tall
slenderness looked well in anything that fell in long
lines, even if made by the most *petite* of *petite*
couturières, as the gray silk had been. The white
fichu covered deficiencies of fit, and left free the
exquisite line of her throat. Her head, in its attitude of quiet listening, struck Odd with the old
sense of a beauty significant, not the lovely mask of
emptiness.

" Come and sit by me, Hilda," he said from his
place on the sofa, " you can hear better at this distance."

The quick turn of her head, her pretty look of
willingness were charming, he thought.

" I like to see you in that dress," he said, as she
sat down beside him on the sofa, "there isn't a
whiff of paint or palette about it, except that, in it,
you look like a picture, and a prettier one than even
you could paint."

"That is a very subtle insult!" Hilda's smile
showed a most encouraging continuation of the
pretty willingness.

"You see," said Odd, "you are not fair to your
friends. You should paint fewer pictures, and be
more constantly a picture in yourself." She showed
a little uneasy doubtfulness of look.

"I am afraid I don't understand you. I am afraid I am stupid."

"You should *be* a little more, and *act* a little less."

"But to act is to be," said Hilda, with a sudden laugh. "We are not listening to Schumann," she added, a trifle maliciously. Her face turned toward him in a soft shadow, a line of light just defining the cheek's young oval, the lovely slimness of the throat affected Odd with a really rapturously artistic appreciation. The shape of her small head, too, with its high curves of hair, was elegant with an intimate elegance peculiarly characteristic. An inner gentle dignity, a voluntary submission to exterior facts of existence resulting in a higher freedom, a more perfect self-possession, seemed to emanate from her; the very poise of her head suggested it, and so strong and so sudden was the suggestion that Odd felt his curiosity intolerable, and those groping suspicions outrageously at sea.

"Hilda," he said abruptly, "I went to your studio the other afternoon. You were not there."

Her finger flashed warningly to her lip, and her glance towards her mother turned again to him, pained and beseeching.

"She—they can't hear," said Odd, in a still lower voice.

"No, I was not there," Hilda repeated.

"And your father, your mother, Katherine, think you are there when you are not. Is that wise? Don't be angry with me, my dear Hilda. You may have confidence in me. Tell me, do you work somewhere else?"

"*No.* I am not angry. You startled me." Her

look was indeed shaken, but sweet, touched even.
" Yes, I work somewhere else."
" And you keep it a secret ? "
She nodded.
" Is it safe to keep secrets from your father and
mother? Or is it a secret kept for their sakes,
Hilda ? " Peter had made mental combinations,
yet he suspected that in this one he was shooting
rather far from the mark. No matter. Hilda
looked away, and seemed revolving some inner
doubt. Her hesitation surprised him ; he was more
surprised when, half unwillingly, she whispered,
" Yes," still not looking at him.

" For their sakes," repeated Odd, his curiosity
redoubled. " Come, Hilda, please tell me all about
it. For *their* sakes ? "

" In one way." Hilda spoke with the same air
of half-unwilling confidence. But that she should
confide, that she should not lock herself in stubborn
silence, was much.

" And as you need not keep it for my sake, you
may tell me," he urged; " I may be able to help
you."

" Oh ! I don't need help." She turned a slightly
challenging look upon him. " It is no hardship to
me, no trouble to keep my little secret."

" You are really unkind now, Hilda."

" No,"—her smile dwelt on him meditatively ;
"but I see no reason, no necessity for telling you.
I have nothing naughty to confess ! " and there was
a touch of pride in her laugh.

" Yes, you are unkind, for you turn my real anxiety to a jest."

"You must not be anxious." Her eyes still rested on his, sweetly and gently.

"Not when I see you surrounded by an atmosphere of carping criticism? When I see you coming home, night after night, worn out, too fatigued to speak? When I see that you are thin and white and sad?"

Hilda drew herself up a little.

"Oh, you are mistaken. But—how *kind* of you!" and again the irradiated look lit up her face.

"Does *that* surprise you? Hilda, Katherine is in the dark about this too?"

"Katherine knows; but please don't ask her about it."

"She does n't approve, then?"

"Not exactly. Besides, it might hurt her. Please don't ask me either. It really is n't worth any mystery, and yet I must keep it a secret."

Odd was silent for a moment, a baffling sense of pitfalls and hiding-places upon him.

"But Katherine ought to tell me," he said at last, smiling.

"Now you are pushing an unfair advantage. She thinks, probably, that it might hurt *me*. Really, *really*," she added urgently, "it is n't so serious as all this seems to make it. The one serious thing is that it *would* hurt mamma, and that is why I make such a mountain out of my mole-hill. How mystery does magnify the tiniest things!"

"Tell me, at least, where you go in the afternoon. I mean to what part of Paris, to what street."

"I go to several streets," said Hilda, smiling resignedly, "since you *will* be so curious."

"Where are you going to-morrow? Give me just an idea of your prowess."

"I go to-morrow to the Rue d'Assas."

"Near the Luxembourg Gardens?"

"Yes."

"I fancied you were walking yourself to death. And next day?"

"Next day—the Rue Poulletier."

"And where may that be? I fancied I knew my Paris well."

"It is a little street in the Île St. Louis. That is my favorite walk; home along the quays. I get the view of Notre Dame from the back, with all the flying buttresses, and the sunset beyond."

"No wonder you are tired every night. You always walk?"

"Usually. I have Palamon with me, and they would not take him in a 'bus. But from the Île St. Louis I often take the boat, and that is one of the treats of Paris, I think, especially when the lights are lit. And on some days I go to the Boulevard St. Germain. There; now you shall ask me no more questions."

Odd made no further comment on the information he had received, but he resolved to be in the Rue d'Assas to-morrow. He did not intend to spy, but he did intend to walk home with Hilda, and to make her understand that one of the brotherly offices he claimed was the right to protecting companionship. He revolved the *rôle* and its possibilities, as he lay back in the sofa watching Hilda's profile, and listening to Schumann—a *rôle* that could, at all events, not last long, since Allan Hope arrived on Wednesday. Allan's arrival would put an end to mysteries, to a need for brotherly protection. Odd felt a certain curiosity on this point; indeed his attitude towards Hilda was one of continual curiosity.

"So Allan Hope turns up Wednesday week," he said. "I shall be glad to see Allan again."

Hilda's silence might imply displeasure, but Odd, in an attitude of manly laziness, one leg crossed over the other, one hand holding an ankle, thought a little gentle teasing quite allowable.

"Will you go bicycling with him, unkind Hilda?" He was not prepared for the startled look she turned on him.

"When I would not go with *you?*" Her own vehemence seemed to embarrass her. "I hardly know how to bicycle at all," she added lamely; "I would have gone with you if I had had time." She looked away again, and then, taking a book from the table beside her—

"Have you seen the last volume of *décadent* poetry? Isn't the binding nice?" Odd felt himself justly, but rather severely, reproved; yet the gentle candor of her eyes was kind and soothing. Katherine was playing the "Chopin" from Schumann's "Carnaval," and Peter, still holding his ankle and feeling rather like a naughty little boy forgiven, did not look at the fantastic volume she held, but at Hilda herself. How blue the shadows were on the milky whiteness of her skin. Odd's eyes followed the thick, soft eddies of hair about her forehead.

"Aren't the margins generous?" said Hilda,

turning the pages; " a mere trickle of print through the whiteness. Some of the verses are really very pretty," and she talked gayly, in her gentle way, as they went through the pages together.

CHAPTER IV

IT was just past four when Peter walked up the Rue Bonaparte and stationed himself at the corner of the Rue Vavin and the Rue d'Assas, opposite the Luxembourg Gardens.

From this point of vantage he could look up and down the street, and there would be no chance of missing her. She rarely reached home till past six, and, even allowing for very slow walking, he was if anything too early.

He felt, as he opened his umbrella—it had begun to rain—that his present position might look foolish, but was certainly justifiable. He would ask Hilda no questions, force in no way her confidence, but really on the gray dreariness of such a day she ought not to reject but rather to be glad for his proffered and unexpected companionship. The combined dreariness of the afternoon with its cold rain, the gray street, the desolate-looking branches of the trees in the Luxembourg Gardens, inspired him with a painful sympathy for Hilda's pursuits. She was, probably, working in one of these tall, severe houses ; perhaps with some atelier chum fallen beneath the ban of Mrs. Archinard's disapproval, and clung to with a girl's enthusiasm. Disobedient of Hilda, very. The chum might be masculine. This was a new and disagreeable supposition ; a Marie Bash-

kirtseff, Bastien Lepage affair; Bohemia gloried in
such audacities; it was difficult to associate Hilda
with such feats of independence. There was a mystery somewhere, however, and if not mountainous,
it must be more than mere mole-hill. It was very
windy, and the rain blew slantingly. Katherine
would find the situation amusing. A vision of the
sympathetic amusement was followed by the realization that to betray his Quixotism might be to betray Hilda's confidence. Yet Hilda had made no
confidence. Peter rebelled at the mere suggestion
of concealment. Knowing all, Katherine could
surely know that he had been admitted into the
outer courts of the mystery. He had ample time
for every variety of reflection, for he had been standing in the rain for over an hour, when Hilda appeared not far from him, stepping from the door of
one of the largest and most dignified of the gray
houses. She paused on the wet pavement to open
her umbrella, and Peter had a glimpse of the wide
red lips and small black beard of an unpleasant-look-
ing French youth, who seemed to loiter behind her
with a certain air of expectancy. It was impossible
to connect his commonplace vulgarity of aspect
with Bohemian friendships or with Hilda, and, indeed, she gave him a mere nod, not looking at him
at all, and came walking up the street, her skirt
raised in one hand, showing slim feet and ankles.
Odd, as he contemplated her advance, was reminded
of the light poise of a Jean Goujon nymph. Her
umbrella, lowered against the wind, hid him from her.
"Well, Hilda," he said amicably, when she was
almost beside him—the umbrella tilted back over
157

her shoulder, and the rain fell on her startled face—
" Here I am."

Her stare of utmost amazement was very amusing,
but she looked white and tired.

" I must get a *fiacre*, I have n't your taste for
plodding through rain and mud, and you 'll be kind
enough to forego the enjoyment for one day, won't
you ? " Her stupefaction at last resolved itself into
one word : " Well ! " she exclaimed with emphasis,
and then she laughed outright.

" By Jove, child, you look done up. I 'm glad
you 're not angry, though. You would n't laugh if
you were angry, would you ? Here is a *fiacre*."
He hailed the approaching vehicle ; the *cocher's*
hat and cape, the roof of the cab, the horse's waterproof covering glistened with rain in the dying light.

"You are very, very kind," Hilda said, rather
gravely now, as they stood side by side on the curb
while the *fiacre* rattled up to them.

" I always intend to be kind, Hilda, if you will let
me. Jump in." He followed her, slamming the
door with relief, and depositing the two dripping
umbrellas in a corner.

" You must be drenched," said Hilda solemnly.

" Imitation is the sincerest flattery, I believe ;
your fondness for drenchings inspired me. You are
not one bit angry, then ? You see I ask you no
questions."

" Angry ? It was too good of you ! " Her voice
was still meditative.

" I am much relieved that you should say so. I
was only conscious of guilt."

" How long did you wait ? "

" About an hour."

" And it was *pouring !* "

" Oh no, not pouring. I have suffered far worse
drenchings for far less pleasure. One has no umbrella in Scotland on the moors."

" One has, at least, the scenery." Hilda smiled.

" Yes; the Rue d'Assas is n't particularly inspir-
ing. I don't disclaim honor; that corner was most
wearing. Only the irritation of waiting for my
mysterious little truant kept me from finding it
dreary."

" Don't call me mysterious, please."

" But you are mysterious, Hilda; very. However, I promised myself, and I promise you, to say
no more about it, to ask no questions."

" You are so kind, so good." There was deep
feeling in her voice; she looked at him with a certain wistful eagerness. " You really do care, don't
you? Shall I tell you? I should like to. It seems
silly not to tell you, and I think you have a right to
know—after to-day."

" I really care a great deal, Hilda; but—I don't
want to take an unfair advantage, you know; I
really have no right whatsoever. Wait till this impulse of unmerited gratitude has passed."

" But it is nothing to tell, really nothing. You
see—I make money. I have to—I teach. There;
that is all."

Peter looked at her, at the white oval of her face,
at the unfashionable little hat, at the shabby coat
and skirt. A lily of the field who toiled and spun.
And a hot resentment rose within him as he thought
of the father, the mother, the sister.

"Why *have* you to?" he asked, in a hard voice.

"We are so dreadfully poor, and we are so dreadfully in debt."

"But why you alone? What can *you* do?"

"I can do a good deal. I have been very lucky. I love my work too, and I make money by it, so it is natural. Mamma, of course, would think it terrible, degrading even; but I can't agree with mamma's point of view; I think it is quite wrong. I see nothing terrible or degrading."

"No; nothing terrible or degrading, I grant you."

"You think I am right, don't you?"

"Yes; quite right, dear, quite right."

Odd paused before adding: "It is the incongruity that is shocking."

"The incongruity?" Hilda's voice was vague.

"Between your life and theirs; yes."

"Oh, you don't understand. I love my work; it is my pleasure. Besides, they don't know; they don't realize the necessity either."

"Why the teaching? I thought your pictures sold well."

"And so they do, often; but I took up the teaching some years ago, before I had any hope of selling my pictures; it is very *sure*, very well paid, and I really find it a rest after five hours of studio work; after five hours I don't feel a picture any longer."

"Yet they must know that the money comes from somewhere?"

Hilda's voice in replying held a pained quality; this attack on her family very evidently perplexed her.

" Mamma thinks it comes from papa, and papa,
I suppose, does n't think about it at all; he knows,
too, that I sell my pictures. You must n't imagine,"
she added, with a touch of pride and resentment,
" that they would let me teach if they knew; you
must n't imagine that for one moment. And I don't
mean to let them know, for then I could n't help
them; as it is, my help is limited. The money
goes, for the most part, towards *guarding* mamma.
She could not bear shocks and anxiety."

Odd said nothing for some moments.

" How did it begin? how did you come to think
of it?" he asked.

" It began some years ago, at the studio where
I worked when I first came to Paris. There was
a kind, dull French girl there; she had no talent,
and she was very rich. She heard my work praised
a good deal, and one day, after I had got a picture
into the Salon for the first time, she came and asked
me if I would give her lessons. Fifteen francs an
hour." Hilda paused in a way which showed Odd
that the recollection was painful to her.

" It seemed a *very* strange thing to me at first,
that she should ask me. I had, I'm afraid, rather
silly ideas about Katherine and myself; as though
we were very elevated young persons, above all the
unpleasant realities of life. But my common sense
soon got the better of my pride; or rather, I should
say, the false pride made way for the honest. We
were *awfully* poor just then. Papa, of course, never
could, never even tried to make money; but that winter he went in for exasperated speculation, and really
Katherine and I did not know what was to become

of us. To keep it from mamma was the great thing. Katherine was just beginning to go out, and no money for gowns and cabs; no money, even, for mamma's books. Keeping up with current literature is expensive, you know, and mamma has a horror of circulating libraries. The thought of poor mamma's empty life soon decided me. I remember she had asked one day for John Addington Symonds's last book, and Katherine and I looked at one another, knowing that it could not be bought. I realized then, that at all events I could make enough to keep mamma in books and Katherine in gloves. You can't think how nasty, how egotistic my vulgar hesitation seemed to me. My life so full, so happy, and theirs on the verge of ruin. There is something very selfish about art, you know; it shuts one off so much from real life, makes one so indifferent to scrapings and pinchings. I realized that, with my shabby clothes and apparent talent, it was most natural for the French girl to think I should be glad of her offer; and indeed I was. It was soothing, too, to have her so eager. She wanted me very much, so I yielded gracefully." Hilda gave a little smile of self-mockery. " I have taught her ever since. She lives in that house in the Rue d'Assas; rich, bourgeois people, common, but kind. She has no talent "—Hilda's matter-of-fact manner of knowledge was really impressive—" but I don't feel unfair in going on with her, for she really does see things now, and that is the greatest pleasure next to seeing and accomplishing ; and, indeed, how rarely one accomplishes. Through her I have a great many pupils, for other girls at the studio heard of

her progress with me, and wanted private lessons
too. All my afternoons are taken up, and, with
fifteen francs an hour, you can see what a lot I make.
It rather annoys me to think of people far cleverer
than I am who can make nothing, and I, just because I have had luck, making so much. But among
my pupils, I really have quite a *vogue ;* and I *am* a
good teacher, I really think I am."

" I am sure your pupils are very lucky. You have
a great many, you say ? "

" Yes, quite a lot. Sometimes I give three lessons in an afternoon. With Mademoiselle Lebon,
my first pupil, I spend all the afternoon twice a
week. She has a gorgeous studio." Hilda smiled
again. " It is very nice working there. To-morrow
I go for two hours to an old lady ; she lives in the
Boulevard St. Germain ; she is a dear, and a great
deal of talent too ; she does flowers exquisitely ; not
the dreadful feminine vulgarities one usually asso-
ciates with women's flower-painting ; why all the
incompetents should fall back on those loveliest and
most difficult things, I never could understand. But
my pupil really sees and selects. Only think how
funny ! Katherine met her son at a dance one
night—the Comte de Chalons—insignificant but
nice, she said ; how little he could have connected
Katherine with his mother's teacher ! Indeed, he
never saw me," and Hilda's smile became decidedly
clever. " I suppose the comtesse—she really is a
dear, too—thinks that for a penniless young teacher
I am too pretty. Well, I make on an average thirty
francs an afternoon. I give Mademoiselle Lebon
and Madame de Chalons double time for their

money, as old pupils. It would be easier to have a class in my studio, of course, but I would lose many of my most interesting pupils, who don't care about going out; then, too, it would be almost impossible to keep my misdoings undiscovered. And there is all the mystery!" She leaned forward in the dusk of the cab to smile at him playfully. "I am glad to get it off my mind ; glad, too, that you should know why I am so often cross and dull; by the time I reach home I am tired. I always bring Palamon, unless it is as rainy as to-day, and of course he puts omnibuses out of the question; omnibuses mount up, too, when one takes them every day. Excuse these sordid details."

"I should think that a young lady who earns thirty francs an afternoon might afford a cab." Odd found it rather difficult to speak. She was mercifully unaware of the aspect in which her drudging, crushed young life appeared to him.

"And then, what would Palamon and I do for exercise!" said Hilda lightly; "it is the walking that keeps me well, I am sure."

His silence seemed to depress her gayety, for after a moment she added: "And really you don't know how poor we are. I have no right to cabs, really. As it is, it often seems wrong to me spending the money as I do when we owe so much, so terribly much. Thirty francs is a lot, but we need every penny of it, for mere everyday life. I have paid off some of the smaller debts by instalments, but the weekly bills seem to swallow up everything."

His realization of this silent struggle—the whole

weight of her selfish family on her frail shoulders—
made Odd afraid of his own indignation. The re-
membrance of Mrs. Archinard's whines, the Captain's
taunts, yes, and worst of all, Katherine's gowns and
gayety, almost overcame him. He took her hand
in his and held it as they rolled along through the
wetly shining streets. His continued silence rather
alarmed Hilda. The relief of full confidence was so
great that she could not bear it impaired by any
misinterpretation.

"You do understand," she said; "you do think I
am right? My success seems unmerited to you,
perhaps? But I try to give my best. I seem very
selfish and unkind to mamma, I know, but I really
am kind—don't you think so?—in keeping the truth
from her and letting her misjudge me. I know you
have thought of me that I was one of those selfish
idiots who neglect their real duties for their art;
but I can do more for mamma outside our home.
And I read to her in the evening. Oh, how con-
ceited, egotistic, all that sounds! But I do want
you to believe that I try to do what seems best and
wisest."

"Hilda! Hilda!" he put her hand to his lips and
kissed the worn glove.

"You simply astound me," he said, after a moment; "your little life facing this great Paris."

"Oh, I am very careful, very wise," Hilda said
quickly.

"Careful? You mean that if you were not you
might encounter unpleasantnesses?"

She looked at him with a look of knowledge that
went strangely with her delicate face.

"Of course one must be careful. I am young—
and pretty. I have learned that."

" My child, what other things have you learned ? "
And Odd's hold tightened on her hand.

" That terrifying things might happen if one were
not brave. Don't exaggerate, please. I really have
found so few lions in my path, and a girl of dignity
cannot be really annoyed beyond a certain point.
Lions are very much magnified in popular and conventional estimation. A girl can, practically, do
anything she likes here in Paris if she is quiet and
self-reliant."

Odd stared at her.

" Of course I have always been a coward, after a
fashion ; I was frightened at first," said Hilda. He
understood now the look of moral courage that had
haunted him ; natural timidity steeled to endurance.
" The greatest trouble with me is that I am too
noticeable, too pretty." She spoke of her beauty
in a tone of matter-of-fact experience ; " it is a pity
for a working woman."

" My child," Odd repeated. He felt dazed.

" Please don't exaggerate," Hilda reiterated.

" Exaggerate ? Tell me about these lions. How
have you vanquished them ? "

" I have merely walked past them."

His evident dismay gave her a merry little moment
of superior wisdom.

" They frightened me and that was all. One was
the husband of a person I taught. He used to lie
in wait for me in the dining-room." Hilda gave
Odd a rather meditative glance. " You won't be

angry? Angry with *me* for keeping on in my path of independence?"

"No; I won't be angry with you." Odd felt that his very lips were white.

"Well, he gave me a letter one day." Hilda paused. "What a despicable man!" she said reflectively; "I taught his wife! I tore the letter in two, gave it back to him, and walked out. Naturally, I never went back again." Her voice suddenly broke. "Oh! it was horrible! I felt—"

"What did you feel?"

"I felt as though I were for evermore set apart from *my* kind of girl, from girls like Katherine. I felt smirched, as though some one had thrown mud at me. That was morbid. I got over it."

"Heavens!" Odd ejaculated. "Katherine knows this too?" he asked bitingly.

"Oh no, no! Mr. Odd, you are the only person. Never speak of it, will you? Never, never! Poor Kathy! It would drive her mad!"

"And she knows of your work?"

"Yes; I had to tell her of that. She felt dreadfully about it. She wanted me to go out with her, and have pretty dresses, and meet the clever people she meets. You should have seen how happy she was in London last spring! To have me with her! Wrenched away from my paint! Of course I could not give up my work, even if there had been money enough. I made her see that, and I can't say I made her agree, but I made her yield. She takes a false view of it still, and worries over it. She wants me to give up the teaching and paint pictures only; but that would be too risky, they don't sell so surely. I have several on my hands. But Katherine knows nothing of lions and unpleasant: ness. I must keep such things secret, or I should not be allowed to go on."

"You think I am safe. I must allow you, I suppose?"

"Yes, you must." She smiled a very decided little smile, adding gravely, " I have confided in you."

"Trust me." There was silence in the cab for some moments. The tall trees of the Cours la Reine dripped in a misty mass on one side ; on the other was the Seine with its lights.

"And the young man I saw at the door as you came out to-day?" said Odd.

"Oh, that is nothing, I hope. He is Mademoiselle Lebon's brother. A harmlessly disagreeable creature, I fancy." Odd resumed his brooding silence. "What are you thinking of so solemnly?" she asked.

"Of you."

" Why so solemnly? I am afraid you are laboring under all sorts of false impressions. I have told my story stupidly."

" The true impression has stupefied me. Good heavens ! Theoretically I believe in the development of character at all costs, and you have certainly developed a *rara avis* in the line ; but practically, practically, my dear little girl, I would have you taken care of in cotton-wool, guarded, protected ; you would always be lovely, and you would have been happy. You have been very unhappy."

Hilda was looking at him with that rather vague

look of impersonal contemplation characteristic of her.

"How you exaggerate things," she said, smiling; "I have not been unhappy."

"The pity of it! The pathos!" Odd pursued, not heeding her comment. Hilda looked at him rather sadly.

"You mean that I should have lost my ignorance? Yes, that made me feel badly," she assented. "That is the worst of it. One becomes so suspicious. But, Mr. Odd, that is merely a sentimental regret. I have not lost my self-respect. I am not ignorant of things I should like to ignore; but one may know a great many things, and be unharmed."

"My dear child, you are probably innocent of things familiar to many modern girls. No knowl-edge could harm you. You have a right to more than self-respect. You are a little heroine. Your unrewarded, unrecognized fight fills me with amazement and reverence. I did not know that such self-forgetful devotion existed."

"Oh, please don't talk like that! It is quite ridiculous! We must have money, and I can make it easily. I would be quite a monster if I sat idly at home, and saw mamma in squalid misery. I merely do my duty." Hilda spoke quite sharply and decisively.

"Merely!" Odd ejaculated.

A thought of the near future, of Allan Hope, kept him silent, otherwise he might have indulged in reckless invective. He still held her hand, and again he raised it to his lips.

169

"That is a very stubborn and unconvinced salute, I am afraid," Hilda said good-humoredly.

"May I come and get you now and then?" he asked.

"You think it would be wise?"

"How do you mean wise, Hilda?"

"I might be found out. I have given you my secret. You must help me to keep it."

"I may speak of it to Katherine—since she knows?"

"Oh, of course, to Katherine. But don't *egg* her on to worry me!" laughed Hilda; "and speak to her with *reservations*—there are things she must not know."

Peter wondered if the child-friendship, the brotherly relations, entitled him to seal the compact with a kiss upon her lips. He looked at her with a sudden quickening of breath. Her dimly seen face was very beautiful. This realization of her beauty's attraction at that moment struck him with a sense of abasement before her. Surely no such poor tie held him to this lovely soul. And, at the turn of his own thoughts, Odd felt a vague stir of fear.

CHAPTER V

ODD was to take a walk in the Bois with Katherine the next morning, and he found her waiting for him in hat and coat and furs, a delightfully smart and wintry little figure. Katherine never failed in elegance, in well-groomed finish—her low-heeled little boots, her irreproachable snowy gloves, bore the same unmistakable stamp of the *cachet* that costs, that is not to be procured ready made. Odd, as a rich man, had given very little thought to the power of money, and little thought to Katherine's garments except as charmingly characteristic symbols of good taste; but to-day his eye noted the black fur that fell about her shoulders and trailed lustrous ends to her very feet, more for its richness than its becomingness.

Her bright though slightly grave smile failed to restore him to his usual attitude of *bon camaraderie*. He smiled and kissed her, but he was conscious of underlying soreness, conscious, too, that he might lose his temper with Katherine; he had never lost it with Alicia. Katherine's very superiority made it imperative to have things out with her. Kindly resignation was an impossibility. He realized that not to admire Katherine would make life with her intolerable. She would immediately perceive reservations and she would revolt against them. He

171

wondered whether he should be the one to broach the subject of Hilda's ill-treatment, and was amazed at a certain embarrassed shrinking, as from a feeling too deep for words, that kept him silent as they walked along, taking a short cut to the Place de l'Etoile, where the Arc stood in almost cardboard clearness on the pale cold sky. It was Katherine who spoke—

" Hilda told me of your kindness yesterday. It touched her very much."

In some subtle way it irritated Odd to hear Katherine vouch for Hilda's feeling.

" And Hilda told you that I had been admitted into the mystery of the Archinard family?" His voice was even enough, but it held a certain keenness that Katherine was quick to recognize.

" You don't think their mystery creditable, do you? Nor do I, Peter. But mamma knows nothing of it, nor papa; and I have tried to dissuade Hilda from the first."

" My dear Katherine, the child has worked like a galley-slave for you all! Your necessities were more potent facts than your dissuasions, I fancy!"

Katherine gave a look at the fine severity of the profile beside her. She felt herself arraigned, and her impulse was towards rebellion. However, her voice was gentle, submissive even, as she answered him—

" I know it must look badly to you—cruel even. But, Peter, don't you know—you do know—how things *grow* around one? One can hardly tell where the definite wrongdoing comes in, or rather the definite submission to a wrong situation." This

was so true, that Katherine felt immediately the
mollified quality of his voice as he answered—

"I know. I know submission was forced upon
you, no doubt. But I had rather you had not submitted when once the situation grew definite. And
I wish, Katherine, that you had helped her in making the situation easier. Granting that you could
give her no material aid—granting that her faculty
is good luck—still the actual burden might have
been lightened."

Odd paused; he could not say his thoughts outright—tell her that the comparative luxury of her
life and her mother's was outrageous, shocking to
him now that he understood its source.

"It is part of Hilda's good luck that her pleasures
are not costly, or rather that she can herself defray
their cost," said Katherine quietly. "She has always lived in her art—seemed to care for nothing
else. My life would indeed have been dreadful had
I not accepted the interests that came into it. I
have always felt, too, that in following the natural
bent of my own character, I was laying foundations
that might some day repay Hilda for everything.
If she has friends—a public—it is owing to me. It
was I who persuaded her to come to London last
spring. I, therefore, who assured her future, in a
sense, for there Allan Hope fell in love with her.
I have felt that I have been doing my duty, in my
own far less conventionally fine way, but doing it
nevertheless. I make a circle for mamma; I brighten
her life and my own and Hilda's, as far as she will
let me. Certain *tools* are necessary—Hilda needs
brushes and canvases and studios; I, a few gowns,

a few cabs, and a supply of neat boots and gloves. Still the contrast is uncomplimentary to me, I own; but when Hilda proposed this work of hers, I entreated her to give up the idea—I said we would all starve together rather. She insisted, and how can I interfere?"

"I can understand, Katherine, that everything you say is most convincing to yourself; I see the perfect honesty of your own point of view. But, my dear girl, it is slightly sophistical honesty. Hilda denies herself the commonest comforts of life, not only to give you the luxuries, but because her high sense of honor rebels against spending on herself money that is owed to others. Don't misunderstand me; I don't ask any such perhaps overstrained sense of responsibility from you. You have, no doubt, been fully justified in living your own life; but could it not have been lived with a little less elegance? I am sure that you would be welcomed everywhere, Katherine, with even fewer gowns and fewer gloves."

Katherine flushed lightly; her flushes were never deep, and always becoming. It certainly cut her now to hear his almost unconscious implication— that from her he expected a less perfect sense of honor than from her sister. She swallowed a certain wrathful mortification that welled up, and answered with some apparent cheerfulness—

"You don't know your world, Peter, if you fancy that even Katherine Archinard would be welcome in darned and dirty gloves!"

Odd walked on silently.

"And might she not be forced into taking some

girlish distraction ? " he said presently. "It came
out yesterday, with that astounding air of *excusing*
herself she has, that she reads to her mother in the
evening! Could not you do that, Katherine, and
let Hilda profit now and then by the *entourage* you
have created for her ? "

Katherine's flush deepened.

" Mamma does n't care for my reading, and Hilda
won't go out; she goes to bed too early."

" And then," Odd continued, ignoring her comment in a way most irritating to Katherine's smart-
ing susceptibility, "you might have gone with her
now and again to these houses where she teaches.
You would have stood for protection. You would
have seen for yourself if, in this drudgery, there
lurked any unpleasantness, any danger. A girl of
her extreme beauty is—exposed to insult."

Katherine gave him a stare of frank astonishment.

" Oh, you must not give way to unpleasant ro-
mancing of that sort! Things like that only happen
in novels of the silliest sort—even to beauties! And
Hilda would have told *me*. She tells me *everything*.
Really, Peter, she must have given you a wrong impression; she enjoys her life! "

" So she tried to convince me," said Odd, with a
good deal of sharpness; " there was no hint of complaint, regret, reproach, in Hilda's recountal; don't
imagine it, Katherine."

Katherine was telling herself that never in all her
life had she experienced so many rebuffs. She contemplated her own good temper with some amazement ; she also wondered how long it would last.
By this time they were half-way down the Avenue

du Bois ; the day was fine and clear, and the wintry trees were sharply definite against the sky.

" I have never even seen her in a well-made gown," said Odd.

" Hilda scorns the fashion-plate garment, as I do. We are both original in that respect."

" Your originality takes different forms."

" Because it must adapt itself to different conditions, Peter. I won't be scolded about my dresses. Men like you imagine that, because a woman looks well, she must spend a lot. It is n't so with me. My dresses last forever, and, to go into details, Hilda by no means clothes me. Papa has money—now and then. Even Hilda could not support the family, and her money mainly goes for mamma's books and oysters and hot-house grapes. If she will not spend it on herself, and if, now and then, I accept some of it, I cannot consent to feel unduly humiliated."

There was a decisiveness in Katherine's tone that warned Peter to self-control. Indeed the situation had been created for her. She had owned up frankly to her distaste for it, her realization of its wrong.

" I am not going to ask undue humiliation of you, my dear Katherine. Don't think me such a priggish brute ; but I am going to ask you to help me to put an end to this." Katherine's smiles had returned.

" Allan Hope will."

Peter walked on, looking gloomy.

" You won't realize that Hilda's life is the one that gives her the greatest enjoyment. I have always envied Hilda till *you* came ; and even now " —Katherine's smile was playful—" Allan Hope is very nice ! Take patience, Peter, till Wednesday."

" Yes ; we must wait."

" I have waited for so long ! Hilda could not have minded what you call the ' drudgery.' She had only to lift her finger to end it."

" Hilda would not be the girl to lift her finger."

" You appreciate my Hilda, Peter ; I am glad." Katherine gave his abstracted countenance another of her bright contemplative glances. There was nothing sly in Katherine's glances, and yet underlying this one was a world of kindly, though very keen analysis ; disappointment, rebellion, and level-headed tolerance. This was decidedly not the man to be fitted to her frame. He could not be moulded to a clever woman's liking, for all his indefiniteness. On certain points of the conduct of life, Katherine felt that she would meet an opposition sharply definite. Katherine understood and was perfectly tolerant of criticism, but she did not like it ; nor did she like being put in the wrong. That Peter now considered her very much in the wrong was evident. She was also aware that the sophistry of her explanation had deceived herself even less than it had deceived him. That Hilda spent her life in drudgery, and that she spent hers in pleasure-seeking, were facts most palpable to Katherine's very impartial vision. She knew she was wrong, and she knew that only frank avowal would meet Peter's severity and touch his tenderness and humor. If she heaped shame on her own head, he would be the first to cry out against the injustice.

Yet Katherine hesitated to own herself wrong. She was not sure that she cared to place her lover in the sheltering and leading attitude of the Love

12   177

in the "Love and Life." The meek, trembling look
of Life had always irritated her in the picture.
Katherine felt herself quite strong enough to stand
alone, and felt that she would like to lead in all
things. It was with a deep inner sense of humiliation that she said—

" Please don't be cross with me, Peter. Please
don't scold me. I have been naughty—far naugh-
tier than I dreamed of—you have made me realize
it, though you are not quite just. But you must
comfort me for my own misdoings."

As Katherine went on she felt an artistic impul-
siveness, almost real, and which sounded so real that
Peter met the sweet pleading of her eyes with a
start of self-disgust.

Peter was very tender-hearted, very sympathetic,
very prone to self-doubt. Katherine's look made
him feel a very prig of pompous righteousness.

" Why, Katherine ! " he said, pausing in his walk.
" My dear Katherine ! as if I could not appreciate
the slow growth of necessity ! I only hope you
may never have to comfort me for far worse sins ! "

This was satisfactory. But Katherine's pride still
squirmed.

Odd went to meet Hilda on Thursday, Saturday,
Monday, and Tuesday. The distances were always
great, and he insisted on cabs for the return trip.
Palamon must be tired, even if Hilda were not.
He was too old for such journeyings ; and Hilda
had smilingly to submit. Wednesday would end it
all definitely ; Peter thought that he saw the end
with unmixed satisfaction, and yet when Allan
Hope walked into his rooms early on Wednesday

morning, this Perseus of Hilda's womanhood gave the Perseus of her childhood a really unpleasant turn of the blood. There was something irritating in Allan Hope's absolute fitness for the *rôle*, emphasizing, as it did, Peter's own unfitness, his forty years, and his desultory life.

Active energy, the go-ahead perseverance that knows no doubts, the honest and loyal convictions which were all arranged for him from his cradle, and which he would bequeath to his children unaltered, all things that make for order and well-being, looked at one from Lord Allan's clear, light eyes. Odd suddenly felt himself to be an uncertain cumberer of the earth; failure personified beside the other's air of inevitable success. He was fond of Hope and Hope fond of him, and they talked as old friends talk, with the intimacy that time brings; an intimacy far removed from the strong knittings of sympathy that an hour may accomplish; for, though Odd understood Allan very well, Allan did not muddle his direct views of things by a comprehension that implied condonation. He thought it rather a pity that Odd had not made more of his life. Odd's books were n't much good that he could see; better do something than write about the things other men have done. Odd felt that Allan was probably quite right. They hardly spoke of Hilda, but in Hope's congratulations on Peter's engagement there was a ring of heartfelt brotherly warmth that implied much, and left Peter in a gloomy rage with himself for feeling miserable. Peter had not analyzed the darks and glooms of the last few days.

Growth does not admit of much self-contempla-
tion. One wakes suddenly to the accomplished
change. If Peter was conscious of developments,
he defined them as morbid enlargements of that
self-doubt which would naturally thrill under the
stress of new responsibilities.

Only from the force of newly formed habit did
he go to the Rue Poulletier that afternoon, hardly
expecting to meet Hilda. But Hilda had, as yet,
not interrupted her usual avocations. She emerged
from the gloomy portals of one of the old disman-
tled-looking *hôtels* that line the Rue Poulletier with
a certain dignity, and she looked toward the corner where he stood with a confident glance. It was
the second time he had met her there, twice in the
Rue d'Assas too.

" It is so kind of you," she said, as she joined him
and they turned into the *quai;* "only you must n't
think that you *must*, you know."

" *May* I think that I *must?* Give me the assurance of necessity. I am always a little afraid of
seeming officious."

Hilda smiled round at him.

" Who is fishing? You know I love to have you
come. You can't think how I look forward to it."
She was walking beside him along the *quai.* The
unobtrusive squareness of the " Doric little Morgue"
was on their left, as they faced the keen wind and
the dying sunset. Notre Dame stood gray upon
a chilly evening sky of palest yellow. "I know
now that I *was* lonely."

" That implies the kindest compliment."

" More than *implies*, I hope."

"You really like to have me come?"

"You know I do. I am only afraid that you will rob yourself—of other things for me."

The candor of her eyes was childlike.

"My little friend." Odd felt that he could not quite trust himself, and took refuge in the convenient assertion.

The cold, clear wind blew against their faces; it ruffled the water, and the gray waves showed sharp steely lights. The leafless trees made an arabesque of tracery on the river and the sky. Hilda looked up at the kind, melancholy face beside her, a faint touch of cynicism in her sad smile; but the cynicism was all for herself, and it was not excessive. She accepted this renaissance gratefully, though the disillusions of the past were unforgetable.

"Tell me, Hilda, that you will be my friend whatever happens—to you or to me."

"I have always been your friend, have I not?"

"Have you, Hilda, always?"

"I am dully faithful." Hilda's smile was a little baffling; it gave no warrant for the sudden quickening of the breath that he had experienced more than once of late.

"I feel as if I had *found* you, Hilda."

"Did you *look* for me, then?"

The smile was now decidedly baffling and yet very sweet.

"You know," she added, "I liked you from that first moment when you fished me out of the river. It seems that you are fated to act always the chivalrous part toward me."

" I would ask no better fate. Hilda, you have seen Allan Hope? Not yet?"

"No; not yet." Hilda's face grew serious. " He is coming to tea this afternoon."

" But you must be there."

" Yes, I suppose I must." This affectation of girlish indifference seemed to Odd more significant than noticeable shyness.

" We must take a cab," he said, trying to keep his voice level.

" Oh, it makes no difference. Cabs, you see, are never reckoned with in my arrivals. I am warranted to be late."

" But you must not be late."

" But if I want to? " There was certainly a touch of roguery in her eyes.

" If you want to and if I want you to, it shows that you are cruel and I conscienceless. Here is a cab. Away with you, Hilda. *Au revoir.*"

" Are n't you coming too? " asked Hilda, pausing in the act of lifting Palamon.

" Not to-day; I can't." Odd knew that he was cowardly. " I shall see you to-morrow? I suppose not."

" Why, yes, if you come to the Boulevard St. Germain." Hilda had deposited Palamon on the floor of the cab and still stood by the open door looking rather dismayed.

" Really ! "

" I shall go there."

" I too, then. Remember our vow of friendship, Hilda. I wish you everything that is good and happy."

HILDA

There was seemingly a slightly hurt look on Hilda's face as she drove away. In spite of the vow, Peter feared that this was the last of Hilda, of even this rather shadowy second edition of friendship.

He had done his duty ; to hurt oneself badly seems a surety of having done one's duty thoroughly.

HILDA drove home, with Palamon leaning his warm body against her feet as he sat on the floor of the cab. She put out her hand now and then and laid it on his head, but absently. She leaned back presently and closed her eyes, only rousing herself with a little start when the cab drew up with a jerk in the Rue Pierre Charron. Palamon stood dully on the pavement while she spoke to the cabman—but the *monsieur* had paid him, as Hilda had forgotten for the moment. Palamon was evidently tired too, and with a little turn of dread she wondered if the time would come when she must leave Palamon to a lonely day in the apartment. Mrs. Archinard did not like dogs near her. Katherine was always out, and although Rosalie the cook was devoted to the *tou-tou*, Hilda would miss him terribly and he would miss her.

She said to herself that if it came to that she would allow herself a daily cab-fare rather than leave Palamon, and she toiled up the steep stairs carrying him. Taylor opened the door to her.

" Give me the dog, Miss Hilda ; you do look that tired. You are to go at once into the drawing-room, Miss. Lord Allan Hope has been waiting for some time."

Hilda was surprised to find that she had been

184

thinking of Palamon rather than of the ordeal before her. She felt calm now, perfectly, as she walked into the drawing-room, a little taken aback, however, to find Lord Allan there waiting for her and alone.

Katherine was in the next room, her own pretty room, a rather perplexed smile of expectancy on her face. Taylor brought in Palamon, and Katherine gave him a drink and patted him kindly. Palamon would go with Hilda to her new home—dear old Palamon! The thought of Hilda's new home and homes—of the castle in Somersetshire and the shooting-lodge in Scotland, and the big house in Grosvenor Square, deepened the look of perplexity on Katherine's brow.

While Palamon lapped the water, she watched him with an expression of absent-minded concentration. She could hear nothing in the drawing-room, except now and then the slightly raised quiet of Allan Hope's fine voice. Presently there was a long silence, and Katherine paused near the door.

The quizzical lift of her eyebrows spoke her amused inquiry. She could hardly imagine Hilda allowing herself to be kissed, and as the silence continued, Katherine felt a touch of impatience color her sisterly sympathy. Lord Allan's voice, pitched on a deep note of pain, startled her. There followed quite a burst of ardent eloquence. With a little *moue* of self-disapproval Katherine bent her ear to the door. She heard Lord Allan quite distinctly. He was pleading in more desperate accents than she could have imagined possible from him, and Katherine caught, too, the half frightened reiteration of Hilda's voice: " I can't, I can't; really I can't. I am so—*so* sorry, so sorry—" The childishness of this helpless repetition brought a quick frown to Katherine's brow.

" Little idiot ! Baby ! "

She straightened herself and stood staring at the gray houses across the way. Then, at renewed silence in the drawing-room, she walked to the mirror and looked at her amethyst-robed reflection.

Her eyes lingered on the contour of her waist, the supple elegance of the line that fell gleaming from her hip. She met the half-shamed, half-daring glance of her deeply set eyes. The silence continued, and Katherine walked out through the entrance and into the drawing-room.

Hilda was sitting upright on a tall chair, looking at the floor with an expression of painful endurance, and Lord Allan stood looking at her.

He turned his eyes almost unseeingly on Katherine and remained silent, while Hilda rose and put out her hand to him. Hilda had no variety of metaphor; "I am so sorry," she repeated.

She left her hand in his for one moment and then passed swiftly out of the room. Katherine was left facing the unfortunate lover. Katherine showed great tact.

"Lord Allan, don't mind me. Sit down for a moment. Perhaps then you may be able to tell me. Perhaps I can help you."

"No good, Miss Archinard ; it 's all up with me."

Her gentle voice evidently turned aside the current of his frank despair. Instead of rushing out, he dropped on the sofa and looked at the carpet over his locked hands.

" I am not going to talk to you for a little while."
The lamps were lighted and the tea-things all in
readiness on the little table. Katherine lit the kettle
and turned a log on the fire. Lord Allan's silence
implied a dull acquiescence. He did not move
until Katherine came and sat down on the chair
beside him.

"*I* am so sorry, too," she said, with a sad little
smile. "Lord Allan, I thought she cared for you."

" I hoped so."

" And have you no more hope?"

" None—absolutely none. I tell you it's rough
on a fellow, Miss Archinard. I—I *adore* that
child."

" Poor Lord Allan," Katherine gently breathed.
She stretched out her slim hand and laid it almost
tenderly on his. Katherine was rather surprised
at herself, and to herself her motives were rather
confused. " I should have liked you as a brother,
Lord Allan."

" You are awfully kind." He lifted his dreary
eyes and surveyed her absently, but with some
gratitude. " I suppose I had best be going," he
added suddenly, as if struck by the anti-climax of
his position.

" No, no; not unless you feel you must."
Katherine put out her hand again and detained his
rising. " I can't bear to think of you going out
alone like that into the cold. Just wait. You are
bruised. Get back your breath. I am not going
to be tiresome."

Lord Allan leaned back in the sofa with a long
sigh, relapsing into the same half stunned silence,

while Katherine moved about the tea-table, meas-
uring out the tea from the caddy to the teapot,
pouring on the boiling water, and pausing to wait
for the tea to steep. Presently Lord Allan was
startled by a proffered steaming cup.

"Will you?" she said. "I made it for you. It
is such a chilly evening."

"Oh, how awfully kind of you," he started from
his crushed recumbency of attitude, "but you
know I really *can't!*" But at the grieved gentleness of Katherine's eyes he took the cup. "It is
too awfully kind of you. I do feel abominably
chilly." He gulped down the tea, and gave a half
shame-faced smile as she took the cup for replen-
ishment.

"No, don't get up," she urged, as he made an
effort to collect his courtesy; "let me wait on you,"
and she returned with a discreetly tempting plate of
the thinnest bread and butter. She sat down beside him again, looking into the fire with kind, sad
eyes as she stirred her tea. She asked him presently, in the same quietly gentle voice, some little
question about the most recent debate in the
House. Lord Allan had rather distinguished himself in that debate; it was on the crest of that
wave of triumph that he had come to Hilda. From
monosyllabic replies he was led on to a rather dole-
ful recitation of his own prowess; it seemed that
Katherine had followed it all in the newspapers, so
tactfully intelligent were her comments. He found
himself sipping his third cup of tea, enjoying in a
dreary way the expounding of his favorite political
theories to the quiet, purple-robed figure beside

him. He remembered that Miss Archinard had always been interested in his career; she, of course, was the intellectual one, though Hilda's beauty sent a sharp stab of pain through him as he made the comparison; he appreciated now Miss Archinard's kindness and sympathy with a brotherly warmth of gratitude. When he at last rose to go, he was dejected; but no longer the crushed individual of an hour before.

"You have been too good to a beaten man," he said, taking her hand.

"Oh, Lord Allan, by the laws of compensation you must lose *sometimes*. Hilda, poor child, does n't know what she has done; she cannot know. Her little achievements bound the world for her. She does n't see outside her studio walls. *Your* great world of action, true beneficent action, would stun her. Do you leave Paris directly, Lord Allan? Yes! Then won't you write to me now and then? I am interested in you. I won't relinquish the claim of 'it might have been.' May I keep in touch with you—as a sister would?"

"You are too good, Miss Archinard."

"To an old friend? A man I have followed and admired as I have you? Lord Allan, I respect you from the bottom of my heart for the way in which you have borne this knock-down from fate. You are strong, it won't hurt you in the end. Let me know how you get on."

Katherine's eyes were compelling in their candid kindness. Lord Allan said that he would, with emphasis. As he went down the long staircase, the purple-robed figure filled his thoughts with a reviving beneficence. He felt that the blow was perhaps not so bad as he had imagined—might even be for the best ; better for him, for his career. Katherine's words enveloped him in an atmosphere that was soothing.

Left alone, Katherine finished her second cup of tea, and made, as she looked thoughtfully into the fire, a second little *moue* of self-disapprobation.

CHAPTER VII

ODD, as usual, found Katherine in the drawing-room when he called next morning. The Captain and Mrs. Archinard had assumed almost the aspect of illusions of late ; for the regularity of his daily routine—the morning spent with Katherine, and the afternoon with Hilda—excluded the hours of their appearance, and Odd was rather glad of the discovered immunity.

Katherine was reading beside the fire, one slim sole tilted towards the blaze, and she looked round at Odd as he came in, without moving. Odd's face wore a curiously strained expression, and, under it, seemed thinner, older than usual. He looked even haggard, Katherine thought. She liked his thin face. It satisfied perfectly her sense of fitness, as Odd did indeed. It offered no stupidities, no pretences of any kind for mockery to fasten on. The clever feminine eye is quick to remark the subtlest signs of fatuity or complacency. Katherine's eye was very clever, and this morning, in looking at Odd, she was conscious of a little inner sigh. Katherine had asked herself more than once of late whether a husband, not only too superior for success, but morally her superior, might not make life a little wearing. Some such thought crossed her mind now as she met his eyes, and she realized that

191

through Allan Hope's discomfiture she herself was as wrongly placed as ever, and Hilda's drudgery as binding.

Indeed, several thoughts mingled with that general sense of *malaise*.

One was that Allan Hope's smooth, handsome face was rather fatuous; the face that knows no doubts is in danger of seeming fatuous to a Katherine.

Another thought held a keen conjecture on Peter's haggard looks.

She put out her hand to him, and, stooping over her, he kissed her with more tenderness than he always showed. Their engagement had left almost untouched the easy unsentimental attitude of earlier days.

" Well," he said, and Katherine understood and resented somewhat the quick attack of the absorbing subject. She shook her head.

" Bad news, Peter. Bad and very unexpected."

Odd stood upright and looked at her.

" Bad ! " he repeated.

" She refused him," Katherine said tersely, and her glance turned once more from the fire to Peter's face. He looked at her silently.

" She is a foolish baby," added Katherine.

" She refused him—definitely ? "

" Quite. She had to face the music last night, of course. Mamma and papa were rather—shabby— let us say, in their disinterested disappointment." Odd flushed a little at the cool cynicism of Katherine's tone. " She told me, when I removed her from the battlefield, that she does n't love him and never will. So, of course, from every high and mighty point of view she is right, quite right."

Katherine's eyes returned contemplatively to the fire. Odd was still silent.

" She ought to love him, of course ; that is where she is so foolish. I am afraid she has ruined her life. I love you, Peter, and he is every bit as good-looking as you are." Katherine glanced at him with a sad and whimsical smile. Peter, certainly, was looking rather dazed. He stooped once more and kissed her.

" Thank you for loving me, Katherine."

" You are welcome. It *is* a pity, is n't it ? "

" Yes, it is "—Peter seated himself on the sofa, where Allan had sat the night before—" an awful pity," he added. " I·am astonished. I thought she cared for him."

" So did I."

" She cares for some one else, perhaps." Odd locked his hands behind his head, and he too stared at the fire.

" There is no one else she could care for. I know Hilda's outlook too well."

" And she refused him," he repeated musingly.

" Really, Peter, that sounds a little dull—not like you." Katherine smiled at him.

" I feel dulled. I am awfully sorry. It would have been so satisfactory. And what 's to be done now ? "

" That is for you to suggest, Peter. My power over Hilda is very limited. You may have more influence."

" She might come and live with us."

13   193

"That would be very nice," Katherine assented, "and it is very dear of you to suggest it."

Peter was conscious of sudden terrors that prompted him to add with self-scorn—

"What would your mother do?"

"Without her? I don't know."

"Of course," Peter hastened to add, "as far as money goes, you know; you understand, dear, that your mother shall want nothing. But to rob her of the companionship of both daughters?" Peter rose and walked to the window. It needed some heroism, he thought, to put aside the idea of Hilda living with them; he tried to pride himself on the renunciation, while under the poor crust of self-approbation lurked jibing depths of consciousness. Heroism would not lie in renunciation, but in living with her. The cowardice of his own retreat left him horribly shaken.

Katherine watched him from her chair, calmly.

"But Hilda's work must cease at once," he said presently, finding a certain relief in decisive measures. "She won't show any false pride, I hope, about allowing me to put an end to it."

"It would be like her," said Katherine, sliding a sympathetic gloom of voice over the hard reality of her conclusions; conclusions half angry, half sarcastic. Peter was dull after all. Katherine felt alarmed, humiliated, and amused, but she steeled herself inwardly to a calm contemplation of facts. She joined him at the window. "What a burden you have taken on your poor shoulders, Peter." Peter immediately put his arm around her waist, and, though Katherine felt a deeper humiliation, she saw that alarm was needless; a proof of Peter's superiority, a proof, too, of his stupidity; as her own most original and clever superiority was proved by the fact of her calm under humiliation. Could she accept that humiliation as the bitter drop in the cup of good things Peter had to offer her? Katherine asked herself the question; it was answered by another. Just how far did the humiliation go? Peter's infidelity might be mere shallow passion, *passagère;* the fine part might be to feign blindness and help him out of it. *Attendons* summed up Katherine's mental attitude at the moment.

"Don't talk to me of burdens, dear Katherine," said Peter. "Don't try to spoil my humble little pleasure. If I can make you and yours happier, what more can I ask?" He looked at her with kind, tired eyes.

"I won't thwart you, but Hilda will."

"Hilda will find it difficult when we are married. That must be soon, Katherine."

Katherine looked pensively out of the window.

"We will see," she replied, with a pretty evasiveness.

It was fine and cold as Odd walked down the Boulevard St. Germain that afternoon. He walked at a tremendous pace, for human nature hopes to cheat thought by physical effort. Indeed, Peter did not think much, and was convinced that his mind was a comparatively happy blank as he paused before the tall house where Hilda was pursuing her avocations. If he made any definite reflections while he walked up and down between the doorway

and the next corner, they were on his last few conversations with Hilda; and then on rather abstract
points merely. He had drawn the child out. He
had penetrated the reserved mind that acquired
for enjoyment, not for display. He had found out
that Hilda knew Italian literature, from Dante to
Leopardi, almost as well as he himself did, and loved
it just as well. The fiction of Russia and Scandi-
navia was deeply appreciated by her, and the essay-
ists of France. Her tastes were as delicately dis-
criminative as Katherine's, but lacked that metallic
assurance of which lately Peter had become rather
uncomfortably aware. As for the English tongue,
from the old meeting-ground of Chaucer they could
range with delightful sympathy to Stevenson's sweet
radiance.

Peter thought quite intently of this literary survey
and evaded any trespassing beyond its limits. His
reticence was not put to a prolonged test. Hilda
met him before half-a-dozen trips to the corner were
accomplished. She showed no signs of conscious
guilt, though Peter was not sure that she was not a
" foolish baby."

" Let us walk," she said, " it is such a lovely day."

" We will walk at least till the sun goes. We
will just have time to catch the sunset on the Seine."

" Yes; what a *lovely* day ! I wish I were ten, with
short skirts, and a hoop, that I could run and roll."

" You would like a bicycle ride. Come to-morrow
with Katherine and me."

" I can't. Don't think me a prig, but my model
is due and I am finishing my picture. Thanks so
much; and this walk is almost as good."

" If Palamon is tired I will carry him, Hilda."

" Oh, he is n't tired. See how he pulls at his cord. The sunlight is getting into his veins. What delicious air."

" The sunlight is getting into your veins too, Hilda. You are looking a little as you should look."

Hilda did not ask him how she should look. It was an original characteristic of Hilda's that she did not seem at all anxious to talk about herself, and Odd continued, looking down at her profile—

" That 's what you ought to have—sunlight. You are a little white flower that has grown in a shadow." Hilda did not glance up at him ; she smiled rather distantly.

" What a sad simile ! "

" Is it a true one, Hilda ? "

" I don't think so. I never thought of myself in that sentimental light. I suppose to friendly eyes every life has a certain pathos."

" No ; some lives are too evidently and merely flaunting in the sunlight for even friendly eyes to poetize—to sentimentalize, as you rather unkindly said."

" Sunlight is poetic, too."

" Success and selfishness, and all the common-places that make up a happy life, are not poetic."

" That is rather morbid, you know—*décadent.*"

" I don't imply a fondness for illness and wrong-ness. Rather the contrary. It is a very beautiful rightness that keeps in the shade to give others the sunshine."

Hilda's eyes were downcast, and in her look a certain pale reserve that implied no liking for these personalities—personalities that glanced from her to others, as Odd realized.

He paused, and it was only after quite a little silence that Hilda said, with all her gentle quiet—

"You must not imagine that I am unhappy, or that my life has been an unhappy life. It is very good of you to trouble about it, but I can't claim the rather self-righteously heroic *rôle* you give me. I think it is others who live in the shadow. I think that any work, however feebly done, is a happy thing. I find so much pleasure in things other people don't care about."

"A very nicely delivered little snub, Hilda. You could n't have told me to mind my own business more kindly." Odd's humorous look met her glance of astonished self-reproach. He hastened on, "Will you try to find pleasure in a thing most girls *do* care for? Will you go to the Meltons' dance on Monday? Katherine told me I must go, this morning, and I said I would try to persuade you."

"I *did n't* mean to snub you."

"Very well; convince me of it by saying you will come to the dance."

The girlish pleasure of her face was evident.

"Do you really want me to?"

"It would make me very happy."

"It is against my rules, you know. I can't get up at six and go out in the evening besides. But I will make an exception for this once, to show you I was n't snubbing you! And, besides, I should love to." The gayety of her look suddenly fell to hesitation. "Only I am afraid I can't. I remember I have n't any dress."

" *Any* dress will do, Hilda."

" But I have n't any dress. The gray silk is impossible."

Peter's mind made a most unmasculine excursion into the position.

" But you were in London last year. You went to court. You must have had dresses."

" Yes, but I gave them to Katherine when I came back. I had no need for them. Her own wore out, and mine fit her very well—a little too long and narrow, but that was easily altered. Perhaps the white satin would do, if it was n't cut at the bottom ; it could be let down again, if it was only turned up. It is trimmed with *mousseline de soie*, and the flounce would hide the line."

Peter stared at her look of thoughtful perplexity ; he found it horribly touching. " It might do."

" It must do. If it does n't, another of Katherine's can be metamorphosized."

" And you will dance with me ? I love dancing, and I don't know many people. Of course Katherine will see that I am not neglected, but I should like to *depend* on you ; and if I am left sitting alone in a corner, I shall beckon to you. Will you be responsible for me ? " Her smiling eyes met the badly controlled emotion of his look.

" Hilda, you are quite frivolous." Terms of reckless endearment were on his lips ; he hardly knew how he kept them down. " How shall I manœuvre that you be left sitting alone in corners? Remember that if the miracle occurs I shall come, whether you beckon or no."

CHAPTER VIII

ODD was subtly glad of a cold that kept him in bed and indoors for several days. He wrote of his sorry plight to Katherine, and said he would see her at the Meltons' on Monday. Hilda was to come; that had been decided on the very evening of their last walk. He had been a witness of the merry colloquy over the lengthened dress, a colloquy that might, Odd felt, have held an embarrassing consciousness for Katherine had she not treated it with such whole-hearted gayety.

The Archinards had not yet arrived when Odd reached Mrs. Melton's apartment—one of the most magnificent in the houses that line the Avenue du Bois de Boulogne—and after greeting his hostess, he waited for half-an-hour in a condition of feverish restlessness, painfully apparent to himself, before he saw in the sparkling distance Katherine's smooth dark head, the Captain's correctly impassive good looks, and Hilda's loveliness for once in a setting that displayed it. Peter thrilled with a delicious and ridiculous pride as, with a susceptibility as acute as a fond mother's, he saw—felt, even—the stir, the ripple of inevitable conquest spread about her entry. The involuntary attention of a concourse of people certainly constitutes homage, however unconscious of aim be the conqueror. To

HILDA

Odd, the admiration, like the scent of a bed of helio-
trope in the turning of a garden path, seemed to fill
the very air with sudden perfume. "Her dear little
head," "Her lovely little head," he was saying to
himself as he advanced to meet her. He naturally
spoke first to Katherine, and received her condo-
lences on his cold, which she feared, by his jaded
and feverish air, he had not got rid of. Then, turning to Hilda—

"The white satin *does*," he said, smiling down at
her. Katherine did not depend on beauty, and need
fear no comparison even beside her sister. She was
talking with her usual quiet gayety to half-a-dozen
people already.

"See that Hilda, in her *embarras de choix*, does n't
become too much embarrassed," she said to Peter.
"Exercise for her a brotherly discretion."

The Captain was talking to Mrs. Melton—a pretty
little woman with languid airs. She had lived for
years in Paris, and considered herself there a most
necessary element of careful conservatism. Her
exclusiveness, which she took *au grand serieux*,
highly amused Katherine. Katherine knew her
world; it was wider than Mrs. Melton's. She
walked with a kindly ignoring of barriers, did not
trouble herself at all how people arrived as long as
they were there. She was as tolerant of a millionaire *parvenu* as might be a duchess with a political
entourage to manipulate; and she found Mrs.
Melton's anxious social self-satisfaction humorous
—a fact of which Mrs. Melton was unaware, although she, like other people, thought Katherine
subtly impressive. Mrs. Melton was rather dull

too, and a few grievances whispered behind her fan in Katherine's ear *en passant*—for subject, the unfortunate and eternal *nouveau riche*—made pleasant gravity difficult; but Katherine did not let Mrs. Melton know that she found her dull and funny.

Hilda for the moment was left alone with Odd, and he seized the opportunity for inscribing himself for five waltzes.

" I will be greedy. I wrest these from the hungry horde I see advancing, led by your father and Mrs. Melton."

He had not claimed the first waltz, and watched her while she danced it—charmingly and happily as a girl should. She was beautiful, surprisingly beautiful. A loveliness in the carriage of the little head, with its heightened coils of hair, seemed new to Odd. No one else's hair was done like that, nor grew so about the forehead. The white satin was a trifle too big for her. A lace sash held it loosely to her waist, and floated and curved with the curves of her long flowing skirt. His waltz came, and he would not let his wonder at the significance of his felicity carry him too far into conjecture.

" Are you enjoying yourself?" he asked, as they joined the eddy circling around Mrs. Melton's ball-room.

" So much; thanks to you." Her parted lips smiled, half at him, half at the joy of dancing. " I had almost forgotten how delicious it was."

" More delicious than the studio, is n't it?"

" You shall not tempt me to disloyalty. How pretty, too! De la Touche could do it—all light and movement and color. I should like to come

out of my demi-tints and have a try myself! What
pretty blue shadows everywhere with the golden
lights. See on the girls' throats. There is the
good of the studio! One sees lovely lights and
shadows on ugly heads! Is n't that worth
while?"

Odd's eyes involuntarily dropped to the blue
shadow on Hilda's throat.

"Everything you do is worth while—from painting to dancing. You dance very well."

The white fragility of her neck and shoulders, in
the generous display of which he recognized the
gown's quondam possessor, gave him a little pang
of fear. She looked extremely delicate, and the
youthfulness of cheek and lip pathetic. That
wretched drudgery! For, even through the happy
candor of her eyes, he saw a deep fatigue—the
long fatigue of a weary monotony of days. But
in neither eyes nor voice was there a tinge of the
aloofness—the reserve that had formerly chilled
him. To-night Hilda seemed near once more;
almost the little friend of ten years ago.

"You dance well, too, Mr. Odd," she said.

"I very seldom waltz."

"In *my* honor then?"

"Solely in your honor. I have n't waltzed five
times in one evening with one young woman—for
ages!"

"You have n't waltzed five times with me yet. I
may wear you out!"

"What an implied reflection on my forty years!
Do I seem so old to you, Hilda?"

"No; I don't think of you as old."

"But I think of you as young, very young, deliciously young."

"Deliciously?" she repeated. "That is a fallacy, I think. Youth is sad; doesn't see things in *value;* everything is blacker or whiter than reality, so that one is disappointed or desperate all the time."

"And you, Hilda?"

Her eyes swept his with a sweet, half-playful defiance.

"Don't be personal."

"But you were. And, after the other day—your declaration of contentment."

"Everything is comparative. I was generalizing. I hate people who talk about themselves," Hilda added; "it's the worst kind of immodesty. Material and mental braggarts are far more endurable than the people who go round telling about their souls."

"Severe, rigid child!" Odd laughed, and, after a little pause, laughed again. "You are horribly reserved, Hilda."

"Very sage when one has nothing to show. Silence covers such a multitude of sins. If one is consistently silent, people may even imagine that one is n't dull," said Hilda maliciously.

"You are dull and silent, then?"

"I have few opinions; that is, perhaps, dulness."

"It may be a very wide cleverness."

"Yes; it may be. Now, Mr. Odd, the next waltz is yours too, you know. You have quite a cluster here. Let us sit out the next. I should like an ice."

Odd fetched the ice and sat down beside her on a small sofa in a corner of the ballroom. Katherine passed, dancing; her dark eyes flashed upon them a glance that might have been one of amusement. Odd was conscious of a painful effort in his answering smile.

Hilda's eyes, as she ate her ice, followed her sister with a fond contemplation.

"Isn't that dress becoming to her? The shade of deepening, changing rose."

"Your dress, too, Hilda, is lovely."

"Do you notice dresses, care about them?"

"I think I do, sometimes; not in detail as a woman would, but in the blended effect of dress and wearer."

"I love beautiful dresses. I think this dress is beautiful. Have you noticed the line it makes from breast to hem, that long, unbroken line? I think that line the secret of elegance. In some gowns one sees one has visions of crushed ribs, don't you think?"

Odd listened respectfully, his mouth twisted a little by that same smile that he still felt to be painful. "And is not this lace gathered around the shoulders pretty too?" Hilda turned to him for inspection.

"You will talk about your clothes, but you will not talk about yourself, Hilda." Odd had put on his eyeglasses and was obediently studying her gown.

"The lace is mamma's. Poor mamma; I know she is lonely. It does seem hard to be left alone when other people are enjoying themselves. She has Meredith's last novel, however. I began it with her. Mr. Odd, I am doing all the talking. *You* talk now."

"About Meredith, your dress, or you?"

"About yourself, if you please."

"It has seemed to me, Hilda, that you were even less interested in me than you were in yourself."

Hilda looked round at him quickly, and he felt that his eyes held hers with a force which almost compelled her—

"No; I am very much interested in you." Odd was silent, studying her face with much the same expression that he had studied her gown—the expression of painfully controlled emotion.

"There is nothing comparably interesting in me," he said; "I have had my story, or at least I have missed my chance to have a story."

"What do you mean?"

"Well, I mean that I might have made a mark in the world and did n't."

"And your books?"

"They are as negative as I am."

"Yet they have helped me to live." Hilda looked hard at him while she spoke, and a sudden color swept into her face; no confusion, but the emotion of impulsive resolution. Odd, however, turned white.

"Helped you to live, Hilda!" he almost stammered; "my gropings!"

"You may call them gropings, but they led me. Perhaps you were like Virgil to Statius, in Dante. You know? You bore your light behind and lit my path!" She smiled, adding: "I suppose you think you have failed because you have reached no dogmatic absolute conclusion. But you yourself praise noble failure and scorn cheap success."

"I did n't even know you read my books."
"I know your books very well; much better than I know you."
" Don't say that. I hope that any worth in me is in them."
" One would have to survey your life as a whole to be sure of that. Perhaps you *do* even better than you write."
"Ah, no, no; I can praise the books by that comparison." His voice stumbled a little incoherently, and Hilda, rising, said with a smile—
" Shall we dance?"
In the terribly disquieting whirl of his thoughts, which shared the dance's circling propensities, Odd held fast to one fixed kernel of desire; he must hear from Hilda's lips why she had refused Allan Hope.

An uneasy consciousness of Katherine crossed his mind once and again with a dull ache of self-reproach, all the more insistent from his realization that its cause was not so much the infidelity to Katherine as that Hilda would think him a sorry villain.

Katherine seemed to be dancing and enjoying herself. She knew that his energy this evening was on Hilda's account; he had claimed the responsibility for Hilda. Katherine would not consider herself neglected, of that Peter felt sure, relying, with perhaps a display of the dulness she had discovered in him, upon her confidence and common sense. Outwardly, at least, he would never betray that confidence; there was some rather dislocated consolation in that.

Hilda was a little breathless when he came to

claim her for the second cluster of waltzes. It was near the end of the evening.

" I have been dancing *steadily*," she announced, "and twice down to supper! Did you try any of the narrow little sandwiches? So good ! "

" And you still don't grudge me my waltzes ? "

" I like yours *best !* " she said, smiling at him as she laid her hand on his shoulder. They took a few turns around the room and then Hilda owned that she was a little tired. They sat down again on the sofa.

" Hilda ! " said Odd suddenly, " will you think me very rude if I ask you why you refused Allan Hope? "

Hilda turned a startled glance upon him.

" No ; perhaps not," she answered, though the voice was rather frigid.

" You don't think I have a right to ask, do you ? "

" Well, the answer is so evident."

" Is it ? " Hilda had looked away at the dancers; she turned her head now half unwillingly and glanced at him, smiling.

" I would not have refused him if I had loved him, would I ? You know that. It doesn't seem quite fair, quite kind, to talk of, does it ? "

" Not to me even ? I have been interested in it for a long time. Katherine told me, and Mary."

" I don't know why they should have been so sure," said Hilda, with some hardness of tone. " I never encouraged him. I avoided him." She looked at Odd again. " But I am not angry with you ; if any one has a right, you have."

" Thanks ; thanks, dear. You understand, you

know my interest, my anxiety. It seemed so—
happy for both. And you care for no one else?"

"No one else." Hilda's eyes rested on his with
clear sincerity.

"Don't you ever intend to marry, Hilda?" Odd
was leaning forward, his elbows on his knees, and
looking at the floor. There was certainly a tension
in his voice, and he felt that Hilda was scanning
him with some wonder.

"Does a refusal to take one person imply that?
I have made no vows."

"I don't see—" Odd paused; "I don't see why
you should n't care for Hope."

"Are you going to plead his cause?" she asked
lightly.

"Would it not be for your happiness?" Odd sat
upright now, putting on his eyeglasses and looking
at her with a certain air of resolution.

"I don't love him." Hilda returned the look
sweetly and frankly.

"What do you know of love, you child? Why
not have given him a chance, put him on trial?
Nothing wins a woman like wooing."

"How didactic we are becoming. I am afraid I
should really get to loathe poor Lord Allan if I had
given him leave to woo me."

"I suppose you think him too unindividual, too
much of a pattern with other healthy and hearty
young men. Don't you know, foolish child, that a
good man, a man who would love you as he would,
make you the husband he would, is a rarity and very
individual?"

Odd found a perverse pleasure in his own paternally admonishing attitude. Hilda's lightly amused but touched look implied a confidence so charming that he found the attitude sublimely courageous.

" I suppose so," she said, and she added, " I have n't one word to say against Lord Allan, except—" She paused meditatively.

" Except what ? " Odd asked rather breathlessly.

" He does n't really *need* me."

"Does n't *need* you ! Why, the man is desperately in love with you ! "

" He needs a wife, but he does n't need *me*."

" You are subtle, Hilda."

" I don't think I am *that*."

"You are waiting, then, for some one who can satisfy you as to his *need* of you ? "

" I shall only marry that person."

Hilda jumped up. " But I'm not waiting at all, you know. *Dansons maintenant !* Your task is nearly over ! "

It was very late when Odd gave Hilda up to her last partner, and joined Katherine in a small antechamber, where she was sitting among flowers, talking to an appreciative Frenchman. This gentleman, with the ceremonious bow of his race, made away when Miss Archinard's *fiancé* appeared, and Odd dropped into the vacated seat with a horrible sinking of the heart. The dull self-reproach was now acute, He felt meanly guilty. Katherine looked at him funnily—very good-humoredly.

" I did n't know you had it in you to dance so well and so persistently, Peter. You have done honor to Hilda's ball."

" I hope I was n't too selfishly monopolizing."

"Oh, you had a right to a certain monopoly since, owing to you only, she came," and Katherine added, smiling still more good-humoredly, "I am *not* jealous, Peter."

He turned to look at her. The words, the playful tone in which they were uttered, struck him like a blow. His guilty consciousness of his own feeling gave them a supreme nobility. She was *not* jealous. What a cur he would be if ever he gave her apparent cause for jealousy. The cause was there; his task must be to keep it hidden.

"But suppose *I* am?" he said; "you have n't given me a single dance."

Katherine's smile was placid; she did not say that he had not asked for one. Indeed they had rarely danced together.

"I think of going to England in a day or two, Peter," she observed. "The Devreuxs have asked me to spend a month with them."

Peter sat very still.

"A sudden decision, Kathy?"

"No, not so sudden. Our *tête-à-tête* can't be prolonged forever."

"Until our wedding day, you mean? Well, the wedding day must be fixed before you go."

"I yield. The first part of May."

"Three months! Let it be April at least, Kathy."

"No, I am for May."

"It's an unlucky month."

"Oh, *we* can defy bad luck, can't we?" Katherine smiled.

"If you go away, I shall," said Odd, after a moment's silence.

" Why, I thought you would stay here and look after mamma—and Hilda," said Katherine slowly, and with a wondering thought for this revealment of poor Peter's folly. Peter then intended to heroically sacrifice his infidelity. That he should think she did not see it!

"I am not over this beastly cold yet. A trip through Provence would set me right. I should come back through Touraine just at the season of lilacs. I am afraid I should be useless here in Paris. I see so little of your mother—and Hilda. Arrange that Taylor shall go for her after her lessons."

" I am afraid that mamma can't spare Taylor."

Peter moved impatiently.

" Katherine, may I give you some money? She would take it from you. Persuade her to give up that work. You could do it delicately."

" As I have told you, you exaggerate my influence. She would suspect the donor. She would not take the money.

" I could speak to your father; lend him a sum."

Katherine flushed.

" It would make him very angry with her if he knew. And the lessons are a fixed sum; only a steady income would be the equivalent."

" Oh dear! " sighed Peter. He suddenly realized that of late he had talked of little else but Hilda in his conversations with Katherine.

" When do you go to London, dear? " he asked.

" The day after to-morrow." Katherine, above the waving of her fan, smiled slightly at his change of tone. " Will you miss me, Peter? "

"All the more for being cross with you. It is very wrong of you to play truant like this."

"It will be good for both of us." Katherine's voice was playful, and showed no trace of the bitterness she was feeling. "I might get tired of you, Peter, if I allowed myself no interludes. Absence is the best fuel to appreciation. I shall come back realizing more fully than ever your perfection."

"What a sage little person it is! Sarcastic as well! May I write to you very often?"

"As often as you feel like it; but don't force feeling."

"May I describe châteaux and churches? And will you read my descriptions if I do?"

"With pleasure—and profit. Let me know, too, how the book gets on. Can I do anything for you at the British Museum?"

It struck Katherine that the change in their relation which she now contemplated as very probably definite might well allow of a return to the first phase of their companionship. A letter from Allan Hope which she had received that morning, though satisfactory in many respects, was not quite so from an intellectual standpoint. An intellectual friendship with Peter Odd was a pleasant possession for any woman, and Katherine perhaps, with an excusable malice, rather anticipated the time when Peter might have regrets, and find in that friendship the solace of certain disappointments from which Katherine had almost decided not to withhold him.

"I shall try to keep you profitably yoked, then, even in London, shall I?" said Odd, in reply to an offer more generous than he could have divined.

" Discipline is good for a rebellious spirit like yours. Don't be frightened, Kathy. Go and look at the Elgin Marbles if you like. I shall set you no heavier task."

" They are so profoundly melancholy in their cellared respectable abode, poor dears! I know they would have preferred dropping to pieces under a Greek sky. A cruel kindness to preserve them in an insulting immortality. The frieze especially, stretched round the ugly wall like a butterfly under a glass case !" Odd laughed with more light-heartedness than he had felt for some time. It rejoiced him to feel that he still found Katherine charming. There must certainly be safety in that affectionate admiration.

" I won't even ask you to harrow your susceptibility by a look at the insulted frieze, then ; you must know it well, to enter with such sympathy into its feelings. Only you must write, Katherine. I shall be lonely down there. A daily letter would be none too many."

" I can't quite see why you are exiling yourself. Of course, the weather here is nasty just now. I have noticed your cough all the evening. Come and say good-bye to-morrow. I shall be very busy, so fix your hour."

" Our usual hour ? In the morning?"

" You will not see Hilda then."

" Hilda has had enough of me to-night, I am sure. You will kiss her *au revoir* for me."

Odd felt a certain triumph.

Katherine's departure could be taken as a merciful opportunity for makeshift flight. After a month or two of solitary wrestling and wandering, he might find that the dubiously directed forces of Providence were willing to help one who helped himself.

His mind fastened persistently on the details of the suddenly entertained idea of escape from the madness he felt closing round him. The disclosure of his passion for Hilda stared him in the face. And how face the truth? A man may fight a dishonoring weakness, but how fight the realization that a love founded on highest things, stirring highest emotions in him, had, for the first time, come into his life, and too late? A love as far removed from the wrecking passion of his youth as it was from the affectionate rationality of his feeling toward Katherine; and yet, because of that tie, drifted into from a lazy indifference and kindness for which he cursed himself, capable of bringing him to a more fearful shipwreck.

Hilda's selflessness was rather awful to the man who loved her, and gave her a power of clear perception that made sinking in her eyes more to be dreaded than any hurt to himself.

And Peter departed for the South without seeing her again.

215

CHAPTER IX

A N April sky smiled over Paris on the day of
Odd's return. A rather prolonged tour had
tanned his face, and completely cured his lungs.

He expected to find Katherine already in Paris;
her last letters had announced her departure from a
Surrey country house, and had implied some anxiety
in regard to a prolonged illness of Mrs. Archinard's.
Katherine had written him very soon after their
parting, that the Captain had gone on a yachting
trip in the Mediterranean, and that she knew that
he had left Hilda with money, so Peter need not
worry. Peter had seen to this matter before leaving
Paris, and had approved of the Captain's projected
jaunt. He surmised that her father's absence would
lighten Hilda's load, and hoped that the sum he
placed in the Captain's hands—on the understanding
that most of it was to be given to Hilda—but *from*
her father, would relieve her from the necessity for
teaching. Peter called at the Rue Pierre Charron
early in the afternoon, but the servant (neither
Taylor nor Wilson, but a more hybrid-looking individual with unmistakable culinary traces upon her
countenance) told him that Mademoiselle Archinard
had not yet arrived. Madame still in bed " *toujours
souffrante*," and " Mademoiselle 'Ilda "—Odd had

hesitated uncomfortably before asking for her—
was out. "*Pas bien non plus, celle-là,*" she volunteered, with a kindly French familiarity that still
more strongly emphasized the contrast with Taylor
and Wilson; "*Elle s'éreinte, voyez-vous monsieur, la
pauvre demoiselle.*" With a sick sense of calamity
and helplessness upon him, Odd asked at what hours
she might be found. All the morning, it seemed
"*Il faut bien qu'elle soigne madame, et puis elle m'aide.
Je suis seule et la besogne serait par trop lourde,*" and
Rosalie also volunteered the remark that "*Madame
est très, mais très exigeante, nuit et jour ; pas moyen
de dormir avec une damé comme celle-là.*"

Odd looked at his watch ; it was almost five. If
Hilda had kept to her days he should probably find
her in the Rue d'Assas, and, with the angriest feelings for himself and for the whole Archinard family,
Hilda excepted, he was driven there through a sudden shower that scudded in fretful clouds across the
blue above. He was none too soon, for he caught
sight of Hilda half-way up the street as they turned
the corner. The sight of him, as he jumped out of
the cab and waylaid her, half dazed her evidently.

"You ? I can hardly believe it !" she gasped,
smiling, but in a voice that plainly showed overwrought mental and physical conditions. She was
wofully white and thin ; the hollowed line of her
cheek gave to her lips a prominence pathetically,
heartrendingly childlike ; her clothes had reached
a pitch of shabbiness that could hardly claim gen-
tility ; the slits in her umbrella and the battered
shapelessness of her miserable little hat symbolized
a biting poverty.

" Hilda ! Hilda ! " was all Odd found to say as he put her into the cab. He was aghast.

" I *am* glad to see you," she said, and her voice had a forced gayety over its real weakness; " I have n't seen any of my people for so long, except mamma. An illness seems to put years between things, does n't it ? Poor mamma has been so really ill. It has troubled me horribly, for I could not tell whether it were grave enough to bring back papa and Katherine; but Katherine is coming. I expected her a day or two ago, and mamma is much, *much* better. As for papa, the last time I heard from him he was in Greece and going on to Constantinople. I am glad now that he has n't been needlessly frightened, for he will get all my last letters together, and will hear that she is almost well again. And you are here ! And Kathy coming ! I feel that all my clouds are breaking."

Odd could trust his voice now; her courage, strung as he felt it to be over depths of dreadful suffering, nerved him to a greater self-control.

" If I had known I would have come sooner," he said ; " you would have let me help you, would n't you ? "

" I am afraid you could n't have *helped* me. That is the worst of illness, one can only wait; but you would have cheered me up."

" My poor child ! " Odd inwardly cursed himself. " If I had known ! What have you been doing to yourself, Hilda ? You look—"

" Fagged, don't I ? It is the anxiety; I have given up half my work since you left; my pictures are accepted at the Champs de Mars. We 'll all go to the *vernissage* together. And, as they were done, I let Miss Latimer have the studio for the whole day. That left me my mornings free for mamma."

" Taylor helped you, I suppose ? "

" Taylor is with Katherine. She went before mamma was at all ill, and indeed mamma insisted that Katherine must have her maid. I was glad that she should go, for she has worked hard without a rest for so long, and, of course, travelling about as she has been doing, Katherine needed her." There was an explanatory note in Hilda's voice; indeed Odd's silence, big with comment, gave it a touch of defiance. "It made double duty for Rosalie, but she is a good, willing creature, and has not minded."

" And Wilson ? "

" He went with papa. I don't think papa could live without Wilson."

" Oh, indeed. I begin to solve the problem of your ghastly little face. You have been house-maid, *garde-malade*, and bread-winner. Had you no money at all ? " Hilda flushed—the quick flush of physical weakness.

" Yes, at first," she replied ; " papa gave me quite a lot before going, and that has paid part of the doctor's bills, and my lessons brought in the usual amount."

" Could you not have given up the lessons for the time being ? "

" I know you think it dreadful in me to have left mamma for all those afternoons." Her acceptation of a blame infinitely removed from his thoughts stupefied Odd. " And mamma has thought it heartless, most naturally. But Rosalie is trustworthy and kind. The doctor came three times a day and I can explain to *you* "—Hilda hesitated—" the money papa gave me went almost immediately—some unpaid bills."

" What bills ? " Odd spoke sternly.

" Why, we owe bills right and left ! " said Hilda.

" But what bills were these ? "

" There was the rent of the apartment for one thing ; we should have had to go had that not been paid ; and then, some tailors, a dressmaker ; they threatened to seize the furniture."

" Katherine's dressmaker ? "

" Yes ; Katherine, I know, never dreamed that she would be so impatient ; but I suppose, on hearing that Katherine had gone to England, the woman became frightened." Peter controlled himself to silence. The very fulness of Hilda's confidence showed the strain that had been put upon her. " And then," she went on, as he did not speak, " some of the money had to go to Katherine in England. Poor Kathy ! To be pinched like that ! She wrote, that at one place it took her last shilling to tip the servants and get her railway ticket to Surrey."

" Why did she not write to me ? Considering all things—"

" Oh ! " said Hilda—her tone needed no comment —" we have not quite come to that." She added presently and gently, " I had money for her."

Odd took her hand and kissed it ; the glove was loose upon it.

" And now," said Hilda, leaning forward and

smiling at him, "you have heard me *filer mon chape-let*. Tell me what you have been doing."

" My lazy wanderings in the sun would sound too grossly egotistic after your story."

" Has my story sounded so dismal? *I* have been egotistic, then. I had hoped that perhaps you would write to me," she added, and a delicately malicious little smile lit her face. Odd looked hard at her, with a half-dreamy stare.

"I thought of you," he said ; " I should have liked to write."

" Well, in the future do, please, when you feel like it."

Mrs. Archinard was extended on the sofa in the drawing-room when they reached the Rue Pierre Charron. The crisp daintiness of pseudo-invalidism had withered to a look of sickly convalescence. She was much faded, and her little air of melancholy affectation pitifully fretful.

" You come before my own daughter, Peter," she said ; " I don't *blame* Katherine, since Hilda tells me that she did not let her know of my dangerous condition."

" Not *dangerous*, mamma," Hilda said, with a patient firmness not untouched by resentment, a touch to Odd most new and pleasing. " The doctor had perfect confidence in me, and would have told me. I should have sent for papa and Katherine the moment he thought it advisable. Under the circumstances they could have done nothing for you that I did not do." Hilda had, indeed, rather distorted facts to shield Katherine. What would Mrs. Archinard have said had she known that Katherine,

in answer to a letter begging her to return, had replied that she *could* not? Even in Hilda's charitable heart that "*could* not" had rankled. Odd's
despairing gloom discerned something of this truth,
as he realized that the uncharacteristic self-justification was prompted by a rebellion against misinterpretation before *him*. Mrs. Archinard showed some
nervous surprise.

"Very well, very well, Hilda," she said, "I am
sure I ask no sacrifices on *my* account. One may
die alone as one has lived—alone. My life has
trained me in stoicism. You had better wash your
face, Hilda. There is a great smudge of charcoal
on your cheek," and, as Hilda turned and walked
out, "I have looked on the face of the King of Terrors, Peter. Peter! dear old homely name! the
faithful ring in it! It is easy for Hilda to talk! I
make no complaint. She has nursed me excellently
well—as far as her nursing went. But she has a
hard soul! no tenderness! no sympathy! To leave
her dying mother every afternoon! To sacrifice
me to her *painting!* At such a time! Ah me!"
Large tears rolled down Mrs. Archinard's cheeks,
and her voice trembled with weakness and self-pity.
Odd, in his raging resentment, could have exploded
the truth upon her; the tears arrested his impulse,
and he sat moodily gazing at the floor. Mrs.
Archinard raised her lace-edged handkerchief and
delicately touched away the tears.

"I have given my whole life, my whole life,
Peter, for my girls! I have borne this long exile
from my home for their sakes!" At Allersley Mrs.
Archinard had never ceased complaining of her re-

stricted lot, and had characterized her neighbors as "yokels and Philistines." Speaking with her handkerchief pressed by her finger-tips upon her eyelids, she continued, "I have asked nothing of them but sympathy; *that* I have craved! And in my hour of need—" Mrs. Archinard's *point de Venise* bosom heaved once more. Odd took her hand with the unwilling yet pitying kindness one would show towards a silly and unpleasant child.

"I don't think you are quite fair," he said; "Hilda looks as badly as you do. She has had a heavy load to carry."

"I told her again and again to get a *garde-malade*, two if necessary." Mrs. Archinard's voice rose to a higher key. "She has chosen to ruin her appearance by sitting up to all hours of the night, and by working all day in that futile studio."

"*Garde-malades* are expensive." Odd could not restrain his voice's edge.

"Expensive! For a dying mother! And with all that is lavished on her studio—canvases, paints, models!"

The depths of misconception were too hopelessly great, and, as Mrs. Archinard's voice had now become shrilly emphatic, he kept silence, his heart shaken with misery and with pity, despairing pity for Hilda. She re-entered presently, wearing on her face too evident signs of contrition. She spoke to her mother in tones of gentle entreaty, humored her sweetly, gayly even, while she made tea.

"You know I cannot touch cake, Hilda."

"There are buttered *brioches*, mamma, piping hot."

"Properly buttered, I hope. Rosalie usually

places a great clot in the centre, leaving the edges uneatable."

" Mamma is like the princess who felt the pea through all the dozens of mattresses, isn't she?" said Hilda, smiling at Odd. " But *I* buttered these with scientific exactitude."

"Exactitude! Ah! the mirage of science! More milk, more milk!" Mrs. Archinard raised herself on one elbow to watch with expectant disapproval the concoction of her tea, and, relapsing on her cushions as the tea was brought to her, " I suppose it *is* milk, though I prefer cream."

" No, it 's cream." Hilda should know, as she had herself just darted round the corner to the *crêmerie.* Odd sprang up to take his cup from her. He thought she looked in danger of falling to the ground.

" Do sit down," he said in a low voice ; "you look very, very badly."

" Have you read Meredith's last?" asked Mrs. Archinard from the sofa. " Hilda is reading it to me in the evenings. We began it, ah! long, long ago. I have sympathy for Meredith, an *intimité!* It is so I feel, see things—super-subtly. Strange how coarsely objective some minds are! Did you order the oysters for my dinner, Hilda, and the ice from Gagé's—*pistache?* I hope you impressed *pistache.* You will dine with Hilda, of course, Peter; I have my dinner here; I am not yet strong enough to sit through a meal. And then you must talk to me about Meredith. I always find you most suggestive—such new lights on old things. And Verhaeren, too ; do you care for Verhaeren? Morbid? Yes, perhaps, but that is a truism—not like

you, Peter. '*Les apparus dans mes chemins*,' poor,
modern, broken, bleeding soul! We must talk of
Verhaeren. Just now I feel very sleepy. You will
excuse me if I simply *sans gêne* turn over and take
a nap? I can often sleep at this hour. Hilda, show
Peter the Burne-Jones Chaucer over there. Hilda
does n't find him limpid, sweet, healthy enough for
Chaucer; but *nous sommes tous les enfants malades*
nowadays. There is a beauty, you know, in that.
Talk it over."

Hilda and Peter sat down obediently side by side
on the distant little *canapé* before the Burne-Jones
Chaucer. They went over the pages, not paying
much attention to the woodcuts, but looking down
favorite passages together. The description of
" my swete " in " The Book of the Duchess," the
complaint of poor Troilus, and, once more, Arcite's
death. The quiet room was very quiet, and they
looked up from the pages now and then to smile,
perhaps a little sadly, at one another. When the
dinner was announced Hilda said, as they went into
the dining-room—

" If your courage fails you, just say so frankly.
I have very childish tastes and childish fare."

Indeed, half a cold chicken and a dish of rice
constituted the repast. A bottle of claret stood by
Odd's place, and there was a white jar filled with
buttercups on the table; but even Rosalie seemed
depressed by the air of meagreness, and gave them
a rather *effaré* glance as they sat down. Odd suspected that the cold chicken was in his honor. He
had come to the conclusion that Hilda was capable
of dining off rice alone.

" Delightful!" he said. The chicken and rice were indeed very good, but Hilda saw that he ate very little.

" I make no further apologies," she said, smiling at him over the buttercups; "your hunger be upon your own head."

" I am not hungry, dear."

Hilda had to do most of the talking, but they were both rather silent. It was a happy silence to Hilda, full of a loving trust.

When he spoke, it was in a voice of the same gentle fatigue that his eyes showed; but as the eyes rested upon her she felt that the past and the present had surely joined hands.

CHAPTER X

ODD went in the same half-dreamy condition through the morning of the next day. He walked and read, but where he walked and what he read he could hardly have told.

He was to fetch Hilda from the Rue d'Assas and go home to tea and dinner with her. His love for Hilda had now reached such solemn heights that his late flight seemed degrading.

So loving her, he could not be base.

The Rue d'Assas was dreary in a fine drizzling rain. In the Luxembourg Gardens the first young green made a mist upon the trees.

It was only half-past four when Odd reached his accustomed post, but hardly had he taken a turn up and down the street when he saw Hilda come quickly from the Lebon abode. She was fully half-an-hour early, but Odd had merely time to note the fact before seeing in a flash that Hilda was in trouble. She looked, she almost ran toward him; and he met her half-way with outstretched hands.

"O Peter!" It was the first time she had used his name, and Odd's heart leaped as her hands caught his with a sort of desperate relief. "Come, come," she said, taking his arm. "Let us go quickly." Peter's heart after its leap began to thump fast. The white distress of her face gave

227

him a dizzy shock of anger. What, who had distressed her? He asked the question as they crossed the road and entered the gardens. Tears now streamed down her face.

He had only once before seen Hilda weep, and as she hung shaken with sobs on his arm, the past child, the present Hilda merged into one; his one, his only love.

" Let us walk here, dear," he said ; " you will be quieter."

The little path down which they turned was empty, and the fine rain enveloped but hardly wet them. They came to a bench under a tree, circled by an unwet area of sanded path. Odd led the weeping girl to it and they sat down. She still held his arm tightly.

" Now, what is it? "

" O Peter! I can hardly tell you! The brother, the horrible brother."

" Yes?" Peter felt the accumulations of rage that had been gathering for months hurrying forward to spring upon, to pulverize " the brother."

" He made love to me, said awful things! " Odd whitened to the lips.

" Tell me all you can."

" I wish I were dead! " sobbed Hilda, " I am so unhappy."

Peter did not trust himself to speak ; he took her hand and held it to his lips.

" Yes ; you care," said Hilda. She drew herself up and wiped her eyes. " I never thought he would be unpleasant. At times I fancied that he came a good deal into the studio where we worked

and, behind his sister's back, looked silly. But he
never really annoyed me. I thought myself unkindly suspicious. To-day Mademoiselle Lebon
was called away and he came in. I went on painting. I did not dream—! When, suddenly he
put his arms around me—and tried to kiss me!"
Hilda gave an hysterical laugh. " Do you know, I
had my palette on my hand, and I gave him a great
blow with it! You should have seen his head!
Oh, to think that I can find that funny now! His
ear was covered with cobalt!" Hilda sobbed
again, even while she laughed. " He was very angry
and horrible. I said I would call his mother and
sister if he did not leave me at once, and then—
and then "—Hilda dropped her face into her hands
—" he jeered at me; ' You must n't play the prude,'
he said."

Odd clenched his teeth.

" Hilda, dear," he said, in a voice cold to severity,
" you must go home; I will put you in a cab. I
will come to you as soon as I have punished that
dog."

" Peter, don't! I beg of you to come *with* me.
You can do nothing. I must bury it, forget it."
She had risen as he rose.

" Yes, bury it, forget it, Hilda. He, at least, shall
never forget it."

Odd's fixed look as he led her into the street
forced her to helpless silence.

" Peter, *please!* " she breathed, clasping her
hands together and gazing at him as he hailed a
fiacre.

" I will come to you soon. Good-bye."

And so Hilda was driven away.

It was past six when Odd reached the Rue Pierre Charron. Rosalie opened the door. Madame was in bed, she had had a bad day. Mademoiselle? she is lying down. She seemed ill. "*Et bien malade même*," and had said that she wanted no dinner.

" I should like to see her, if only for a moment; she will see me, I think," said Odd, walking into the drawing-room. Hilda entered almost immediately.

She had been crying, and the disorder of her hair suggested that she had cried with her head buried in a pillow, after the stifled feminine fashion. Her face was most pathetically disfigured by tears; the disfigurement almost charming of youth and loveliness; but she looked ill, too. The white cheek and the heavy eyelids, the unsteady sweetness of her lips showed that an extreme of physical exhaustion, as well as the tempest of grief, had swept her beyond all thought of self-control, beyond all wish for it. The afternoon's unpleasantness had been merely the last straw. The long endurance of the past month—the past months indeed—that had asked no pity, had been hardly conscious of a claim on pity—was transformed by her knowledge of near love and sympathy to a quivering sensibility. There was no reticence in her glance. He was the one she turned to, the one she trusted, the only one who understood and loved her in the whole world. Odd saw all this as the supreme confidence of a supremely reserved nature looked at him from her eyes.

He met her, stooping his head to hers, and, like a child, she put up her face to be kissed. When he had kissed her, he drew back. A sudden horrible weakness almost overcame him.

"Sit down, dear; no, I will walk about a bit. I have been playing the fiery *jeune premier* to such an extent this afternoon that dramatic restlessness is in keeping."

Hilda smiled faintly, and her eyes followed him as he took a few turns up and down the room.

"You look so badly," he said, pausing before her; "how do you feel?"

"Not myself; or, perhaps, too much myself." Hilda tried to smile, stretching out her arms with a long shaken sigh. "I feel weak and foolish," she added, clasping her hands on her knee.

"It is all right, you know. He apologized profusely."

"How did you make him do that?"

"I told him the truth, including the fact of his own despicableness."

"And he believed it?"

"I helped him to the belief by a pretty thorough thrashing."

"Oh!" cried Hilda.

"He deserved it, dear."

"But—I had exposed myself to it; he thought himself justified."

"I had to disabuse him of that thought. He bawled out something like a challenge under the salutary lesson, but when I promptly seconded the suggestion—insisted on the extreme satisfaction it would give me to have a shot at him—the bourgeois

strain came out. He fairly whined. I was disappointed. I had bloodthirsty desires."

" Oh, I am very glad he whined then! Don't
speak of such horrors. You know I am hysterical."

Odd still stood before her, and Hilda put out her
hand.

" How can I thank you ? " He put her hand to his
lips, not looking at her but down at the heavy folds
of her white dress ; it had a shroud-like look that
gave him a shudder. Hilda's life seemed shroud-
like, shutting her out from all brightness, from all
love—love hers by right, and only hers.

" You know, you know that I would do anything
for you," he said.

The hand he kissed drew him down beside her,
hardly consciously, and he yielded to the longing
he felt in her for comforting kindness and nearness ;
yielded, too, to his own growing weakness ; but
he still held the hand to his lips, not daring to look
at her. This childlike trust, this dependence, were
dreadful. The long kiss seemed to his troubled
soul a momentary shield. He found her eyes on
him when he raised his own.

" I never thought it would come true—in this
way," she said.

" What come true? "

" That you would really care for me,"

Her pure look seemed to flutter to him, to fold
peaceful wings on his breast ; its very contentment
constituted a caress. The child was still a child,
and yet in the look there were worlds of ignorant
revelation. A shock of possibilities made Odd
dizzy, and the certain strain of weakness in him

made it impossible for him to warn and protect her ignorance.

He was conscious of a quick grasp at the transcendental friendship of which alone she was aware. "My little friend, I care for you dearly, dearly." But with the words, his hold on the transcendental friendship slipped, fundamental truths surged up; he took both her hands, and clasping them on his breast, said, hardly conscious of his words—

"Sweetest, noblest—dearest," with an emotion only too contagious, for Hilda's eyes filled with tears. The sight of these tears, her weakness, the horrible unfairness of her position, appealed, even at this moment, to all his manliness. He controlled himself from taking her into his arms, and his grasp on her hands held her from him.

"I understand, Hilda, I understand it all—all you have suffered; the loneliness, the injustice, the dreary drudgery. I know, dear, I know that you have been unhappy."

"Oh yes! I have been unhappy! so unhappy!" The tears rolled down her cheeks while she spoke, fell on Odd's hands clasping hers. "No one ever cared for me, no one. Papa, mamma, Katherine even, not really; is n't it cruel, cruel?" This self-pity, so uncharacteristic, showing as it did the revulsion in her whole nature, filled Odd with a sort of helpless terror. "That is what I wanted; some one to care; I thought it must be my fault." The words came in sighing breaths, incoherent: "I have been so lonely."

"My child! My poor, poor child!"

"Let me tell you everything. I *must* tell you

now since you care for me. I have been so fond of you—always. You remember when I was a child?" Odd held her hands tightly and mechanically. Poor little hands; they gave him the feeling of light spars clung to in a whirling shipwreck. "Even then I was lonely, I see that now; and even then it weighed upon me, that thought that I was not to the people I loved what they were to me. I felt no injustice. I must be unworthy. It seems to me that all my life I have struggled to make people love me, to make them take me near to them. But you! You were near at once. Do I explain? It sounds morbid, does n't it? But it isn't, for my loneliness was almost unconscious, and I merely felt that with you I was happy, that things were clear, that you understood everything. You did, didn't you? Only I don't think you ever quite understood my gratitude, my utter devotion to you." Hilda's tears had ceased as she went on speaking, and she smiled now at Odd, a quivering smile.

"And then you went away, and I never saw you again. Ah! I can't tell you what I suffered."

Odd bent his head upon the hands clasped in his.

"But how could you have known?" said Hilda tenderly; "I was really very silly and very unreasonable. I thought you would come back *because* I needed you. I needed the sunshine. Perhaps you were right about the shadow. But for years I waited for you. I felt sure you knew I was waiting. You said you would come back you know; I never forgot that." She paused a moment: "It all ended in Florence," she went on sadly; "such a bleak, bitter day, just the day for burying an illusion. I see the cold emptiness of the big room now; oh! the melancholy of it! where I was sitting alone. All came upon me suddenly, the reality. You know those crumbling shocks of reality. I realized that I had waited for something that could never come; that you had never really understood, and that it would have been impossible for you to understand. I was a pretty, touching little incident to you, and you were everything to me. I realized, too, how silly it would all seem to any one; how it would be misinterpreted and smiled at as a case of puppy-love perhaps. A sort of cold shame crept through me, and I felt really alone then. Do you know what that feeling is?" Her hand under his forehead lifted his head a little as though to question his face, but putting both her hands over his eyes he would not look at her.

"You are so sorry?" Odd nodded. "But you have had that feeling? Imprisoned in oneself; looking, longing for a voice, a smile,—and silence, always, always silence. A thing quite apart from the surface intercourse of everyday life, not touched by it. You have so many friends, so many windows in your prison, you can't know."

"I know."

"Really?"

"Yes, yes."

"And you call out for help and no one hears. Oh, I can't explain properly; do you understand?"

"I understand, dear."

"Well, after that day in Florence, the last cranny of my prison seemed walled up. And—oh, then our troubles came, worse and worse. Responsibilities braced me up—far healthier, of course. And your books! Their strength; their philosophy—don't tell me I might find it all in Marcus Aurelius; your way of saying it went more deeply in me. Just to do one's duty; to love people and be sorry for them, and not snivel over oneself. Ah! if you knew all your books had been to me! Would you like it, I wonder?" Again the tenderness, almost playful, in her voice. Odd raised his head and looked at her.

"And when I came at last, what did you think?" The loving candor of her eyes dwelt on him.

"When you came?" she repeated. "Then I saw at once that you were Katherine's friend, and that your books were the nearest I should ever get to you." Hilda's voice hesitated a little; a doubt of the exactitude of her perceptions from this point showed itself in a certain perplexity of tone. "And —I don't quite understand myself, for I did n't plan anything—but just because I felt so much I was afraid that you would imagine I made claims on you. I was resolved that you should see that I had reached your standpoint—that I had forgotten— that the present had no connection with the past."

"But I had not forgotten," Odd groaned.

"No?" Hilda smiled rather lightly; "it would have been very strange if you had n't. Besides, as I say, I saw at once that you were Katherine's, and that it was right and natural. Your books taught me, too, the true peace of renunciation, you see! Not that this called for renunciation exactly," and again Hilda paused with the faint look of perplexity. "There was nothing to renounce since you were

hers, except I must have felt a certain disappointment. I felt a little frozen. Such dull egotism!"
She turned her eyes away, looking vaguely out into
the dusky room. "But even on that first day I
meant that you should see, and that she should see,
that I knew that the past made no bond: in my
heart it might, not in yours, I knew, for all your
kindness."

"Go on, Hilda," said Odd, as she paused.

"Well, you know all the rest. When you were
engaged and she more than friend, I had hoped for
it, and I saw that my turn might come; that I
might step into Kathy's vacated shoes, so to speak;
that we might be friends, and all my dreams be fulfilled after all. I began then to let myself know
that I did care, for I had tried to help myself before
by pretending that I did n't. I would n't do anything to make you like me. If you were to like me,
you would of yourself; all the joy of having you
care for me would be in having made no effort.
And the dream did come true. I saw more and
more that you cared. To-day I feel it, like sunshine." Odd still stared at her, and again through
sudden tears she smiled at him. "Only—is n't it
strange?—things are always so; it must be, too,
that I am weak, overwrought, for I feel so sad, as
though I were at the bottom of the sea, and looking
up through it at the sun."

"Great heavens!" muttered Odd. He looked at
her for a silent moment, then suddenly putting his
arm around her neck, he drew her to him.

He did not kiss her, but he said, leaning his head
against hers—

"And I—so unworthy!"

"No, no," said Hilda, and with a little sigh, "not unworthy, dear Peter."

"I, dully stumbling about your exquisite soul," Peter went on, pressing her head more closely to his. "Ah, Hilda! Hilda!"

"What, dear friend?"

"I cannot tell you."

"Unkind; I tell you everything."

"You can tell me everything. You can tell me how much you have cared for me, how much you care. I cannot tell you how much I care. I cannot tell you how infinitely dear you are to me." He had spoken, her face hidden from him in its nearness; now, turning his head he kissed her hair, and frowning, he looked at her and kissed her on the lips. Hilda drew back and rose to her feet. A subtle change, perplexity deepened, crossed her face, but, standing before him, she looked down at him and he saw that her trust rose as to a test. She put her hands out as though from an impulse to lay them on his shoulders ; then, as an instinct within the impulse seemed to warn her, though leaving her clear look untouched, she clasped them together and said gravely—

"You may tell me. You are infinitely dear to *me*."

Odd still frowned. Her terrible innocence gave him a sense of helpless baseness.

"I may tell you how much I love you?" and he too rose and stood before her.

"I have always loved you," said Hilda, with her grave look. "I love you now as much as I did when I was a child."

The impossible height where she placed him beside her made Odd's head swim. He felt himself caught up for a moment into the purity of her eyes, and looking into them he came close to her.

" My angel! My angel! " he hardly breathed.

" Dear Peter," and the tears came into the pure eyes. And, at the sight, the heaven brimmed with loveliest human weakness, the love unconscious but all revealed, Odd was conscious only of a dizzy descent from impossibility, the crash of the inevitable.

One step and he had taken her into his arms, seeing as he did so, in a flash, the white wonder of her face ; he could almost have smiled at it—divinely dull creature ! Holding her closely, the white folds of the shroud-like dress crushed against his breast, his cheek upon her hair, he could not kiss her and he could not speak, and in a silence as unmistakable as word or kiss, his long embrace forgot the past and defied the future.

The painful image of a bird he had once seen, wings broken, dying of a shot and feebly fluttering, came to him as he felt her stir ; her hands pushing him away.

" Dearest—dearest—dearest."

Her effort faltered to resistless helplessness.

Stooping his head he looked at her face ; it wore an almost tranquil, a corpse-like look. Her eyes were closed and the eyebrows drawn up a little in a faint, fixed frown ; but the childlike line of her mouth had all the sad passivity of death. Odd tremblingly kissed the gentle sternness of the lips.

She loved him, but how cruel he was.

"Oh, my precious," he said, "look at me. Forgive me; I love you."

He had freed her hands, and she raised them and bent her face upon them.

"You don't hate me for telling you the truth?" And as she made no sign: "No, no, you don't hate me; you love me and I love you. I have loved you from the beginning. Oh, my child, my child, why did you let me think you did not care? Look at me, dearest."

"What have I done?" said Hilda. She still kept her face hidden in her hands.

"You have done nothing; it is I, I who have done it!"

"I never could have believed it of you," she said, and he felt it to be the simple statement of a fact.

"O Hilda—I have only told you the truth, that is my crime."

"You told me because of what I said? You love me because of what I said?"

"Good God! I have been madly in love with you for months!"

"For months?" she repeated dully.

"For years, perhaps, who knows!"

"I did not know that I—that you—"

"You knew nothing, my poor angel."

He enfolded her again. Her look seemed to stumble and grope for an entreaty; her very powerlessness in the grasp of her realized love enchanted him.

"How base! how base!" she moaned.

"Am I a cruel brute? Ah! Hilda, you love me, and I cannot help myself."

"No—you cannot help yourself. I love you and I told you so."

"You did not mean *this*."

"I did not mean it. Oh, I trusted you. I did not doubt myself. I am wicked." The strange revulsion from her long selflessness had reached its height in poor Hilda; but, in her eyes, the discovered self was indeed wicked, a terrible revelation.

Her head fell helplessly against his shoulder.

"O Peter, Peter!"

"What, my darling child?"

"That we should be so base!"

"Not *we*, Hilda. Not *you!*"

"Yes, I—for I am happy—think of it, happy! Peter, I love you so much." She wept, her head upon his shoulder. "Keep me for a moment, only a moment longer. As I am wicked, let me have the good of it. I am glad that you love me. No; don't kiss me. Tell me again that you have loved me for a long time."

"From the moment I saw you again, I think. I knew it when I began meeting you after your lessons. Do you remember that first day in the rain? I do; and your little hat with the bow on it, the hole in your little glove, your white little face. I went away to the South because I could not trust myself with you. I did not dream that you loved me, but I felt—ah! I felt—that I could have made you love me!"

"And yet—you loved Katherine!"

The anguish of the broken words pierced him.

"Hilda, you cannot find me baser than I find myself. I did not love her."

" Peter ! Peter ! "

" Believe me, my precious child, when I tell you that you are the only one—my only love ! "

" O Peter ! "

" I never thought that I loved Katherine, but I had no fear of injustice to her, for I never thought that love would come into my life ; and, hardly was the cruel stupidity consummated, when the truth crept upon me. Friendly comradeship on the one hand, and on the other—O Hilda !—a passion that has transformed my life. The truth fell upon you like a thunderbolt ; my love for you crashed in upon your heavenly dreaming ; but you see—be brave enough to acknowledge what it all means, your dream and my love that needed no thunderbolt to wake it,—be brave enough to own that it is inevitable, that from the time that you put your hand in mine ten years ago, dated that rarest, that divinest thing, a love, a sympathy infinite. Dear child, be brave enough to own that before it, mistakes may be put aside without dishonor."

" Peter, Peter, let me go. Without dishonor ! We are both already dishonorable, and oh ! it is that that breaks my heart ; that you, that you who should have helped me, protected me from the folly of my ignorance, that you should be dishonorable ! "

" O Hilda ! "

" Yes," she said wildly, " yes, yes, Peter ; and I am wicked—wicked, for I love you. Yes—kiss me ; there, now I am thoroughly wicked. Now let me go."

Odd, white and shaken, still locked his arms about her.

"I was base if you will, too base for your loveliness; but you, my darling, have not a shadow on you; you were impossibly noble. Remember, that if there is dishonor, I am dishonored, not you; remember that *I* have done this!"

As he spoke, holding Hilda in his arms, the door opened and Katherine entered.

243

KATHERINE closed the door swiftly behind her and looked at them, not with a horror of surprise for the betrayal, but a strange, stiffened look. She had on her travelling hat and coat, a wrap on her arm, and the thumping of her boxes was heard outside on the stairs.

Katherine had schemed and success was hers, but this unlooked-for achievement struck her like a dagger and made triumph bitter.

Fate had played for her; Fate and not she was the heroine. Katherine felt herself struck down from her masterly eminence, saw herself reduced to a miserable position, a tool with the other tools— Peter and Hilda.

To see Hilda thus was an undreamed-of shattering of ideals and pierced even her own humiliation, for Katherine almost unconsciously had looked up to Hilda. She was to use her, play her game with her, but for Hilda's own advantage; she, not Fate, was to put her in Peter's arms, unspotted and innocent of the combinations that had led her there. All Katherine's plans in England had prospered and, in Paris, a nobly frank part awaited her. Avowal to Peter of incompatibility, her generous perception of his love for Hilda—a brave, manlike part—to which she had looked forward as to an

244

atonement for the ulterior motives. And Katherine
had almost persuaded herself that there would be
little acting needed. Had she not seen, guessed,
the truth? Had the truth not pained her, humiliated her? Had she not risen finely above her pain
and wished them happiness? In moments of self-
scorn, the ulterior motives, her own cautious look
before leaping, had filled her with impatient scorch-
ings, and Katherine could scorch herself as well
as others in the pitiless flame of clear-sighted analysis. But was her own rebellion from the irksome
standards of a higher nature—a rebellion that had
carried her into such opposition as to fall below herself to a hard matter-of-fact ambition, touched with
a sense of revenge upon her own disappointment,
—was that rebellion, that ambition, so base, so
pitiful?

Perhaps even the clearest analysis becomes sophistical if carried too far, and Katherine found ex-
cuses that explained for herself. But now all was
base, all pitiful, and she, in contrast with Hilda's
fall, had risen. On this lowered platform, the advantage was hers, terribly hers, and it was good,
good to lose self-scorn in her scorn for them.

She laid down her wrap on a table and began to
slowly draw off her gloves.

" My return was inopportune." The icy steadi-
ness of her voice pleased her own sense of fitness.
" Or opportune? " She directed her eyes upon
Odd, and indeed his attitude assumed all the igno-
bility of the situation. He welcomed responsibility;
to heap shame upon his own head was all he prayed
for. With a kind of desperate sincerity he kept his

arm around Hilda, and almost defiantly he had placed himself before her; he felt that Hilda's look of frozen horror gave him the advantage.

" Opportune, Katherine," he said ; "now at least I shall not have to lie to you. You can see the whole extent of my baseness."

" Such sudden baseness too. How long have we been engaged ?"

It was good to turn on him those daggers of her own humiliation ; to feel his disloyalty justify hers, nay, more than justify, give absolution, for she had not been disloyal, thinking he loved her.

" Katherine," said Odd, " I can only beg you to believe that I have struggled—for your sake, for her sake. Until this evening I thought that neither of you would ever know the truth."

This bracketing of Hilda's injury with hers stank in Katherine's nostrils. She controlled a quivering rage that ran through her, and, speaking a little more slowly for the tension she put upon herself—

" I can imagine no greater humiliation than the one you were so chivalrously preparing for me," she said. " Marriage with an unloving man ! I can imagine nothing more insulting. I deserved the truth from you, and how dared you think of degrading me by withholding it?" The white indignation of her own words almost impressed Katherine with their sincerity. She had seen the truth, and Peter's futile efforts to withhold it from her had filled her with an almost kindly scorn for his stupidity. But in the light of his present relapse from fidelity, the retrospect grew lurid.

" Katherine," said Odd gloomily, " I would not so

have insulted you after this. As long as I kept my secret there would have been no insult."

" I think I should have preferred the jilting before. You might have waited, Peter."

Until now Katherine had steadily kept her eyes on Odd, and there had been growing in her a certain sense of loss, most illogical, most painful. Hilda had won, and she had never gained. Katherine hardly knew for jealousy the sudden desire for vengeance as she turned her eyes upon her sister.

"So at last your long fidelity has been rewarded, Hilda," she said.

Hilda's wild wide gaze, her parted lips of mute agony, gave her the stricken look of a miserable animal with the fangs of a pack of hounds at its throat. Odd sickened at the sight; it maddened him too, and long resentments, long kept under, sprang up fierce and indifferent to cruelty.

" Katherine, say anything—anything you will to me," and Odd's voice broke a little as he spoke, " but not one word to her ! Not one word ! It comes badly from you, Katherine, badly ; for you have played the vampire with the rest of them ! This child has given you all her very life." He held Hilda to him as he spoke ; his look, his gesture those of a man driven to fury by the hint of an attack on his best beloved ; and Katherine, her head bent, looked at them both from under her straight eyebrows, breathing quickly.

" Her life has been one long self-immolation. It was too much for me this evening. I realized what she had never told me, the past years and this past month of drudgery and loneliness and insult !

247

She nursed your mother; she did the work of the servants you and your father took with you ; she earned the money for the bare necessaries of life— you and your father having the luxuries ; she bore insult, as I said. And once, and once only, I saw her crushed, and like the brute I am, like the dastard I am, I too joined the ranks of the egotists, I too heaped misery upon her ; I told her I loved her, and I took her into my arms as you saw us."

" Yes; as I see you." Katherine's very lips were white.

Hilda gave a sudden start and almost roughly she thrust Odd away ; the terror on her face had hardened to that look of resolution ; Odd remembered it. From the very extremity of anguish she passed to the extremity of self-control.

" Katherine," she said, " he is trying to shield me. It did not happen like that. I told him that I loved him. I told him that I had always loved him."

" Oh ! did you ? " said Katherine, with a withered little laugh.

" My child ! " cried poor Odd, a horrid sense of helplessness before this assumption of incredible humiliation half paralyzing him—" my child, what are you saying ? What madness ! "

" I am not mad, I am saying the truth. I told you that I loved you."

" In reply to an avowal of love on my part, a love you misunderstood. You know, as I knew when you spoke, that the affection you owned so finely, so nobly, so purely, was the child's love, the love of the loyal sister for her friend, the love of an angel."

" I am not sure," said Hilda.

"Oh!" cried Odd, looking at her with savage tenderness, "this is unbearable."

It was as if they had forgotten, each in the mutual justification of the other, Katherine standing there a silent spectator.

But Odd was conscious of that outraging contemplation.

"Hilda," he said appealingly and yet sternly, "at the very height of your trust in me I betrayed it. Your nobility had reached its climax. I had kissed you and you retreated, but without a shadow of doubt; and I, from the base wish to try your trust to the utmost, said that I loved you. You never faltered from your innocent outlook in replying; it was I who saw the truth, not you."

"Katherine," Hilda repeated, "he is trying to shield me. We are both base, yes; but I forced him to baseness. I longed for him to love me, and when he took me in his arms, I was glad."

"Good God!" cried Peter.

Katherine averted her eyes from her sister's face.

"I must own, Peter," she said, "that your position was difficult. Hilda evidently painted the pathos of her life to you in most touching colors —she herself very white on the background of our black depravity. That in itself is enough to shake a rather emotional heart like yours. And then, Hilda being very beautiful, and you not a Galahad I fear, she confesses her love for you, retreating delicately before your kisses. Of course those kisses she received as platonic pledges—from the man engaged to her sister. Trying for the man, very; I quite recognize it. Under such tempting circumstances the struggle for loyalty and honor must have been difficult. As you could hardly solve the difficulty, she solved it for you, very effectually, very courageously. When you took her in your arms—how often we repeat that phrase—the 'truth' at last flashed upon you. Even devoted friendship could hardly account for such yielding unconventionality, and Hilda's hidden love won the day."

During these remarks, Odd felt himself shaking with rage. If Katherine had been a man he would have knocked her down; as it was, his voice was the equivalent of a blow as he said, clenching his hand on the back of a chair—

"You despicable creature!"

He and Katherine glared at one another.

"Only the higher nature can put itself so hideously in the power of the lower," Odd went on; "and you dare!"

"No, no; all she says may be true!" moaned Hilda. She dropped upon the sofa and hid her face in her hands, adding brokenly: "And how can *you* be so cruel? so cruel to her? She loves you too!"

Katherine turned savagely upon her sister, and then, impulse nipped by quick reflection—

"You need not allow for a woman's jealousy, Mr. Odd. Don't, no indeed you must not, flatter yourself with my broken heart. I don't like humiliation for myself or for others. I don't like to scorn my sister whom I trusted, whom I loved. I could have killed the person who had told me this of her! My humiliation, my scorn, make me too bitter for charity. But I give you back your word without one regret for myself. You have killed my love very effectually."

"Was there ever much to kill, Katherine ?"

"That is ignoble, quite as ignoble as I could predict of you. Hilda's lesson must necessarily make the past look pale."

"I can only hope that you do yourself an injustice by such base speeches, Katherine."

"Your example has been contagious."

"Let me think so by proving yourself more worthy than you seem. Ask your sister's forgiveness—as I ask yours—humbly. She has not feared humiliation."

"I do not find myself in a position to fear or accept it. I found Hilda in the dust, and I cannot forgive her for having fallen there. Her poor confession was no atonement. And now, Mr. Odd, I make an exit more apropos than my entrance, and leave you with her." Katherine took up her wrap and walked out without looking again at Hilda.

"And *I* have done this," said Odd. Hilda lay motionless, her face upon her arms, and he approached her. There was a strange effect of no Hilda at all under the heavy folds of the gown; in the dark it glimmered with a vacant whiteness; it was as though the cruel words had beaten away her body and her soul.

"Hilda!" said Odd, broken-heartedly, hesitating as he paused beside her, not daring to touch the still figure. "Hilda!" he repeated; "if only you will forgive me; if only you will own that it is I, ·I only who need forgiveness, and unsay those mad words that gave her the power! Oh! that she

should have had the power! She has made remorse impossible!" Odd added, addressing himself
rather than Hilda, whose silence offered no hint of
sympathy.

"Why did you put yourself under her feet and
make me powerless?" he asked; "you know that
your gentle reticence had for months kept my love
in check; you knew that had I kept at your level,
you would have never realized that you loved me."
He bent above her and kissed her hand. "Precious
one! Dearest, dearest child."

"Oh, don't!" said Hilda. She drew her hand
away, not lifting her head. "Her heart is broken.
I am all that she said."

"Her heart is not broken!" cried Odd, in rather
desperate accents. "I could swear to it! She is a
cruel, heartless girl!"

"What would you have asked of her? You were
cruel to her."

"I am glad of it." And as Hilda made no reply
to this statement, he stooped to her again, imploring:
"Will you not look at me? Look up, dearest; tell
me again that you love me."

"I am already in the dust," said Hilda, after a
pause.

"You shall not sink to a morbid acceptance of
that venom!" cried Odd; he took her by the
shoulders with almost a suggestion of shaking her.
"Sit up. Listen to me," he said, raising her and
looking down at her stricken face, his hands on her
shoulders. "I have loved you passionately for
months. She was right in one thing; I had better
have told her, not have fumbled with that fatally

misplaced idea of honor. You may have loved me,
but I was as unconscious of it as you were. To-day
you were worn out, terrified, miserable. Just see it
with one grain of common charity, of common
sense, psychology, physiology if you will, for you
are ill, wretchedly weak and off balance, my darling
child!" Odd added, sitting down beside her; and
he would have drawn her to him, but Hilda
repeated—

" Don't."

" You felt my pity, my sympathy," Odd went on,
holding her hands. " You felt my love, poor little
one, unconsciously. You turned to me like the
child you were and are. You were starving for
kindness, consolation—for love—you came to your
friend, the friend you trusted, and you found more
than a friend. The love you owned so beautifully
was a truth too high for the hearer."

" Oh! I did not dream that you loved me. I did
not dream that I *loved* you!" Hilda wailed suddenly.

" Thank God that you own to that!" Odd
ejaculated.

" That does not clear me," she retorted. " No,
no ; I was a fool. You, the man engaged to my
sister! I should have felt the danger, the disloyalty of your interest. I was a fool not to feel
it! And that appeal I made to you—it was no
more or less that sickening self-pity, that das-
tardly whine over my own pathos, that morbid
sentimentality! I see it all, all! I was trying to
make you care for me, love me. I suppose crimes
are usually committed by people off balance physi-
cally, but crimes are crimes, and I am wicked. I

hate myself!" she sobbed, bending again her face upon her hands.

"Hilda," said Odd, trying to speak calmly and reasonably, "you could not have tried to make me fond of you, since I had plainly proved to you for months that I adored you. You complain! You gain pity! When your cold little air of impersonality blinded even my eyes; when only my love for you gave me the instinctive uneasiness that led me, step by step—you retreating before me—to the final realizations; and final they are not, I could swear to it! Ah! some day, Hilda, some day I shall get at the real truth. I shall worm it from you. You shall be forced to tell me all that you have suffered." Hilda interrupted him with an "Oh!" from between clenched teeth.

"Katherine was right," she said, "I have painted myself in pathetic colors. What a prig! What an egotist!" Her voice trembled on its low note of passionate self-scorn.

"An egotist!" Odd burst into a loud laugh. "That caps the climax. Come, Hilda," he added, "don't be too utterly ridiculous. Facts are, happily, still facts; your toiling youth and utter sacrifice among them. As I say, I have n't yet sounded the depths of your self-renunciation, and, as I say, some day you will tell me, my Hilda; my brave, splendid, unconscious little child." Odd put his arms around her as he spoke, but Hilda's swift uprising from them had a lightning-like decision.

"You dare speak so to me! After this! After our baseness! You dare to speak of some day? There will never be any day for us—together."

"I say there will be, Hilda."

"You think that I could ever forget my sister's misery; my shame and yours?"

"You are raving, my poor child. I think that common sense will win the day."

"That is a placid term for such degradation."

"I see no degradation in a love that can rise above a hideous mistake."

"You will find that hideous mistakes are things that cling. You can't mend a broken heart by marching over it."

"One may avoid breaking another."

"You make me scorn you. I am ashamed of loving you. Yes; there is the bitterest shame of all. I love you and I despise you. You are nothing that I thought you. You are weak, and cruel, and mean."

"You, Hilda, are only cruel—unutterably cruel," said Odd brokenly.

"I never wish to see you again." Hilda stared with dilated eyes into his eyes of pitiful appeal. "You have robbed my life of the little it had; you have robbed me of self-respect."

"Shall I leave you, Hilda?"

"You have broken her heart, and you have broken mine. Yes, leave me."

"Good-bye," said Odd. He walked towards the door like a man stabbed to the heart, and half-unconscious.

"Peter!" cried Hilda, in a hard voice. He turned towards her. She was standing in the middle of the room looking at him with the same fixed and dilated eyes.

"What is it, my child?" Odd asked gently.

"Kiss me good-bye!"

He came to her, and she held out her arms. They clasped one another.

"Must I leave you?" he asked, in a stammering voice.

"Yes, yes, yes. Kiss me."

He bent his head and their lips met. Hilda unclasped her arms and moved away from him, and he made no attempt to keep her. Looking at her with a characteristic mingling of suffering and rather grimly emphatic humor, he said—

"I will *wait.*"

And turning away, he walked out of the room.

CHAPTER XII

FOR two whole weeks—strange cataclysm in the Archinard household—Hilda stayed in bed really ill. Taylor waited on her with an indignant devotion that implied, by contrast, worlds of repressed antagonism ; for Taylor had highly disapproved of her trip with Katherine, and when she announced to Hilda on the day after the great catastrophe that Katherine had returned to England, she added with emphasis—

" But I don't go this time, Miss Hilda. It 's your turn to have a maid now."

The news took a weight of dread from Hilda's heart. She shrank from again seeing her own guilt looking at her from Katherine's tragic eyes. She did not need Katherine to impress it ; during long days and dim, half delirious nights it haunted her, the awful sense of irremediable wrong, of everlasting responsibility for her sister's misery. With all the capability for self-torture, only possessed by the most finely tempered natures, she scourged her memory again and again through that blighting hour when she had appealed for and confessed a love that had dishonored her. She dwelt with sickening on the moment when she had said : " I love you, too ! " Her conscience, fanatically unbalanced, distorted it with cruellest self-injustice. Indeed, such moments in life are difficult of analysis; the unconsciously spoken words followed by a consciousness so swift that in perspective they merge. In periods of clearer moral visions she could place her barrier, but only for mere flashes of relief, turned from with agony, as the dreadful fact of Katherine's ruined love surged over all and made of day and night one blackness.

Hilda's love for Odd now told her that for months past it had been growing from the child's devotion, and, with the new torture of a hopeless longing upon her—for which she despised herself—she saw in the whole scene with him the base self-betrayal of a love-sick heart.

Only a few days after Katherine's departure, the Captain returned.

Hilda felt, as he would come in and look at her lying there with that weird sense of distance upon her, that her father was changed. He walked carefully in and out on the tips of the Archinard toes, and, outside the door, she could hear him talking in tones of fretful anxiety on her behalf.

He hardly mentioned Katherine's broken engagement, and, for once in her life, Hilda was an object of consideration for her family. Even Mrs. Archinard rose from her sofa on more than one occasion to sit plaintively beside her daughter's bed ; and it was from her that Hilda learned that they were going back to Allersley.

Her father, then, must have enough money to pay mortgages and debts, and Hilda lay with closed eyes while her forebodings leaped to possibilities and to probabilities. The Captain's good fortune showed to her in a dismal light of material depend-

ence, and she could guess miserably at its source.
She could guess who encompassed her feeble life
with care, and who it was that shielded her from
even a feather's weight of gratitude—for the Captain
made no mention of his good luck.

"Yes, we are going back to the Priory," Mrs.
Archinard said, her melancholy eyes resting almost
reproachfully upon her daughter's wasted face. "It
would be pleasant were it not that fate takes care to
compensate for any sweet by an engulfing bitter.
Katherine to jilt Mr. Odd, and you so dangerously
ill, Hilda. I do not wonder at it, I predicted it
rather. You have killed yourself *tout simplement;*
I consider it a simple case of suicide. Ah, yes, indeed! The doctor thinks it very, very serious. No
vitality, complete exhaustion. I said to him, '*Doc-
teur, elle s'est tuée.*' I said it frankly."

Mrs. Archinard found another invalid rather confusing. She had for so long contemplated one only,
that, insensibly, she adopted the same tones of
pathos and pity on Hilda's behalf, hardly realizing
their objective nature.

By the beginning of May they were once more in
Allersley. It was like returning to a prior state of
existence, and Hilda, lying in a wicker chair on the
lawn, looked at the strange familiarity of the trees,
the meadows, the river between its sloping banks of
smooth green turf, and felt like a ghost among the
unchanged scenes of her childhood.

Mrs. Archinard found out, bit by bit, that it was
tiresome to keep her sofa now that there was an
opposition faction on the lawn; she realized, too, to
a certain extent, what it was that Hilda had been

to that sofa existence; without the background of Hilda's quiet servitude, it became flat and flavorless, and Mrs. Archinard arose and actually walked, and for longer periods every day, drifting about the house and garden in pensive contemplation of tenants' havoc. She sighed over the Priory and said it had changed very much, but, characteristically, she did not think of asking how the Priory had come to them again. The Captain vouchsafed no hint. He went rather sulkily through his day, fished a little—the Captain had no taste for a pleasure as inexpensive as fishing—and read the newspapers with ejaculations of disgust at political follies.

When Hilda sat in the sunshine near the river, her father often walked aimlessly in her neighborhood, eyeing her with almost embarrassed glances, always averted hastily if her eyes met his. Hilda had submitted passively to all the material changes of her life; she saw them only vaguely, concentrated on that restless inner torture. But one day, as her father lingered indeterminately around her, switching his fishing-rod, looking hastily into his fishing-basket, and showing evident signs of perplexity and indecision very clumsily concealed, a sudden thought of her own egotistic self-absorption struck her, and a sudden sense of method underlying the Captain's manœuvres.

" Papa, come and sit down by me a little while. I am sure the fish will be glad of a respite. Isn't it a little sunny to-day for first-class fishing? " Hilda pointed to the chair near hers, and the Captain came up to her with shy alacrity.

" Even first-class fishing is a bore, *I* think," he

observed; not taking the chair, but laying his rod upon it, and looking at his daughter and then at the river.

"Feeling better to-day, are n't you? You might take a stroll with me, perhaps; but no, you 're not strong enough for that, are you? Fine day, is n't it?"

Now that the moment looked forward to, yet dreaded, might be coming, the Captain vaguely tried to avert it after the procrastinating manner of weak people. Hilda did not seem to have anything particular to say, and the absent-minded smile on her face reassured him as to immediate issues.

"How are *you* feeling?" she asked; "I have been looking at the trees and grass for so long that I had almost forgotten that there are human beings in the world."

"Oh, I 'm very well; very well indeed." The Captain was again feeling uncomfortable. An inner coercion seemed to be forcing him to speak just because speaking was not really imperative at the moment. A little glow of self-approbation suddenly prompted him to add: "You know, I know about it now. That is to say, I was n't exactly to speak of it, if it might pain you; but I don't see why it should do *that*. Upon my word," said the Captain, feeling warmly self-righteous now that the ice was broken, "it 's more likely to pain me, is n't it? Rather to my discredit, you know; though, intrinsically, I was as innocent as a babe unborn. Of course you helped me over a tight place now and then, but I thought the money came to you with a mere turn of the hand, so to speak; and, as for your teaching—wearing yourself out—well, I don't know which I was angrier with first, you or myself. I never dreamed of it, it never entered into my head. And then, *my* daughter and low French cads! Well, *he* saw to that, and so did I. I saw the fellow too; thought it best, you know; for, naturally, Odd couldn't have my weight and authority. I was simply stupefied, you know. It quite knocked me over when he told me. Odd told me—"

The Captain took up his rod, examined the reel, and then switched its limber length tentatively through the air. It was embarrassing, after all, this recognition of his daughter's life.

"Now your mother doesn't know," he pursued; "Odd seemed rather anxious that she should; rather unfeeling of him too, I thought it. There was no necessity for that, was there? It would have quite killed her, wouldn't it? Quite."

"You need neither of you have known." All she was wondering about, trying to grasp, made Hilda pale. "It came about most naturally; and, if mamma's illness and that other unpleasant episode had not broken me down, my modest business might have come to an end—no one the wiser for it. Mr. Odd exaggerated the whole thing no doubt."

"Well, I don't know." The Captain now sat down on the chair with a sigh of some relief. "It's off my mind at all events. I wanted to express my —pain, you know, and my gratitude—and to say what a jolly trump I thought you; that kind of thing."

"Dear papa, I don't deserve it."

"Ah, well, Odd isn't the man to make misstatements, you know. A bit of dreamer, unpractical, no doubt. But he sees facts as clearly as any one, you know. He showed it all clearly. Rather cutting, to tell you the truth. Of course he 's very fond of you; that's natural. This sad affair of Katherine's; if it had n't been for that, you and he would be brother and sister by this time."

It was Hilda's turn now to draw in a little breath of relief. At all events her father was no ally. No other secret had been told, and she saw, now that the dread had gone, that any cause for it would have involved an indelicacy towards Katherine of which she knew Odd to be incapable.

"Where is he—Mr. Odd?" she asked, steeling herself to the question.

The look of gloom which touched the Captain's face anew, confirmed Hilda in her certainty of infinite pecuniary obligation.

"Not at home. Travelling again, I believe. A man can't sit down quietly under a blow like that."

A flush came over Hilda's face. Part of her punishment was evident. She must hear Katherine spoken of as the fickle, shallow-hearted, while she, guilt-stained, answerable for all, went undiscovered and crowned with praises. Yet Katherine herself —any woman—would choose the part Odd had given her—the part of jilt rather than jilted; and she, Hilda, was helpless.

"Papa," she asked, driving in the dagger up to the hilt—she could at least punish herself, if no one else could punish her—"where is Katherine? Is she not coming to stay with us?" The Captain swung one leg over the other with impatience.

"I've hardly heard from her; she is with the Leonards in London. Odd spoke very highly of her; seemed to think she had acted honorably; but, naturally, Katherine must feel that she has behaved badly."

"I am sure she has not done that, papa. She found that she would not be happy with him."

"Pshaw! That's all feminine folly, you know. She probably saw some one she liked better, some bigger match. Katherine isn't the girl to throw over a man like Odd for a whim."

Hilda's flush was now as much for her father as for herself. She felt her cheeks burning as she said, her voice trembling—

"Papa, papa! How can you say such a thing of Katherine! How can you! I know it is not true. I know it!"

"Oh, very well, if you are in her secrets. I know Katherine pretty well though, and it's not unimaginable. I don't imply anything vulgar." The Captain rose as he spoke and swung his basket into place; "that's not conceivable in my daughter. But Katherine's ambitious, very ambitious. As for you, Hilda—and all that, you know—I am awfully sorry, you understand." The Captain walked away briskly, satisfied at having eased his conscience. Odd had made it feel uncomfortably swollen and unwieldy, and the Captain's conscience was, by nature, slim and flexible.

Hilda lay in her chair, and looked at the river running brightly beyond the branches of the lime-tree under which she sat. The flush of misery that her father's cool suppositions on Katherine's conduct had seemed to strike into her face, only died slowly. She had to turn from that shame resolutely, contemplation would only deepen its helplessness. She looked at the river, and thought of the time when she had stood beside it with Odd and recited Chaucer to him. She thought of the humorous droop of his eyelids, the kind, comprehensive clasp of his hand on hers; the look of the hand too, long, brown, delicate, the finger-tips too dainty for a man, and the dark green seal on his finger. Hilda turned her head away from the river and closed her eyes.

"Allone, withouten any companye," that was the fated motto of her life.

CHAPTER XIII

BY the end of June, returning physical strength gave Hilda the wish to seek self-forgetful effort of some kind. She tried to busy herself with something—with anything—and experienced the odd sensation of a person upon whom duty has always pressed and crowded, in a futile search for duty. The stern, sweet helper eluded her, the unreality of manufactured, unnecessary activity appalled her. She regretted the strenuous days of labor that meant something. Taking herself to task for a weak submission to circumstance, she fitted up a large room at the top of the house with artistic apparatus; nice models were easily lured from the village; she told herself that art at least remained, and tried to absorb herself in her painting; but the savor of keen interest was gone; the pink cheeks and staring eyes of her village girl were annoying. Hilda felt more like crying than trying to select from and modify her buxom charms.

Mrs. Archinard had suddenly assumed an active *rôle* in life most confusing to her daughter. Even mamma did not need her. Mrs. Archinard drove out in the pony-cart to see people; she held quite a little *côterie* of callers every afternoon. Mrs. Archinard's little *Causeries de Mardi*, her society for little weekly dinners—only six chosen members

266

—*les Élites*—stirred Allersley to the quick with æsthetic thrills and heart-burnings. Mrs. Archinard laughed prettily and lightly at her own feats, but Allersley was awestricken, and got down its Sainte-Beuve trembling, resolved on firm foundations.

Hilda was not one of *les Élites.* " Just for us old people, trying to amuse ourselves," Mrs. Archinard said, and at the *Causeries* Hilda was an anomalous and silent onlooker ; indeed the *Causeries* were quite Sainte-Beuvian in their monologic form, Mrs. Archinard *causant* and Allersley attentive, but discreetly reticent, no one caring to risk a revelation of ignorance. The Captain carefully avoided both the *élites* and the *mardis*, and devoted himself to more commonplace individualities whose dinners were good, and then one was n't required to strain one's temper by listening to fine talk.

Mary Apswith spent a week at the Manor, and one fresh sunny morning she came to see Hilda. She found her in the garden standing between the rows of sweet-peas, and filling with their fragrant loveliness the basket on her arm. Mary's mind had been given over to a commotion of conjecture since Peter's flying visit to her in London. He had told her much and yet not enough ; though what he had told insured sympathy for Hilda. Mary was generous, and the sight of Hilda's white sunlit face completed Peter's work. She found that she had kissed Hilda—she, so undemonstrative—and standing with her arms around the girl's slight shoulders, she said, looking at her with a grave smile, in which the slight touch of playfulness reminded poor Hilda of Peter—

"You will see *me*, won't you?"

Hilda still held in her hands the last long sprays she had cut—palest pink and palest purple, "on tiptoe for a flight."

"How kind of you to come," she said.

"Kind of you to say so, since I come from the enemy's camp. That reckless brother of mine!"

"Did he send you?" Hilda asked, fright in her eyes.

"Send me? Oh no, he did n't send me; but after what he has told me, I came naturally of my own free will." Hilda smiled faintly in reply to Mary's smile.

"What has he told you?"

"Why, simply that he had been in love with you almost from the day he proposed to Katherine; indeed he implied an even remoter origin. Really Peter ought to be whipped! He almost deserves the sacking you are giving him!"

Hilda winced at the humorous tone.

"That he had made love to you most cruelly; that Katherine had come in upon the love scene; that she, too, was cruel—natural, though, was n't it? Peter is rather hard on Katherine. And, to sum up, that you had been badly treated by the world in general, by himself in particular, and that he was very desperate and you painfully perfect, and—oh, a great many things."

"Did he tell you that I loved him?" Hilda asked, looking down at her sweet-peas with, if that were possible, an added pallor. She wondered if it was demanded of her that she should humiliate herself before Peter's sister—tell her that she had made love to him.

"My dear child," Mary's voice dropped to a graver key, "Peter trusts me, you know, and he ought to trust me. He told me that when he made love to you, you and he together found out that fact."

Even Hilda's morbid self-doubt could not deny the essential truth of this point of view.

"And now you won't marry him," Mary added, but in a matter-of-fact manner, and as if the subject were folded up and put away by that conclusive statement.

"Let us walk along the path, my dear Hilda. What a delightful garden this is. I must have a pansy border like that in mine. Tell me, Hilda, why have you always so persistently and doggedly effaced yourself? Why did you never let anybody know you, and subside passively into the background *rôle*? *I* never knew you, I am sure, and if it had n't been for Peter I should n't have known you now. He made me see things very clearly. The poor little caryatid cowering in a dark corner, and holding up a whole edifice on its shoulders."

"How could he! Why will he always see things so? It makes me miserable."

"Well, well; perhaps Peter's point of view would seem to you exaggerated. But, as I say, why did you never let me get a glimpse of you?"

"I never tried to hide. Circumstances kept me apart. I loved my work."

"Yes; it must have been charming work, in all its branches." Mary gave her a gravely gay glance.

"When you did emerge from your shadows, why did you never talk—make an effect, like Katherine?"

"Katherine makes effects without trying. She is effective, and people like her for herself. I was fitted for the dark corner. That is why I stayed there."

"No, my dear, one can't explain the injustices of fortune by that comfortably, or uncomfortably, fatalistic philosophy. Noble natures get oddly jumped on in this world," Mary added reflectively. "The tragedy, of course, lies in being too noble for one's *milieu*, for then, not only does one renounce, but one is expected to, as a matter of course. Forgive me, Hilda, if I am a little coarsely frank. I am speaking, for the moment, with gloves off; I know the truth, and you may as well face it. It's a pity to be too noble; one should have just a spice of egotistic rebellion, else one is squashed flat to one's corner."

"Peter found me," said Hilda, with a sad smile that evaded the "coarse" frankness.

They walked silently along the little path under the sunlit shade of the fruit-trees. Mary stopped at a turning.

"Yes; that is encouraging. Reminds one of Emerson and optimism. Peter did find you." Her large clear eyes looked an exhortation into Hilda's. "Peter found you, my dear child; let Peter keep you, then."

"He always will keep—what he found," said Hilda, trembling. "I love him. I shall always love him."

" My dear Hilda ! "

" But I cannot marry him. I cannot."

" You are a foolish little Hilda."

" We made Katherine miserable."

" And therefore all three must be miserable. For Peter to have kept faith with Katherine—loving you —might have called down a far worse tragedy."

Hilda gazed widely at her—

" Yes ; I deserve that suspicion."

"Oh, you foolish, foolish child!" cried Mary, laughing ; and she kissed her. "Come, come ; say that you will be good to my poor brother?"

"I love him, but I cannot ground my happiness on a wrong."

"Your happiness would be grounded on a right ; the wrong was a mere incidental. Peter must wait, I see. Perhaps you will own some day that that was ample expiation."

CHAPTER XIV

ONE October day Hilda received a queer little note from Katherine. That Katherine had spent a month in Scotland and was now on a yacht with a party of friends, Hilda knew, and the note was dated from Amalfi.

"Why don't you marry Peter, you little goose?" was all it said.

Hilda trembled as she read. Katherine's scorn and Katherine's nobility seemed to breathe from it.

"I am not as base as you think," was her answer.

Katherine received this answer in Amalfi. She had come in from a walk with Allan Hope along the road that runs above the sea between Amalfi and Sorrento, and one of the yachting party, a girl who much admired Katherine, was waiting for her before the hotel holding the letter, an excuse for the excited whisper with which she gave it to her.

"Dear Miss Archinard, *he* is here!"

"What 'he,' Nelly?" asked Katherine; she looked down at the writing on the envelope of her letter, and the becoming flush that her walk through the warm evening had brought to her cheeks faded a little.

Allan Hope had gone on into the hotel, and Nelly's excited eyes followed him till he was safely out of sight.

"Mr. Odd," she said with dramatic emphasis. "Of course he did n't know."

"Oh, he is here!" Katherine's eyes were still on the writing. "No, of course he did n't know."

"You are n't afraid of his meeting Allan?" Nelly was Allan Hope's cousin. "Is there no danger, Miss Archinard? He must be feeling so—dreadfully!"

"What a romantic little pate it is! I really believe you were looking forward to a duel. No, no, Nelly, there is nothing of an exciting nature to hope for!"

"But won't it be terrible for you to meet him? The first time, you know! And engaged to Allan!" said Nelly.

"We are not at all afraid of one another. Don't tremble, Nelly."

Katherine read her letter standing on the terrace before the hotel. The dying evening seemed to throb softly in the southern sky, arching solemnly to the horizon line. Katherine looked out at the sea—it was characteristic of her deeply set eyes to look straight out and seldom up. She stood still, holding the letter quietly; Katherine had none of the weakness that seeks an outlet for the stress of resolution in nervous gesture. She did not even walk up and down; indeed the resolution was made and meditation needless. Turning after a moment, she went into the hotel and asked at the office whether Mr. Odd were to be found.

"Yes, he was in his room; he had only arrived an hour ago.

Katherine requested the man to tell Mr. Odd that

18   273

Miss Archinard was on the terrace and would like to see him. In two minutes Peter was walking out to meet her.

Peter's eyes, as they shook hands, were rather sternly steady; Katherine's steady, but more humorous.

"*Sans rancune?*" she inquired, with some lightness, and then, sparing him the necessity for a reply that might be embarrassing for both of them—

"I want to ask you a question; pardon abruptness; why don't you marry Hilda? Won't she? There are two questions!"

"I don't marry her because she won't. And there is the evident reply, Katherine."

"Do you despair?" she asked.

"I can't say that. Time may wear out her resistance."

"I know Hilda better than you do—perhaps. You see I have got over my jealousy." Katherine's smile had all its charm. "She won't if she said she would n't; if she has ideals on the subject."

"Then I must resign myself to hopeless wretchedness."

"No; you must not. *I* am going to help you. Don't look so gloomily unimpressed. I am going to help you. I am going to do penance, and I don't believe you will consider it an expiation either! Just encourage me by a little appreciation of my dubious nobility." Odd looked questioningly at her.

"Peter, when I came back that night I was engaged to Allan Hope."

"Oh!" said Peter. They looked at one another through the almost palpable dusk of the evening.

" I 'll give you the facts—draw your own conclusions. I 'll give you facts, but don't ask self-
abasement put into words. You really have n't the
right, have you, Peter?"

"No; I suppose not. No, *I* have n't the right."

" You put yourself in the wrong, you see. You
must allow me to flaunt that ragged superiority.
Peter, very soon after our engagement you began
to dissatisfy me because I realized that I should
never satisfy you. The more you knew me the
more you would disapprove, and your nature could
never understand mine to the extent of pardoning.
Once I 'd seen that, everything was up. It would n't
do; and the knowledge grew upon me that the impossibility was emphasized by the fact that Hilda
would do. *I* saw that you loved her, Peter; stupid,
stupid Peter! And poor little Hilda! She was
ground between two stones, was n't she? your ignorance and my knowledge. I give you leave to offer
me up as a burnt sacrifice at her altar, only don't
let me hear myself crackling. Yes; I saw that you
were in love with her, and that she would be in love
with you if it could come—as it should have come—
as I intended it to come—foolish, hasty Peter! No;
no comments, please! I know everything you can
say. I took precious good care of myself, no doubt;
my generosity was n't very spontaneous; perhaps I
thought you 'd get over it; perhaps I wanted you to
get over it; perhaps even while seeing that Allan
Hope would do—for I satisfy him most thoroughly
—I kept a tiny indefinite corner in my motives for
possible reactions; I give you leave to draw your
inferences, but don't ask me to dot my i's and cross

my t's too cold-bloodedly. I accepted Allan Hope on the understanding that the engagement was to be kept secret for a few months. I told Allan that you did not love me; that I did not love you; that our engagement was broken. I told him that when I saw his love for me struggling with his loyalty to you. It was the truth from my point of view; but from his, from yours, it was a lie—and own that at least I am generous in telling you! Too generous perhaps. I came back to Paris to tell you that I had discovered it would n't do, and to make you and Hilda happy. And, when I saw you together, both as bad as I was—at least I thought so at the time —both disloyal—I forgot my own self-scorn; I felt a right to a position I had repudiated. I *had* to be cruel, for, Peter, I was jealous; I hated her for being the one who would satisfy you thoroughly and forever."

There was silence between them. If she had satisfied him as only Hilda could satisfy him, she would not have gone to Allan perhaps. Odd with a quick throb of sympathy understood the intimation, understood both her courage and her reticence. He had seen her at her noblest, yet there was much not touched upon, far from noble.

The half avowal of a disappointed love flawed her loyalty to Allan. Such love deserved disappointment and was of a doubtful quality. Peter respected her frankness but was not deceived by it. His manliness was touched by the possibility she had hinted at. He understood Katherine and he forgave her —with reservations.

There seemed to be nothing to say, and he did

not seek words. He and Katherine walked slowly
to the end of the terrace.

Then Katherine told him of her note to Hilda and
handed him Hilda's reply.

" I shall go to England to-morrow, Katherine,"
said Odd, when he had read it.

" You will have to fight, you know. She will say
that my wrong did not excuse hers. She will say
that nothing excused you. She *is* a little goose."

" I 'll fight."

They had walked back to the entrance of the
hotel and here they paused ; there was a fitness in
farewell.

" Katherine," said Odd, " it would have been very
base in you to have kept silence, and yet, in spite of
that, you have been very courageous this evening."

"You are a hideously truthful person, Peter.
Why put in that damaging clause ? Have I merely
escaped baseness ? "

" No, for you have never been finer."

" That is true. I 'll never reach the same heights
again," and Katherine laughed.

" Understand that *I* understand. Your story has
not absolved *me*."

" There is the danger with Hilda. You must
make my holocaust avail."

" I hope that a good thing is never lost," Peter
replied.

CHAPTER XV

THE October day was deliciously warm at Allersley, a fragrant autumnal warmth, limpid
with sunshine, and the woods all golden.

Odd was walking through the woods, the sunshine
of home and hope in his blood, his mood of reso-
lute success tempered by no more than just a touch
of trembling.

In the distance lay the river, a glitter here and
there beyond the tree trunks; the little landing-
wharf where he had first seen Hilda was no doubt
still unchanged and worth a pilgrimage on some
later day, but now he must take the most direct way
to the Priory ; he had only arrived an hour before,
but a minute's further delay would be unbearable.
This day must atone for all the past failure of his
life, and make his autumn golden. He walked
quickly, following, he remembered, almost the same
path among the trees that he and Hilda had gone
by that night, ten years ago; the memory emphasized the touch of trembling. To dwell on her dear-
ness made fear tread closely. The gray stone wall
wound among the woods, Peter caught sight of it,
and, at the same moment, of the fluttering white of
a dress beyond it that made his heart stand still.

He could not have hoped to find Hilda here with

no teasing preliminaries, no languid mother or sulky father to mar the fine rush of his onslaught.

Such good luck augured well, for—yes, it was Hilda walking slowly among the trees—and at the clear sight of her, Peter wondered if the breathing space of a conventional preliminary would not have been better, and felt that he had exaggerated his own courage in picturing that conquering impetuosity.

She wore no hat, and her head drooped with an air of patient sadness. Her hands clasped behind her, she walked aimlessly over the falling leaves and seemed absently to listen to their rustling crispness as her footsteps passed through them. There was a black bow in the ruffled bodice, and with her black hair she made on the gold and gray a colorless silhouette.

Odd jumped over the wall, and, as he approached her, the rustling leaves under his feet, their falling patter from the trees, seemed to fill the air with loud whisperings. Hilda turned at this echo of her own footfalls, and Odd could almost have smiled at the weary unexpectancy of her look transformed to a wide gaze of recognition. But his heart was in a flame of indignant tenderness, for, all chivalrous comprehension conceded, Katherine's confession had been cruelly tardy and Hilda's face was pitiful. She stood silent and motionless looking at him, and Odd, as he joined her, said the first words that came to his lips.

" My child ! How ill you look ! "

The self-forgetful devotion of his voice, his eyes, sent a quiver across her face, but Odd, seeing only its frozen pain, remembered those stabbing words: "You are cruel and weak and mean," which she had spoken with just such a look, and any lingering thought of a fine onslaught was nipped in the bud.

" I may speak to you ? " he asked.

Hilda, for her own part, found it almost impossible to speak; she wanted to throw herself on his breast and weep away all the gnawing loneliness, all the cruel doubts and bitter sense of guilt. The sight of him gave her such joy that everything was already half forgotten—even Katherine ; even Katherine— she realized it and steeled herself to say with cold faintness—

" Oh, yes ; " adding, "you startled me."

" So thin, so pale, such woful eyes ! " He stood staring at her.

"You—don't look well either," she said, still in the soft cold voice.

" I should be very sorry to look well."

Peter was adapting himself to reality ; but if the impetuous dream was abandoned, the courage of humbler methods was growing, and he could smile a little at her.

"Hilda, I have a great deal to tell you. Will you walk with me for a little while ? It is a lovely day for walking. How beautiful the woods are looking."

"Beautiful. I walk here a great deal." She looked away from him and into the golden distance.

"And you will walk here now with me ? " he asked, adding, as the pale hesitation of her face again turned to him, "Don't be frightened, dear, I am not going to force any solution upon you ; I am not going to try to make you think well of me in spite of your conscience."

Think well of him! As if, good or bad, he was not everything to her, and the rest of the world nowhere! Hilda now looked down at the leaves.

"And here is Palamon," said Peter, as that delightful beast came at a sort of abrupt and ploughing gallop, necessitated by the extreme shortness of his crumpled legs, through the heaped and fallen foliage. " He remembers me, too, the dear old boy," and Palamon, whose very absorbed and business-like manner gave way to sudden and smiling demonstration, was patted and rubbed cordially in answer to his cordial welcome.

"It must seem strange to you being here again after such a time," said Odd, when he and Hilda turned towards the river, Palamon, with an air of happy sympathy, at their heels. The river was invisible, a good half-mile away, and the whispering hush of the woods surrounded them.

"It does n't seem strange, no," Hilda replied ; " it seems very peaceful."

"And are you peaceful with it ? " All the implied reserves of her tone made Peter wonder, as he had often wondered, at the strength of this fragile creature ; for, although that conviction of having wronged another was accountable for her haggard young face, the crushed anguish of her love for him was no less apparent in the very aloofness of her glance.

"I feel merely very useless," she said with a vague smile.

"I have seen Katherine, Hilda." Odd waited during a few moments of silent walking before making the announcement, and Hilda stopped short and turned wondering eyes on him.

"It was at Amalfi. She had just received your letter, and she sent for me; she had something to say to me." Hilda kept silence, and Odd added, "You knew that she was on a yachting trip?" Hilda bowed assent. "And that Allan Hope is of the party?"

"I heard that; yes."

"And that he and Katherine are to be married?"

Here Hilda gave a little gasp.

"She does n't love him," she cried. Odd considered her with a disturbed look.

"You must n't say that, you know. I fancy she does—love him."

"She did it desperately after you had failed her; after I had robbed her."

Odd was too conscious of the possibility of a subtle half-truth in this to assert the bold unvarnished whole truth of a negative.

Hilda's loyalty lent a dignity to Katherine's most doubtful motives, a dignity that Katherine would probably contemplate with surprise, but accept with philosophic pleasure.

Had Hilda indeed robbed her unwittingly? Had he failed her long before her deliberate breach of faith? He had, she said, shown his love for Hilda, and would she have turned to Lord Allan's more facile contentment had she been sure of Peter's?

Delicate problem, without doubt. His mind

dwelt on its vexatious tragic-comic aspect, while he stared almost absently at Hilda.

Certainly his disloyalty had been unintentional, guiltless of plot or falsehood ; and Katherine's was intentional, deceitful, ignoble. It would be possible to shock every chord of honor in Hilda with the bold announcement that Katherine had been en-gaged when she came to Paris, and that her cruel triumph had been won under a lying standard.

And that shock might shatter forever, not the sense of personal wrong-doing, but all responsibility towards one so base, all that brooding consciousness of having spoiled another's life. Katherine had abandoned the position, and poor Hilda had merely stumbled on its vacant lie.

Yet Odd felt that there might be some ignoble self-interest in showing the ugly fact with no soften-ing circumstances ; circumstances might indeed soften the ugliness into a dangerously tragic resem-blance to despairing disappointment. Hilda would be horribly apt to think more of the circumstances than of the fact. Odd was consciously inclined to think the fact simply ugly, inclined to believe that the irksomeness of his growing disapproval, rather than the loss of his love, had led Katherine to seek a more amenable substitute ; but with a sense of honor so acute as to be hardly honest, Peter put aside his own advantageous surmises, and prepared to give Katherine's story from a most delicate and selected standpoint. Strict adherence to Kath-erine's words, and yet such artistic chivalry in their setting that even Katherine would find her sacrifice at Hilda's altar painless.

"You shall have her own words," he said, after a long pause. He felt that the inner trembling had grown to a great terror. He became pale before the compelling necessity for exaggerated magnanimity.

To lose his own cause in pleading Katherine's loomed a black probability, yet in his very defeat he would prove himself not unworthy of Hilda's love ; neither cruel nor mean nor weak. Ah ! piercing words ! At least he could now draw them from their rankling. And as they walked together he told Katherine's story, lending to it every charitable possibility with which she herself could not honestly have invested it.

When he had done, taking off his hat, for his temples were throbbing with the stress of the recital, and looking at Hilda with an almost pitifully boyish look, he had emphasized his own unconscious revelation of his love for Hilda, emphasized that hint of broken-hearted generosity in Katherine, he had hardly touched on her lie to Allan or on the glaring fact that she had made sure of him before giving Peter his freedom. The soreness that the revelation of Katherine's selfishness had made between them so soon after their engagement, he had not mentioned.

Hilda walked along, looking steadily down. Once or twice during the story she had clutched her clasped hands more tightly, and once or twice her step had faltered and she had paused as though to listen more intently, but the white profile with its framing eddies of hair crossed the pale gold background, its attitude of intense quiet unchanged.

284

The silence that followed his last words seemed cruelly long to Odd, but at last she lifted her eyes, and meeting the solemn, pitiful, boyish look, her own look broke suddenly into passionate sympathy and emotion.

"Peter," she said, standing still before him, "she didn't love you."

"I don't think she did." Odd's voice was shaken but non-committal.

"Perhaps she loved you more than she could love any one else," said Hilda.

"Yes; perhaps."

Hilda's hands were still clasped behind her, and she looked hard into his face as she added with a certain stern deliberateness—

"I don't believe she ever loved anybody."

Odd was silent. He had not dared to hope for such a clear perception.

"She was very cruel to me," said Hilda, after a little pause, and her eyes, turning from his, looked far away as if following the fading of a lost illusion.

"I don't think she ever cared much for me either," she added.

"Not much; not as you interpret caring."

Peter kept the balance with difficulty, for over him rushed that indignant realization of Katherine's intrinsic selfishness.

"No; I could not have been so cruel to her, not even if she had robbed me of you." It was the most self-assertive speech he had ever heard her utter.

"No; you could not have been so cruel to her," he repeated, "not even loving me as you did and as she did not."

285

There was a pause, a pause in which it seemed to Odd that the very trees stretched out their branches in breathless listening, and Hilda said slowly—

"But that does n't make what I did less wrong. I was as weak, as disloyal, as though Katherine had loved us both as much as I thought she did."

"And I as cruel, as weak, as mean?" Odd asked.

"Ah, don't!" she said, with a look of pain. "You have redeemed yourself," she added, "and have made me more ashamed."

"Then I have made a miserable failure of my attempt."

"No, no ; you have not."

The river was before them now, and the woods sloped down to its curving band of silver. They both stood still and looked at it, and beyond it at the gentle stretches of autumnal hill and meadow.

"Dear Peter," said Hilda gently. He looked down at her and she up at him, putting her hand in his, but so gravely and quietly that the tender little action conveyed nothing but a reminiscence of the child of ten years ago.

So, holding hands, they were both still silent, and again they looked at the river, the meadows, and the blue distance of the hills. Palamon, after running here and there, with rather assumed interest, his nose to the ground, came and sat down before them with an air of dignified acquiescence and appreciative contemplation. In the woods the sudden, sad-sweet twitter of a bird seemed to embroider the silence with unconscious pathos.

"O Peter!" said Hilda suddenly, on a note as

impulsive and as inevitable as the bird's. He looked at her and put his arms around her, saying nothing.

" Oh ! " said Hilda, " I cannot help it. I love you too much, dear Peter. Everything else may have been wrong, but it is right to love you."

He took her face between his hands and looked at her.

" Everything else would be wrong."

" Then kiss me, Peter."

He gave himself the joy of a delicious postponement.

" Not till you tell me that you see that everything else would be wrong." But the kiss was given before her answer.

" I trust you, and you must know."

THE END.